Acknowledgements

The actual events of The Murder of Andrew Sigler are taken from several sources, most notably, the Ironwood Daily Globe, the Montreal River Miner, and the preliminary hearing and trial testimony of Emma Sigler. The Daily Globe and the Miner covered the murder, Andy Anderson's arrest, the trials, and the events following Emma's commitment to Waupun.

I interviewed people who knew Emma and Andrew Sigler and Andy Anderson, including Cyril LaMarche, Sven Sunie and Sigrid Hawley. Larry Peterson, a local historian, encouraged me to write. Virginia Giacomino and Karen Ransanici, the former and current Iron County Clerks of Court, respectively, and Iron County Judge Patrick Madden, helped in directing me to and making available court records about the crime and subsequent trials. The current owners of the building that was the Gogebic Hotel graciously allowed me full access to the building.

Others instrumental in providing documentation and insight into the circumstances of the crime and Andy's and Emma's imprisonment, were the Iron County Historical Society; the Iron County Miner; Harry Miller, a records custodian at the Wisconsin State Historical Society; Andy's parole officer, Lee Wagner; Jann Johnston of the State of Wisconsin Department of Corrections; Pam Garcia of the Waupun Public Library; and Wendy Bruns at Green Bay Correctional Institute.

Andy Anderson's son from his second marriage, Andrew, provided details about his father's life after he left prison.

I want to give special thanks to those relatives of Emma and Andrew Sigler who provided information and family photos, Joe Sigler, a grandson of Andrew and Emma; Sandee Williams, Andrew Sigler's niece; and Vicki Roberts, Lester Sigler's daughter.

My patient wife and editor, Andrée, has had to put up with the facts and minutiae of the Sigler murder for many years.

PART ONE

In 1924, Hurley, Wisconsin, and Ironwood, Michigan, were the largest of many communities that peppered the Gogebic Range, whose production of high-grade iron ore ranked a close second to the giant Mesabi Range of Minnesota.

Iron miners, lumberjacks, saloonkeepers, bootleggers and prostitutes helped build the Gogebic Range, a 30-mile-long stretch of towns, headframes and mining company buildings.

The iron mines of the Gogebic Range were scattered on an east-west line from Iron Belt, Wisconsin, to Wakefield, Michigan, and the underground mines contributed most of the Range's income to the mining barons. The miners contributed a large part of their income to the saloon owners of Hurley.

Mining communities are unique. Each city and town on the Gogebic Range had its individual settlements called "locations", a means of societal and geographical identification located in the shadow of a mining company's shaft and headframe. It was more meaningful to identify one's home as being in Germania or Norrie location, for example, than in Hurley or Ironwood. Each of these small settlements had a family-owned grocery store and a few speakeasies. Many homes in the area housed a family plus several boarders who had come to the Gogebic to work in the mines. They worked in shifts, and when one gang of workers went to work, the miners who worked the shift before came home to sleep in the beds that had just been emptied. Ethnic and cultural distinctions also made each location a separate entity. Several mining companies competed for the ore, and each one tended to recruit miners from specific areas of

Europe. As immigrants arrived, it was only natural that they sought a community of their own language and customs. Thus, locations grew with Finnish or Swedish or Italian, French-Canadian, Austrian or English families.

Only short distances apart, the mining locations were physically separated by stockpiles, vast mountains of deep red ore waiting to be loaded into ore cars by huge steam shovels for the 40-mile train ride to the docks at Ashland, Wisconsin. It was then dumped into ore boats for delivery to the steel mills in Indiana and Ohio via the Great Lakes.

Large depressions in the land, called "caves", the remains of a long-forgotten open pit excavation or an unproductive underground mine that had been deliberately blasted for safety caused a transportation barrier between locations. Shortcuts over the stockpiles and caves were made up of footpaths and railroad grades that crisscrossed the mining company land.

An electric streetcar ran from Iron Belt, Wisconsin, through the downtown areas of Hurley and Ironwood, down Ayer Street to Jessieville Location in Ironwood. The streetcar covered a distance of about 12 miles, and it cost a nickel to ride.

In 1924, Hurley had a population of about 4,000, predominantly Italians and French-Canadians, who supported one of the finest school systems in the state, where 90 percent of its students graduated from high school and 30 percent of those went on to higher education. Its proud citizens sponsored athletics, churches flourished, and a city band played concerts in the park. The fire department had the latest equipment. Small, family homes lined the streets. At the west end of Silver Street, the main thoroughfare, across from the railroad station stood the magnificent, four-story Burton House hotel with 92 guest rooms and a 216-foot veranda. The Burton House would be made famous by Edna Ferber in her book Come and Get It, published a decade later.

There was a seamy side of Hurley, too, where prohibition was mocked and prostitution flourished, a town that had gained a reputation among underworld figures as a safe city, a northern retreat where big-city crime bosses could relax without fear of arrest. They also recognized that Hurley was a town where crime expansion was not welcome. Dubbed "Sin City of the North", more than 75 saloons lined the five blocks of Silver Street; one of these was the Gogebic Hotel operated by Andrew and Emma Sigler.

Prohibition was in effect, but in Hurley it was ignored. A patron only need open the front door of any "shop" along Silver Street, saunter up to the bar, and purchase a drink of quality imported whiskey or less expensive home brew. Hurley saloon owners discovered that the Federal agents who stalked Silver Street looking for indiscretions would not bother them if they were unable to spot anything illegal. The only thing the saloon owners needed to do was keep their windows shaded. Some built dividers inside the door that blocked the view of the inside of the saloon from the street.

Once in a while federal agents were ordered to visit the "ice cream parlors" and "soda fountains" as the saloons had been called since prohibition was enacted. Word rapidly spread through town when a raid was about to take place; doors were padlocked and booze was hidden. When the FBI conducted a raid, they did so with discretion, picking and choosing only those licensed establishments that caused the city, county or the Federal government a problem. Since liquor licenses were not available during prohibition, some saloonkeepers purchased an ice cream parlor or restaurant license for about six dollars. Ironically, once a saloon owner purchased his license, the FBI agents could legally search his establishment at any time. There was no state requirement to buy a license, so saloon owners simply did not purchase one;

a loophole in Wisconsin State law protected them from being raided.

Prostitution was a lucrative trade in Hurley, especially when the spring log drives were over and hundreds of lumberjacks left the woods. An estimated 200 prostitutes practiced their trade in Hurley; the girls usually charged $5 or less and gave half to the house. Every few months, the sheriff raided establishments in an attempt to eradicate prostitution, but it was an exercise in futility. During one raid, the sheriff could locate only 17 of the hundreds of prostitutes who lived in Hurley. The rest of the girls had simply sashayed across the state line to stay in Ironwood or took the train to Ashland or Superior to wait until the heat was off. After a week or two, they came back to Hurley to carry on as though nothing had ever happened.

Just across the Montreal River from Hurley is the city of Ironwood, Michigan.

In 1924, the population of Ironwood was nearly 17,000, made up primarily of first-generation Western European immigrant families. For the most part, these families lived and worked in the mining locations. The well-to-do folks lived on the north side of town, separated from the mine locations by railroad tracks and the main street of Ironwood. On Aurora Street, the newly-completed Masonic Temple building housed the J.C. Penney Co. and Mrs. Frank Reed's restaurant on the first floor and the lodge on the second. The Curry, St. James and Commercial hotels were usually filled with traveling salesmen who arrived and left twice a day on the Chicago-Northwestern passenger train from Chicago and Milwaukee or the Soo Line from Superior, Wisconsin.

Ironwood had its share of illegal saloons scattered among its numerous locations, but Michigan had been a dry state since well before prohibition, so it was far more risky to sell illegal whiskey there, and most of the population took advantage of Hurley's funtime atmosphere.

Mid-April, 1924

"I never killed anybody before, Ray. I never even held a revolver."

"I'm telling you Andy, if you're gonna bump somebody off, you gotta know how to use a gun."

Ray and Andy stopped in a field on the side of the road to Lake Superior a few miles north of Ironwood, Michigan. There was still snow on the ground that the sun melted into muddy puddles. He drove them out in his old Ford roadster, and she had a revolver that she and Emma had bought back in February, a .38 caliber. Emma had given the hardware store owner an extra $10 so he wouldn't register it. Ray had the gun in her hand.

They took six tin cans and planted them at the base of a ridge.

"Watch me," she told him. "All you have to do is aim and shoot." She raised the gun and squinted at the targets. "Best if you squeeze the trigger. You can't jerk it. You have to take a deep breath and keep both eyes open."

Bang! She turned the gun over to Andy.

He raised it and shot at one of the tin cans 30 feet in front of him. The gun kicked, and he missed three feet too high.

"Remember now, you have to aim, hold your breath and squeeze," Ray told him patiently.

Andy did as she said, and this time he hit about a foot left to one of the cans. "Hey, this is okay. Easy when you know how to do it right. This is a real nice piece, Ray. Where'd you learn to shoot, anyhow?"

"My old man taught me."

Andy had spent most of his life behind prison bars, but this was the closest he had ever been to a handgun. He plinked until he had fired the remaining rounds. He gave the gun to Ray who emptied the spent cartridges, reloaded, and proceeded to pick off the cans one by one in rapid succession.

"See. It's all in the breathing," Ray reminded him.

"Yeah, I see what you mean."

Andy was stocky, about five foot eight, and looked strong as a bull. He was 27 years old, but his face bore the marks of years of pain and suffering at the hands of prison guards. Ray thought he was handsome; so did his wife, and so did Emma. He had one gold tooth that flashed when he smiled, something Andy did often. He was smoking a cigar. He wore a red and black mackinaw jacket and a cap with earflaps because it was April, and there was still quite a chill in the air.

Ray was in her early thirties. She had on a long dress and a coat that reached down to her ankles; on her head was a tight-fitting cloche. Her husband had brought her to Hurley just to have some fun, but Ray liked the town so she decided to stay when Jack Rice left town without her one day. She wasn't particularly pretty: thin, with a pointed nose, and her complexion showed the effects of too much bootleg gin. She had wrinkles on her forehead and crow's feet that inched out from her eyes, and she looked like 40 miles of bad road. She had a job at the Gogebic Hotel in Hurley as a maid and occasional baby sitter for the Sigler kids.

After they were finished on that chilly April day and because Emma Sigler had asked them to do it, Ray Rice and Andy Anderson conspired to murder Emma's husband, Andrew.

Friday, May 2, 1924

About two o'clock in the afternoon, Harry La Fave and his wife Mayme were returning to Hurley on Highway 10, known as the Mercer Road. They had gone to the lakes region about 20 miles south of Hurley to pick up Mayme's niece and her friend who planned to stay with the La Faves in Hurley over the weekend to do some shopping and maybe take in a movie.

It was still a little chilly outside, and the three women were bundled up in blankets. It had snowed some, the April kind of snow that was partly freezing rain. Even though the winter snow had not melted from the forest, signs of spring were everywhere. Mayme searched the sides of the road trying to see the new shoots of green grass and trilliums that accompanied the beginning of the season in Oma Township.

The girls were bundled up in the back seat wondering whether they should go to the Rex Theater in Ironwood where Booth Tarkenton's "Penrod and Sam" starring Bennie Alexander was playing. Mayme rode in the front passenger seat.

"Harry, we better hurry before the stores close. The Gogebic Fruit Store has strawberries for twenty-one cents. Should we get some?"

"Huh? What's that?"

"Strawberries. Maybe we should get three."

"Three strawberries? Why just three? What are we going to do with three strawberries?"

The girls in the back seat giggled.

"I can make shortcake, and we can have some strawberry shortcake."

"Oh, right. That's fine." Harry barely paid attention to her over the din of the constant chattering the teen-aged girls and his wife were making. The ice was nearly gone from Pine Lake, he noticed. His thoughts were on walleye fishing rather than moving pictures or strawberries. Harry was a barber, and opening day was just around the corner. He planned to take a week off work.

About a quarter mile past Layman's Creek, Mayme spotted something out of place off the side of the gravel road. "Harry, stop the car will you? It looks like there's a man lying in the grass back there on the right side of the road between those two little hills. Maybe he's hurt and could use some help."

Harry pumped the brakes and put the car into reverse, grinding the new Studebaker's gears as he did so. Then he slowly backed up the large touring sedan.

"There he is on the other side of the ditch," said Mayme as the two girls leaned over to get a better look. The man was lying face down in the grass, wedged between two fallen logs. Harry stuck his head out of the window.

"Hey! You okay?" he shouted in the general direction of the figure. There was no answer.

"Wait here," La Fave said, "I'll go over and have a better look." He got out of the car and jumped the three-foot ditch, being careful not to get his feet wet. He looked down at the man wearing a red and black checked mackinaw coat.

"Hey, fellah, you okay?" Getting no response, he nudged the body with his foot. Then he turned the man's head to have a closer look at him. "Well, I'll be damned!" La Fave muttered to himself when he recognized the dead man.

He turned back to the car and shouted, "Hey! It's Andrew Sigler, and I think he's dead. Guess somebody finally got to that ornery cuss. Been shot through the head!"

Mayme and the two girls got out of the sedan and looked where Harry was standing.

"Do you see anything, Harry?" Mayme asked.

He scanned the area immediately around Sigler's body, first examining the rock where Sigler's head was resting, then the area between two logs where the body was wedged. He looked back at his wife. "Nope. Just the body. I'm going to look around here and see if there's anything like a gun or something. You girls be careful. Maybe you best get back in the car."

La Fave walked about five feet from the body, circled around it, and then headed north where the ground was less swampy. About 20 feet away from the body, he spotted something and reached down to pick it up.

"Well now, look at this. Here's a man's cap. Wonder if it belonged to Sigler or to the guy who shot him?" Harry put the cap in the pocket of his coat.

He jumped over the ditch to the road and clasped his hands together in the small of his back and carefully examined the gravel road ahead of him, his eyes scanning every inch. He had walked about 10 feet when he found an empty cartridge. He picked it up and put that, too, in his coat pocket along with the cap.

Searching further alongside the road, he found three buttons and put those in the pocket where he had stowed the cap and the cartridge. As he continued to search, he heard a car coming from the south. He stepped to the middle of the road and began to shout and wave his arms to stop the car. The driver slammed on his brakes and the car skidded to a halt on the loose gravel.

The driver recognized La Fave and poked his head through the open windshield of the new Hurley Taxi Company automobile.

"What's the matter, Harry? New Studebaker bust down already? Ya should've bought a Ford," Eddie shouted. Eddie had trouble hearing and thought everyone else did, too.

"No, not a problem with the car. It's Sigler, the guy that owns the Gogebic next door to my shop. He's the one got a problem. Been shot dead. Come on over here and have a look."

Eddie got out of his taxi and ran over to where La Fave stood at the side of the ditch. He followed La Fave, and they both jumped the ditch and then looked down at the dead man.

He squatted down to have a closer look at the body and glanced up at La Fave. "Hoo-whee! Looks like somebody tried to blow his head off. Ya know, that bastard Sigler was the meanest guy I ever ran across. Don't know anybody who liked him. But for crying out loud, I can't imagine anybody would murder him. Wonder who it was that blasted him?"

"I sure don't have a clue," said La Fave, "but I know one thing. We darn well need to get the sheriff out here right away. I'll stay here and wait and you drive the women home and then call the sheriff's office from my house, okay?" Harry dug in his coin purse and fished out a quarter. "Here, this should cover the ride. Now be sure and let the sheriff know right away. Make sure you talk to Volant himself."

Eddie nodded his head. "C'mon, ladies, jump in and I'll take you home." Mayme, the niece and her girlfriend packed themselves into the taxi.

Mrs. La Fave looked at her husband as she sat in the front passenger seat. "Please be careful, Harry. The killer might still be in the woods."

"Naw. Uh-uh. A man who kills somebody wants to get away pretty quick. Nope, I think he's long gone by now." La Fave paused and saw the expression of concern on his wife's face. He took her by the hand and said reassuringly, "There's no need to worry, dear. Volant and Kalliomaa will be here soon. Now don't worry because I'll be fine. I'll be home in a little while."

EMMA AND ANDREW

Nobody said life was fair, and Emma Schroth's life certainly wasn't after her marriage to Andrew Sigler.

Emma was born in Washburn, Wisconsin, to Robert and Emelia Schroth on September 19, 1895. She had two brothers, Arthur, William Falkenberg, Emelia's son from a previous marriage, and two sisters, Maty and Emelia.

The Schroth Family. Emma is on the left.

Emma was about 5'3" tall, had light brown hair and a pretty face. She loved to cook, sew and clean. She left school in the seventh grade to stay at home helping her mother raise children and working odd jobs in private homes in the Washburn area.

She visited with her mother's sister in Milwaukee the summer when she was 16 and fell in love with the big city atmosphere. All Emma wanted out of life was a husband and children that she could care for, and Milwaukee was just the place to find a husband. She spoke to her parents, who made arrangements for Emma to live with her aunt and look for work. In early 1913, Emma took the train to Milwaukee and got a job as a domestic, went back to Washburn, packed her meager belongings, and moved to Milwaukee.

Her duties at her new job were to keep the house clean, wash dishes and tend to the owner's children when their live-in baby sitter was off, which left precious little time to meet the husband Emma so desperately wanted. Occasionally on Saturday nights she would go dancing at one of the large public ballrooms on Milwaukee's south side. One evening she met Andrew Sigler, an Austrian immigrant who had arrived in the United States from Neudorf, Austria, in 1908.

Emma was 17 years old when she met the handsome, 29-year-old, blue-eyed, brown-haired immigrant. They seemed to have a lot in common and enjoyed being together when they were courting. She could speak German, the only language in which Sigler could converse. They spent a lot of time together in the early days of their courtship; Emma taught Sigler English, and Sigler taught her fine embroidery, an art he had learned when he was a child in Austria.

He had also learned to be thrifty, and he had what Emma thought was a fortune. They talked of marriage, but Sigler wasn't very keen on the idea. He was intent on making money, and the more he could make, the happier he was. However, Andrew came around, perhaps because he thought that Emma would be a help in his quest to become a successful businessman.

They were married in Milwaukee by a justice of the peace on August 22, 1914, and moved into their new home at 563 Clinton Street.

The newlyweds argued a lot during that first year, but the fighting began in earnest after their first child was born on August 17, 1915. It had been Sigler's dream to own his own business, and he felt that children would only be in the way. It wasn't just having babies that bothered Sigler. He expected that

Andrew and Emma Sigler

he would have a cook and personal housekeeper with Emma around. Now the child was in the way of all that he had been led to believe in the old country, where a woman's place was helping her husband. *How can I run a business with kids around? I need a wife to help me run things. I need a cook and hostess, not a baby machine.* Sigler began to drink heavily, and became cruel and physically abusive to both Emma and Robert. He complained that the baby kept him awake at nights with his crying. He often threatened to strike him or throw him down the stairs. Emma tried in vain to explain that the baby needed to cry in order to expand his lungs, and it was the only way the child was able to express his emotions.

Sigler worked as a bartender and cook in the Milwaukee restaurant where they roomed, but what he wanted most was to own his own place somewhere. He needed more money than he and Emma had managed to save in three years so he quit his job, and they moved to Washburn where his father-in-law helped him get work, and moved in with Emma's family.

With the war going on, Andrew registered for the draft on June 5, 1917, in Washburn. His job at the time was "common laborer" working for the local box factory. Still unable to save money, they moved back to Milwaukee in 1918, but Sigler had a difficult time finding steady work. Even in Milwaukee, with its large German population, Germans had difficulty finding steady, well-paying jobs.

In 1919, Andrew, Emma and Robert moved to Hurley. Sigler got a job as a cook in a restaurant and started to make his presence known around town. Shortly after their arrival, Sigler arranged to manage the Gogebic Hotel and Restaurant, a red brick building near the southwest corner of Second Avenue and Silver Street. Andrew's drinking had already become a problem, and it became worse because of the responsibilities of managing the hotel and the constant quarrels between him and Emma.

The hotel owner and Sigler were happy because the business was making a profit, and Emma was happy that she lived near her parents. She loved her parents, but wanted to raise her family without interference from them. After all, she could visit them any time she felt like it; Washburn was only 40 miles from Hurley.

Soon after they moved into the hotel, Emma discovered she was pregnant again. Sigler wasn't happy about Emma's pregnancy, and during an argument about money and another mouth to feed, he kicked Emma in the stomach, and she mis-

The Gogebic Hotel in 1924 (True Detective Magazine, June, 1932)

carried. She went to the police who advised her to leave. There was nothing they could do, they told her.

Emma went to Washburn and stayed for three weeks to recuperate. She would have been glad to stay longer, but Sigler went to Washburn and turned on the charm.

"Please, Emma. Please come home. I promise to be a good husband, and I'm sorry for the way I've treated you. I'm trying so hard to make it in the business, and I'm fearful of losing everything we are working for. We can buy this business, but I can't do it without you."

Emma did not look at him. "Let me think it over, Andrew. You hurt me bad and I need to think it over. I don't know if I want to go back with you."

"Emma, I'm pleading with you. Please come home."

"No, Andrew. You go back to Hurley without me. I need more time."

Sigler returned to Hurley alone. Emma had a frank discussion with her parents about her ordeal. The Schroths thought it was a better idea for Emma to return to Hurley with their son-in-law rather than stay with them. After all, they told her, a woman's place was with her husband, and divorce was not a thing they wished to discuss.

Andrew drove to Washburn the minute that Emma telephoned him to come for her. After they got home, Emma found that Sigler had hired a couple of prostitutes and was selling bootleg liquor. She was furious, but Sigler told her that it would work out for them.

"Emma, it is a way of life here in Hurley. Don't you know that? It is a way that we can make a lot of money."

"There is a risk. And besides, we should be running a reputable business here, not a place where men can come in and take their pleasures with women. It just isn't right."

"I've made up my mind, Emma. We will have working girls. There is no risk because all the bars in this town have those girls. We will not be left out, and we will have more money than we ever dreamed about."

Emma reluctantly accepted her husband's new venture. She even became friendly with some of women and discovered that many had fallen on hard times and even felt sorry for them when they told her of their misfortunes.

In the fall of 1919, Sigler became ill with pneumonia and almost died. It took him two months to get well while Emma managed the restaurant alone, and the prostitutes went elsewhere for the time being. The major problem with his delayed recovery was that he drank liquor heavily during his recuperation.

Soon after, Emma discovered that she was pregnant again. Sigler was furious.

"I told you there is no place for a baby in the business. You are nothing but a bitch! A sow who is always in heat." Andrew cursed her and beat her throughout her pregnancy.

On June 17, 1920, Joseph Lyle Sigler, who they called "Junior" was born. When Dr. Urquhart delivered the baby, he refused to let Sigler see Emma and the baby because Sigler told him he preferred to kill Emma and Junior rather than have another baby around.

In September, Sigler demanded that Emma take Junior outside and let him crawl around the back yard and in the alley. "Maybe he'll die of exposure or something," he told her.

A year after Junior was born, Emma gave Sigler the news that she was pregnant again. He immediately ran to the drugstore and purchased an abortive of cotton root and wild cherry that Emma refused to take. On October 10, 1921, Sigler got in a fight with Alex McCarl, a 65-year-old lumberjack from Ironwood and threw several pieces of wood at him. The incident occurred while McCarl was delivering a load of wood for the F.G. Brown Company. McCarl drove to the rear of Kelley's Saloon next to the Gogebic Hotel when suddenly Sigler rushed into the yard and yelled at him for some reason or another. McCarl told Sigler that if he had trespassed or had done any damage he would gladly pay for it. While McCarl's back was turned, Sigler threw several chunks of wood at him, breaking his right arm and shoulder. McCarl sued Sigler in circuit court and was awarded $800.

That year, 1921, was a nightmare for Emma. She had two children to care for, was pregnant with twins, and to add to her workload, in November Sigler's parents, Joseph and Theresa, his brother, William, and sister, Theresa, arrived from Austria. Sigler and his brother argued constantly. During one of their numerous fights, he grabbed a rolling pin and broke it on his 19-year-old brother's arm. William was so terrified of Andrew that he slept in bed with his mother and father that night. Sigler didn't have much respect for his younger sister, either. He taught her to swear in English and tried to convince her to stay at the Gogebic Hotel where she could make a lot of money working as a prostitute. When Emma argued that this was all wrong, Sigler told her it was none of her concern and that she should never meddle in his affairs with his family. To make certain that she understood, he beat her with his fists and threatened to kill her with a cooking fork.

Unaccustomed to this behavior, Joseph, Theresa and William and Theresa Sigler moved to a house on Poplar Street, just a few blocks from the Gogebic Hotel. Their daughter, Theresa, left home shortly after.

Later that winter, in a drunken rage Sigler chased Emma, who was dressed only in her nightgown, out into Silver Street. He caught up with her and tore chunks of hair out of her scalp and tried to rape her while she was lying there in a snow bank outside the hotel. Her screams brought cigar maker Vince Clifford and coroner Joe Charbonneau to get Sigler away. Once again, she went to Mayor Lennon's office and pleaded with him to help her, but as before, it was viewed as a domestic dispute, and the authorities did nothing.

On March 3, 1922, Emma had twin boys, Lester and Leslie. Sigler ranted and raved like a madman when the twins were born. "Bad enough they come out one at a time. Now they come out two at a time," Sigler screamed at Emma. When the twins were three months old, Sigler wanted to take them outside, tie them up in a gunny sack and drown them in the river "like they do cats." Emma was horrified.

"Andrew, you are a mean man who cares nothing for your family, and only for yourself!" she shouted at him. "Why, those poor little twins are just babies. I'm ashamed that I ever married you."

"Don't you ever talk that way to me, Emma. I am the man in this house. What I say goes, and you better learn that. I don't want your babies around here. All they do is cry. If you want those babies, then you must do something to keep them quiet!"

"If you do anything to harm these children, I will divorce you, Andrew, and that's the honest truth."

"If you ever divorce me, Emma, I will kill you, and that's the honest truth!"

In April, 1922, Emma requested help from Mayor Lennon, Judge Shemondal and District Attorney Foster. She was advised to start divorce proceedings, but Sigler had told her time after time that he would kill her if she tried to divorce him. Foster suggested to Sigler that he should leave town for six months, but Sigler ignored his advice. He finally did leave for a short time in the fall and went to Superior, Wisconsin, where he met Louise Mason, a 46-year-old widowed, itinerant prostitute. When Sigler returned to Hurley, Louise followed him, turning up at the Gogebic Hotel in October and looking for a job.

When Louise arrived at the Gogebic Hotel that October, she stopped at the bar, ordered a couple of drinks and sat down in the restaurant and asked for Andrew. She had come in holding two yappy little dogs, put them down on the restaurant floor and sat in one of the booths. Sigler sat down across from her.

"Hi, Louise," he said.

"Hi to you," she replied. "I missed you."

Grinning, Sigler said "I've missed you a lot, too, Louise, but now that you are here everything will be wonderful for me."

"It will be for me, too, Andrew."

They chatted for about an hour, and that afternoon Louise moved into the first floor front bedroom of the hotel with two Pekinese, a hatbox, and a trunk loaded with her belongings. One of the dogs bit Junior when he tried to pet it, and when the children's bath water was drawn, Louise gave the dogs a bath first.

There is little doubt that considerable friction developed between Emma and Louise from the start. Emma would become furious whenever Louise bathed her dogs in the children's freshly-drawn bath water, and she certainly didn't appreciate that Sigler confided to Louise while he lied to her, his own wife. After the sheriff ordered Louise to leave town that December for prostitution, Sigler visited her in Superior and purchased a pair of lovebirds and a canary for her. He returned to Hurley to spend Christmas with Emma, the children and his parents.

Not all could have gone well over the next couple of weeks. Whether Emma asked him to leave or the sheriff asked him to leave, Sigler took off again for Superior. In a letter dated February 4, 1923, that Sigler wrote to Emma from Superior, he wrote that he hoped that she would rethink their marriage vows and let him come back to her.

Dear Emma,

You did not answer my last letter therefore I must write again. I do not feel good at all.... I know I have did you injustice, but you know I am hot and I cannot help myself. No doubt you will now start with the divorce and you know, Emma, if you can only forgive me once more I will be an entirely different man. If you take me back I will not beat you any more and also not a bad word for you and the children. Emma, otherwise you were never untrue to me but I know you had to bribe and jazz Foster. Otherwise you would never have gotten me out of the city but I will never throw it up to you. Do not be mad that I am writing this to you. It will be a new world for us when I come back. God be with you until we meet again.

Andrew[1]

Emma gave in to his pleadings. Sigler came back to Hurley and kept to his promise. For awhile.

They finally purchased the hotel on March 22, 1923, for $10,000, but fearing another lawsuit, put it in Emma's name. In April, Andrew and Emma mortgaged the property for a total of $10,144.39 and remodeled the building, adding 21 guest rooms and steam heat. At the rear of the first floor, they added several small single rooms and made the second floor into their living quarters. A two-column, eight-inch display ad was placed in the Ironwood Daily Globe on December 28, 1923, notifying the public that the Gogebic Cafe was open all night "Under New Management".

Inside the Gogebic Hotel and Restaurant. Andrew is behind the bar and Emma is standing.

[1] Verbatim from trial transcript

That spring and summer, the Siglers bought the two lots immediately to the east of the Gogebic Hotel and built an addition, or rather, another whorehouse with yet more rooms.

All seemed fine until November, 1923, when Sigler resumed his drinking and his violent behavior. Toward the end of the month at three in the morning, Sigler went to Emma's bedroom and demanded that she have sex with him. She told Sigler that she couldn't because it was the wrong time of the month. He knocked her off the chair she was sitting on, picked up a wash basin and threw it at her. She ran out the front door to Silver Street as far as the Office Saloon in her nightgown and bare feet. Sigler picked up a lead pipe and took off after Emma.

She saw police officer Jimmy Sommers coming to help her and shrieked, "Help me, Jimmy! Sigler is after me. I need help. He's gonna kill me," she yelled. "Shoot him!"

Sommers drew his gun and Sigler ran back into the Gogebic Hotel and upstairs to their quarters. Emma went into the hotel with Sommers. They found the three-foot-long lead pipe on the floor of the restaurant near the door where Sigler had dropped it. Emma quickly grabbed a blanket, a pair of shoes and a coat and went with Officer Sommers around the corner to the alley, where she slept in the backyard chicken coop until the hired help came at 6:00. The cop kept an eye on the back of the building until dawn, but there was no more trouble from Sigler that night.

The week before Thanksgiving, Sigler placed an ad in the Ironwood Daily Globe looking for an experienced chef, two experienced soda fountain girls and two experienced kitchen helpers.

The menu on Thanksgiving Day as advertised in the Daily Globe was food fit for a king. For a dollar the diners got "roasted Vermont turkey with chestnut dressing, live lobsters and oysters, celery soup and rice, mashed potatoes, stewed corn, English plum pudding and cranberry sauce."

In December, Sheriff Joe Volant and his deputies raided many of the saloons looking for prostitutes, illegal gambling and illegal booze. The Gogebic Hotel was one of the saloons that was raided, and Louise Mason was one of the many whores who were forced to leave town. Although most merely crossed the bridge to Ironwood, Louise took the train back to Superior.

With Louise gone, Emma hoped to get a family picture taken to send to relatives and friends. Sigler refused, telling her that it would "look too much like a sow with a litter of pigs."

By the end of 1923, Emma's mother and father had moved from Washburn to Superior. The Siglers paid them a visit, and Emma stayed with them while Andrew moved in with Louise Mason and her dogs. Andrew and Louise went to a play, had dinner out and had a great time. When they returned to Hurley, while they were eating dinner one evening, Sigler informed Emma that he had a venereal disease.

Junior, Emma, the twins and Robert.

"Well, you didn't get it from me," Emma shouted at him.

"No I didn't. I got it from a toilet seat."

"You can't get the clap from a toilet seat!"

"I did, and I'm going to give you a dose of it right now," Sigler yelled. "Get up to bed."

"I will do nothing of the kind. I don't want anything more to do with you. I'm fed up to here with you and your disgusting behavior."

"You'll do what I tell you to do," Sigler yelled at her and reached for a fork and stabbed her in the arm. Emma did nothing about the stab wound except bandage it.

On Christmas Eve, Robert was playing with Junior, running back and forth in the hallway and up and down the stairs. When Robert accidentally ran into him, Junior began to cry. Sigler got so mad at Robert that he beat him and banged his head against a wall repeatedly, then he hit him over and over with a piece of wood. On Christmas Day, Sigler told Robert that there were no presents for him. Sigler had thrown every gift out. When Robert started to cry, Sigler picked up a chunk of firewood and beat him again.

Emma told Mayor Lennon about the incident, and on the day after Christmas, Robert was taken to Superior by Mrs. Fall, a social worker, to stay with Emma's mother and father for a short time until Sigler cooled down.

On January 9, 1924, Louise Mason returned to the Gogebic Hotel, where she resumed her trade as a prostitute and barmaid. That was about all that Emma could stomach.

At the end of the month, Emma talked to Rachel "Ray" Rice about her problems with her husband. They discussed asking Andy Anderson to murder Andrew Sigler. They couldn't think of a better person to kill Sigler than Andy. Both Emma and Ray thought the world of Andy, and they knew he would do anything for them. Besides that, they reasoned, Andy was experienced. Maybe not with killing, but he knew his way around.

ANDY

Andrew Gudleski, Jr., was born on November 15, 1896, the first child of Polish immigrants Andrew and Maria Gudleski.

Maria's sister had already moved to Hurley a year before, and she wrote to the Gudleskis in Poland and told them to come. Within walking distance from her home there were a grocery store and a butcher shop just down the hill on Copper Street, and the parish church was a couple of blocks away. Silver Street, the main street of Hurley, had a clothing store, a pharmacy, two medical doctors and two dentists. Unfortunately there were also more than 75 saloons and burlesque houses with nude dancing girls. If it hadn't been for that, it would have been perfect. There were too many drunks and too many lights on Silver Street. "There might be some shameful things going on here," she wrote, "but there is plenty of work, and the people are nice."

Maria was pregnant with Andy on the steamship voyage across the Atlantic. The trip was terrible for her; they were berthed in steerage, and the seas were rough. When they arrived at Ellis Island, the crush of the crowds made her nauseous. The Gudleskis were herded off the ship, issued their nametags and placed in a pen along with other immigrants headed for Wisconsin. Maria's stay in the pen was brief. An alert immigration official who noticed that she was about to give birth rushed her through the paperwork and had her moved to the home of a midwife in New Jersey where Andy was born.

They arrived in Hurley shortly thereafter, and they rented a small house, not too far from her sister and her family on Germania Hill, with one large bedroom and a smaller bedroom no bigger than a closet. The kitchen was adequate, they had an outdoor toilet and electricity, and Maria set about making it a home.

The Gudleskis were Catholics in good standing at St. Mary's parish for at least a few years after they arrived in Hurley. Andrew, Sr., got an underground job shoveling ore into tram cars at the Germania mine. Underground mining was dirty and cold, and the miners made just a dollar or two for a 12-hour shift, but there was plenty of work, and payday was every week.

For Andrew, Sr., the good life was not as wonderful as it was painted by Maria's family, and he started to drink heavily. He would take his anger out on Maria and Andy. Andy's friends were no better off. Their fathers also worked long, hard hours in the mines, and many children were victimized by strict, overbearing parents.

Older boys worked when they could find jobs, and after their chores were done, they went swimming in the Montreal River and Lake Lavina, made slingshots and shot sparrows at the Scott and Howe lumber mill in the summer. In the winter, they made skis out of old barrel staves or raced down the hills in a sled or a cardboard box. The young boys would often grab onto the rear of the streetcar and slide to the next stop.

Playing in the red ore piles was heaven for small boys, and Andy was no exception. A gang of four or five would watch for endless hours as the huge wooden derrick hoisted ore from the stockpiles into ore cars. One of their favorite games was to was to hop a moving ore car and ride it until they got caught or until it reached the Ashland, Wisconsin, ore docks on the shore of Lake Superior. They also thought it fun to place a nail on the train tracks, and after the train wheels had flattened the nail, they would imbed the nail into a block of wood and hone their new knife into a sharp blade.

When the Germania mine was forced to lay off workers, Gudleski was unable to find steady work. He could speak Polish, but could neither read, write nor speak English, Italian or Finnish, the main ethnic groups in town. Unemployed, frustrated and angry over not working, Andrew Gudleski, Sr., became despondent and began to frequent the saloons on Silver Street. As his father's drinking increased, Andy's home life deteriorated, and because there was no income aside from what little charity they could get, Andy tried to find odd jobs to help out with expenses.

One morning in 1911, when he was 14 years old, Andy was up early cleaning a Silver Street saloon with another boy, 13-year-old Jack McCauley. The boys stole a gold watch and some cash. McCauley managed to run away, but Andy was caught by the owner and was sentenced to the Industrial School for Boys in Waukesha, Wisconsin, on January 21, 1911. The reform school, as it was popularly called, stressed agricultural knowledge, and became a center for dairy production. It also focused on industrial skills, producing shoes, brooms, chairs, mittens, and socks, among other things.

After two years, he was paroled to work on a farm, but had no sooner arrived there than he was in trouble with the farmer for stealing some food and was sent back to Waukesha.

He stayed there for another year, and then escaped with two other boys and ransacked a local elementary school. He was gone for only three days before the authorities found him not far away, hungry and cold, having decided that he had been better off in the reform school after all. On June 22, 1916, he was sent to the Green Bay Correctional Institution. It was there that he learned the electrician's trade. He became prisoner number 3032 and resided in Palmer House, Cell 26A.

He was at the prison at Green Bay for a year and was paroled during the summer of 1917, to a Mr. Everett in Eagle River to help install the electrical work at his resort. He was allowed to go home to Hurley that winter, but was arrested for drunkenness and disturbing the peace and was returned to the reformatory at Green Bay.

On March 12, 1918, when he was 22, Andy finally got his release and was paroled from the state juvenile system to electrician Louis Niebuhr in Verona, Wisconsin, until November 15. According to the records at Green Bay Correctional Institution, Andy was a model parolee. Niebuhr paid him $40 per month salary plus room and board. In November, after his release from parole, Andy moved back to his home in nearby Hurley with $67.55 in his pocket and soon found a job as an electrician for Friola's Electric Shop.

It appeared that Andy was rehabilitated. His newfound freedom in Hurley got him in trouble only once, when he was put in the Hurley city jail overnight for public drunkenness.

One evening while Andy was having a cup of coffee in at Allen's Quick Cafe, he noticed a young, pretty flapper who had come into the popular ice cream parlor several times before. She was always in the company of several other girls who looked and acted like they were after a good time. He thought she noticed him, too, so he walked over to the ladies and introduced himself. Andy, as usual, was smoking a cigar. The ladies smoked Lucky Strikes, he noticed. "My name is Andy, what's yours?" he asked the prettiest girl.

"I'm Lily, and these are my cousins Amby and Olga. Pleased to meet you, Andy."

"I've seen you in here a few times."

"We often come here for a little soda pop, if you know what I mean. Coffee is pretty good even." The three ladies giggled.

Andy grinned and asked, "So do any of you have my henway?"

"What are you talking about, Andy?" Lily asked.

"You know, my henway."

"What's a henway?"

"Oh, about 3 or 4 pounds."

They all laughed at Andy's joke.

"Lily, there's a dance in Ironwood on Saturday night. Would you want to go with me?" asked Andy.

"Well, I don't know you very well. It's rather soon to ask me out." She looked at her cousins. "Don't you think so, girls?"

"Aw, go on, Lily. Go with him. You've been eyeing him for three weeks now. It isn't as though he's a perfect stranger after all."

Andy and Lily began to keep steady company. They went dancing, partied and had an occasional drop of moonshine. Andy was a very good dancer it turned out, after Lily taught him the steps. Like Andy, Lily had an overly-strict father. Alex Randa was a Finnish immigrant who kept his European values of no card playing, no working on Sunday, and an attitude toward children of "spare the rod and spoil the child," and was a faithful member of the Finnish Temperance Society and a charter member of the Finnish Evangelical Lutheran Church in Ironwood. He had come to the Gogebic Range in 1893 to seek his fortune by working in the underground ore mines, saved his money, and in 1921, he seized an opportunity to invest in the Model Store in downtown Ironwood, a haberdashery and shoe store that catered to Finns.

One evening when Andy and Lily were at a dance, the Hurley police came looking for Andrew Gudleski but arrested young Andy for disorderly conduct instead of his father. It seemed that Andrew, Sr., had been out drinking one night and got into a fight. Andy explained to the Hurley police that it was his father they were looking for and not him. Shortly after, Andy paid $2.00 to legally change his name to Anderson.

Andy and Lily continued to see each other, and on January 14, 1920, when Lily was two months pregnant, he married her. The wedding reception was held in the Randa home on Oak Street in Norrie Location. The inside of the house was decorated with roses and tiny white flowers. All the Randa and Gudleski relations were invited, a blend of Polish Roman Catholics and Finnish Evangelical Lutherans, few of whom spoke English. Andy and Lily appeared to be very happy together; at least they were as happy as a newly-married couple could be while living with her parents, four sisters, 27 Finnish boarders and one maid.

A son, Randall, was born later that year, and Andy and Lily soon decided that her parents' home was far too crowded, so they moved a few blocks away to a rented house in Norrie Location on the corner of Beech and Tamarack Streets.

While Andy worked at his part-time job with Friola Electric, he also cleaned and tended bar at the New Central Saloon on the southeast corner of First Avenue and Silver Street in Hurley, just a block away from the Gogebic Hotel. Lily worked part-time as a clerk at Bostrom's grocery store on the top of Norrie Hill in Ironwood.

Tuesday, April 29, 1924

Louise returned to Hurley on the afternoon train, carrying her two dogs, and Sigler was at the station to greet her.

"Hi, Louise, welcome home," Sigler said.

"Glad to be back, Andrew." Louise took off her hat, brushed her hair out of her face with her hand, and looked at Sigler for a minute. "Is everything okay? You look angry."

"Emma is getting on my nerves again."

"Why? What happened?"

"She is always pushing me. I get so mad at her for telling me what I can or can't do."

"Yes, I have the same problem with her. She is either hot or cold. Honestly, that woman.... I swear she's crazy."

Sigler grabbed her trunk from the baggage cart, and they walked to his car. At the hotel, Louise washed her face and changed into a light dress and went into the kitchen where Emma was washing dishes. Her dogs followed her. When Emma saw the dogs, she scowled, but said nothing about them and tried her best to be cordial.

"Hi, Louise, nice to see you. How have you been?"

"Hi, Emma. I've been better. That train ride takes so long. Damn train stops at every crossing and whistlestop along the way. Too much smoke! All that train did was belch soot! First thing I did when I got here was run to the washroom and clean up."

"Well, you just rest up for a while. Maybe you can help me with these dishes before you do that. Here, take this towel and dry them."

"Guess it won't kill me."

Emma and Louise were finishing the dishes when Sigler came into the kitchen. He told them he was going to walk over to Erspamer's Hardware and buy some nails and a few building supplies for the garage.

After finishing the dishes, Louise went to her room and fell asleep, and Emma went upstairs to wake the twins from their naps.

Emma, Ray, and the children had finished with their supper by the time Sigler came into the restaurant from the back where he had been working on the garage. Robert sat at a table with Emma, but Junior and the twins were running back and forth chasing the barking dogs. Just then, Louise stomped out of her bedroom.

"Emma, can't you control those kids of yours?" Louise said. "I'm going upstairs where I can sleep."

"Look at what you did!" Sigler shouted at Emma. "Louise is angry, and you and those goddamn kids are to blame. Look at this mess! Kids and dogs all over the place. This is not the way to run a business!"

"Andrew, those children need to play and run. They're doing nothing wrong, and those dogs belong to Louise."

"Take them outside and let them run."

"It's dark outside."

"Then go with them! Get out of here, all of you!"

"So you want me to leave and take the children with me?"

"Ya! Ya! Go before I kill you all!" Sigler said, and he went upstairs.

Ray had heard his threats before, but Sigler seemed to be serious this time. She looked at Emma and saw that her face had turned bright red from anger. "Listen, kid, why don't you go over to the Burton House and get yourself a room for the night. I'll see to the children," Ray said.

"I'm scared of Sigler when he gets like that, Ray. I'm afraid he'll kill me and the children. He's crazy. I get so damn mad at him I could kill him myself."

"I don't think you should stay here, Emma. Don't worry about the kids. I'll sleep in their bedroom with them. Sigler won't try anything if I'm with them."

"Maybe I should take the children with me?"

"No, they'll be okay, I'm telling you; don't worry. Now, go get something to wear in the morning."

Emma grabbed some clothes and put on her coat and hat.

"Ma, don't worry. My brothers and me will be okay here. Pa won't hurt us," Robert told her. "Besides, I can help."

"Come here you three," Emma said to Junior and the twins. She took them in her arms. "Now you listen to Mrs. Rice and Robert. I'm going away for the night."

"Where you going, Ma?" Junior asked.

"Burton House."

"Why?"

"Because I'm gonna sleep there."

"Can I come?"

"No, you stay here with your brothers."

Junior started to cry, and the twins began to shriek.

"Go, Emma, and don't forget your handbag," Ray told her, and Emma walked out of the restaurant leaving her crying children and Louise's barking dogs behind.

Wednesday, April 30, 1924

Emma did not sleep well that night. She tossed and turned and heard every sound coming from within the huge hotel. She heard noises from Silver Street: Jimmy Sommers, the cop, walking his beat; the streetcar; the laughter of the whores and drunks.

And there was Louise. Too bad she had to come back from Superior. *Miss High-and-Mighty Painted Lady with her bobbed hair and those yapping dogs of hers peeing and crapping all over the hotel.*

Emma woke at 5 am. as she always did. She got dressed and walked the three short blocks from the Burton House to the Gogebic Hotel and opened up for the day. She went straight to the cast iron cook stove and started a fire and put on a large pot of coffee. Sigler was nowhere in sight, but she could imagine where he was. *I just bet he's sleeping with Louise. That's okay, as long as it's with her and not with me. That's enough of this day-dreaming. I've got to get the kids ready for school.* As soon as the day help came in the back door around 6 am., Emma trotted up the stairs and roused Robert. Robert would turn nine in August.

"Time to get up and get ready for school," she said.

In spite of the many beatings he took from Andrew Sigler over the years, Robert seemed like a normal child, but emotionally he was a wreck.

When Robert came downstairs to the restaurant, he saw Sigler fixing a drain plug on the bar.

"Whatcha doing, Pa?"

"Trying to fix this drain."

"Why? What's wrong with it?"

"Get out of here and quit bothering me while I'm working! Damn kids. Always in the way," Sigler shouted at Robert. He picked up a piece of firewood and threw it at Robert as he ran down the hall to the alley door.

"Stop it, Andrew, you're going to hurt him," Emma shouted.

"Get away from me. I'm busy!"

Emma left the hotel in a huff and wandered over to the New Central saloon. Andy was cleaning, and the place was empty.

"Andy, Sigler is going to kill me. You got to help me with this."

"I will not do it now, Emma."

"I didn't ask you to do it now. Tonight?"

"No, not tonight. Soon."

"Listen, Andy, I told you I'd pay you $2,000 to kill him, and I have $200 with me to show you that I am good to my word." Emma gave Andy the money, and he slipped it in his pocket. Emma went back to hotel, but Sigler had left.

Later that evening, Emma finally heard Sigler coming down the staircase. He had been upstairs washing up after spending much of the day building the garage to house their new automobile. She had swept the floor and was mopping up when Sigler came into the kitchen asking why Ray Rice was not helping her. *Ray is sick with the flu, you bastard. She can't help. She's in bed, you damn fool. She's probably sick of you, too. And that damn Louise always manages to have some excuse for not helping. Either she's too tired or she's in bed with some dirty, smelly lumberjack or miner.* Emma knew Andrew would beat her if she spoke her mind, though. She ignored him, and continued to clean the floor.

"Look at me and answer me when I talk to you! I ask you again, why is that pig, Ray, not here scrubbing floors with you," Sigler shouted in his thick, German accent.

"She's sick in bed. Where's your girlfriend, Louise? Why the hell can't she help out? You know what she did yesterday after she got here?" Emma shouted. "Not a damn thing! She slept all the way from Superior on the train. Oh, she helped me with the dishes once then she went upstairs to sleep! And then all she did last night was sleep, and she's probably still sleeping, because I haven't seen her all day except when she came down for a cup of coffee!"

Sigler went to the bar and poured himself another drink of moonshine and continued to yell at Emma. "I did not ask you why is Louise not here helping. That Ray, she is a good-for-nothing dirty sow. At least Louise, she brings money in!"

Emma scowled and replied sharply to Sigler's ranting and raving. "Shhhh, keep your voice down. The kids are in bed, and you know that we have guests."

"I told you to never talk back to me, you bitch! And I don't give a damn if the guests or the kids hear me."

Sigler grabbed a piece of firewood but thought better of striking Emma. He was too tired. He turned away from her and started for the stairs, taking his drink with him, but instead went to the bar, grabbed a bottle of booze and glared at Emma.

"I'm going to bed. I don't care where you sleep tonight, but I know something for sure. This is your last night in this shack. I want you out of here tomorrow or I'll kill you!" He stomped up the stairs.

Emma finished with her evening chores and went upstairs to tuck the children in for the night. When she got downstairs, Louise was in the restaurant chatting with patrons. Emma walked up to her.

"Come with me for a minute, Louise" Emma said.

Louise followed Emma to the booth next to the kitchen, and they sat down.

"What's the matter?" Louise asked.

"Sigler is worse. He told me that I have to leave, and that tonight is my last night here. He said he'd kill me if I ain't gone tonight."

"Aw, he doesn't mean half the stuff he tells you."

"He means it, all right. Louise, I'm scared. Would it be okay if I slept in your bedroom tonight?"

"I have a better idea. Let's sleep in the front room. There's two beds in there, and all we have to do is make them up."

"That's a swell idea, Louise."

Emma and Louise slept in the front bedroom that night, and they had no trouble from Sigler.

Thursday, May 1, 1924
5:00 am.

Andy Anderson woke up, threw on his clothes and went downstairs. Lily was watching their three-year-old son Randall eat his breakfast.

"Morning, Andy," Lily said.

"Morning," he said as he pecked her on the cheek. He bent down over the boy, screwing up his face and tickling him under the chin.

"Well, good morning to you, Randy. How's Daddy's big boy?" This brought chuckles from the child.

"I was just about to go upstairs and get you."

"Well, I'm here now."

Andy helped himself to some coffee and laced it with two teaspoons of sugar.

"Where's the cream?" he asked. He looked around the small kitchen.

"The cream is in the ice box where it always is." Andy opened the icebox door and poured a little cream in his coffee.

"Any bakery left?" he asked.

"There's a few saffron rolls in the warming oven. Help yourself."

He and Lily sat down at the kitchen table and watched Randy eat.

"You up to anything today, Lily?"

"Not this morning, but Bostrom asked me if I could come in at noon."

Lily paused and glanced at Andy. If there was anything that annoyed him it was when she wasn't home when he got there.

"And then I have singing practice at Helen's house tonight."

"Again? You were just there on Tuesday night. What time are you planning to be home?"

"Oh, about nine or nine thirty, I suppose. We usually chat for awhile after practice. When will you be home?"

"I'll be here at the usual time. Why would you care, anyhow?" he replied sarcastically. "You're never here when I get home. You're always off to chorus practice or whatever you do with those Finlander cousins of yours."

"I enjoy visiting with my cousins. And by the way, when are you going to quit that bartending job and do some electrical work like you were trained to do? Friola sure doesn't give you much work anymore. And there must be other jobs to do that pay better than Shorty gives you at that saloon. Next thing you know, we'll lose this house because we can't pay the rent, and I sure don't want to work for Bostrom the rest of my life. Andy, I love you. Can't you see that? All I want is for us to be happy. I just wish we could leave this lousy city and move to Milwaukee. Maybe we could go to Detroit. The automobile factories there are hiring, I've been told. I would love it if we could get out of this place."

"So would I, but I'd have a tough time finding a better job anywhere else with my prison record."

"Maybe we should take a trip and see what kinds of jobs there are in Milwaukee? We could stay with my sister and her husband. Who knows, maybe Roy could help you find a job."

"Why is it that we have this same talk every goddamn morning? There are times, Lily, when I really miss prison!" he shouted and slammed the door behind him.

Andy trudged through the muddy slush and snow to his car, a brand-new Ford coupe he had bought the day before from the Walter Point Garage in Ironwood, making a down payment with the $200 Emma Sigler had given him.

* * * *

5: 15 AM

When she woke, Emma washed, dressed and went into the restaurant and gazed absent-mindedly out the window. Snow was falling in big flakes that melted when they hit the cobblestones on Silver Street. *God, I wish I could get a chance to sleep. I'm so tired. Every night I've had to put up with him. I'm about at the end of my rope. What am I going to do? I don't think Sigler will kill me. I know he'd like to, but I don't really think he will. I know he'll try to throw me out, though. What will happen to the children? I own the hotel and the restaurant. They're in my name, not his. I'm not going to worry about this. If anybody has to leave it'll be him, and he can take that awful Louise with him. I just wish he'd die.*

Emma lit the fire in the stove and started the coffeepots brewing, then unlocked the front door to the restaurant. *Wonder what kind of mood Sigler will be in this morning. He's so damn unpredictable.* She walked down the hall and opened the bolt on the back door. *The kitchen is a mess, but I don't care. The girls will be here soon to help straighten up.*

Then she sat down in the restaurant and stared blankly out the front window. Silver Street was already busy. She saw the 5:30 streetcar go past on its way to Ironwood and Jessieville with its load of miners and hired girls coming from Cary, Gile and Montreal. She heard the whistle of a train engine as it picked up speed on its way with a load of ore on the way to the ore docks at Ashland. There were a few cars. It was light outside, but the skies were overcast. She looked north over Lake Superior and west toward Ashland and Washburn. *Rain clouds or maybe more snow. Weather sure can change in a hurry this time of year.* The smell of fresh-brewed coffee permeated the room.

Well, guess I gotta get going. Washday again. And so begins another day. Tuesdays and Thursdays were laundry days at the Gogebic Hotel and Restaurant.

The back door opened and Jean Hartley, one of the maids, came in. Soo Ling, the cook, arrived just behind her and headed for the kitchen.

"Good morning, Chinaman." Emma liked her cook because he couldn't speak much English, and he was kind and courteous, besides. Soo Ling bowed his head and smiled. "Morning, Missy."

"Morning, Emma," Jean said.

"Good morning, Jean. How are you today?"

"Fine, thank you, Ma'am." Jean paused, and then glanced around to see if anyone might be nearby.

"Emma," she whispered, "I wonder if I can talk to you about something? Maybe it's nothing, but I thought about it all night."

"Sure, come on and sit down. Oh, bring me a cup of coffee and grab one for yourself."

Jean poured two cups of coffee and brought them to the table and sat down across from Emma. She glanced around the room as if she were expecting to see someone.

"I don't know how to say this, Emma, but it has to do with Mr. Sigler. It's really none of my business. Like I said, it may be nothing, and maybe you already know, but all of us are aware of how he treats you and such, I just thought you ought to be told. Anyhow, yesterday I saw your husband hide a gun."

Emma was startled. "I didn't know that he has a gun! My God, that's all we need around here. He knows I'm deathly afraid of guns around the kids. How was it that you saw him with it?"

"Well, I was in the hallway when I saw him hide it in the crown of that old wood stove in the back of the kitchen, the part that opens on the top where dishes and bakery can be warmed."

"Can you show me the place where he put it?" Emma followed the girl to the kitchen. Jean opened the crown of the old, rusty kitchen stove.

"It's right in here. This is where he put it."

Emma reached in and took out a loaded .32 caliber Colt automatic. She turned the gun over in her hand and examined it. *I've got to do something with this thing. I don't want to throw it away because it might come in handy someday, but I've got to hide it someplace where he can't find it and where the kids can't get at it. Someplace where he'll never dream of looking. And I know just the place.*

"I really want to thank you for telling me, Jean. Honestly, I don't know what I'd do without you and some of the others. You're all so kind to me."

Emma walked down the hall to the laundry room. She stuffed the gun into a baby buggy and covered it with a blanket.

They heard Sigler coming down the stairs. Jean went through the restaurant into the hotel and Emma began to sort clothes.

Sigler mumbled an obscenity and went into the bar to pour himself a drink.

* * * *

After Andy left home that morning, he went directly to the New Central Saloon, cleaned up the floor and bar, checked the supplies, and sat down, put his feet upon a table and read the newspaper. He was finished about noon, and went to La Fave's barber shop to get a shave and a haircut. Then he went next door to the Gogebic Hotel and bought some lunch. Sigler was busy behind the bar and Andy waved to him. Sigler waved back. Emma came out from the kitchen and sat down in the booth across from Andy.

"How's it going, Andy?" she said. Then, when Sigler wasn't looking she whispered, "Meet me at the corner at two o'clock. We need to talk."

"What about?"

"Shhh. We can't talk here. Just be there, okay?"

"Sure," Andy said and continued eating his lunch.

Emma left the booth. "See you, Andy. And take care of that little one," she said as she wandered over to chat with another lunch-time diner.

* * * *

2:00 pm

Emil Erickson sat in the window of his employment agency and saw Emma pacing up and down the sidewalk. After several minutes of watching for him, she saw Andy approach her, and the two went around the corner and walked toward Copper Street.

"Andy, for Christ sakes, when you gonna do the job?" Emma demanded.

"Don't worry, I'll get it done," he replied.

"Sure. When? You told me a month ago that you'd do the job, and Sigler is getting meaner every day. I don't know, but he just may kill me first. I'll find somebody else to do it if you won't."

"Yeah? Who would you get?"

"I have friends. There's a man here in Hurley who would do it for me."

"Yeah? What's his name?"

"I won't give you his name."

"I'll do the job, but I have to wait until the right time."

"I'll do it myself if you won't."

"No, you can't do it because a woman always bungles a job like that."

"I'm desperate, Andy. Please do it. I want to see him gone."

"I know, but the time has got to be right. I'll need some money to get on the lam for awhile. How much did you say you'll pay me for doing the job?"

"Two thousand bucks, but I gave you $200 yesterday. I can give you another $150 if you need it." Emma was excited about the prospect of ridding herself of Sigler forever.

"Can you do it tonight, Andy?"

"I think so. Lily has singing tonight so she won't be the wiser. I think I'll need more dough than $150, though."

"All I can get my hands on is $150. I can get more later on. After Sigler is dead, I'll collect his insurance. Then I'll give you the rest of the two thousand."

"Guess I can make it on $150 then."

"Okay," Emma said. "I'll get the money. Come back here in about 15 minutes. Just hope Sigler doesn't catch me. I've been tucking some cash away in places where he won't look for it."

Emil Erickson, sitting in his window, caught all of this. He couldn't hear what was said, but whatever it was, Emma and Andy held his interest. When Emma turned to go in the Gogebic Hotel, Emil went to get a cup of coffee. He went back to his seat in the window, lit up a Chesterfield and resumed his survey of Silver Street. After a few minutes, he saw Andy leave the New Central at the same time as Emma left the Gogebic Hotel. They went around the corner as they had earlier, staying out of earshot of the cop in the police booth.

Emma handed an envelope to Andy. Inside was the $150 he had been promised.

"What time?" Emma asked him.

"Oh, when I get done at work. Eight or eight thirty I guess," Andy told her.

"Okay. Come by the restaurant. Sigler will be there. Ask him if he would like to go for a ride in your new Ford. Use some excuse. Then take him out someplace and kill him."

* * * *

8:30 pm

Andy drove his new Ford coupe down the alley and parked it in back of the restaurant and went in through the back door. He looked for Emma in the laundry room and the kitchen as he walked down the hallway to the restaurant and bar area, and spotted Sigler in the kitchen.

"Hey, Sigler," he yelled. "Watcha doing tonight?"

"Dunno yet. Why?"

"Wanna take a ride with me in my new car?"

"New car? Where did you get enough money for a new car?"

"I robbed a bank," Andy laughed. "C'mon. Any place you want to go?"

"Well, yes. I think I'll take you up on that. I've been meaning to go to Pence and pick up some girls. And I have to get some chickens in Saxon."

"Well, let's drive out there," Andy said.

Sigler thought a minute and then said, "Sure, I'll go. I'll get my coat and cap from upstairs and tell Emma where I'm going. Why don't you wait in the restaurant? Maybe get a piece of pie. Cook just baked some this afternoon."

Sigler started to walk upstairs, but Andy caught up with him in the hall.

"Hey, Sigler, wait a minute," Andy said. "I can't load chickens and girls in my new car. Not enough room. I'll run over and get the roadster."

It took Andy just a few minutes to drive to the New Central, exchange cars and get back to the hotel. He sat down with a couple of lumberjacks and asked a waitress for a piece of pie and a cup of coffee. He saw Sigler coming down the stairs.

"Emma!" Sigler shouted.

"What? I'm in here!" she shouted back.

Sigler found her with their son Robert in the restaurant eating a piece of pie. Emma was drinking coffee.

"Emma," he said, "I'm going to get some chickens in Saxon with Andy. I'll be back late. And that goddamned pig, Ray Rice, better not be here when I get back. You got that?"

Emma didn't answer. *I'll see you dead before I tell Ray to leave.*

Sigler went back to the booth in the front of the restaurant where Andy was sitting chatting with the lumberjacks. "I'll just be a minute," he told Andy.

"Okay, I'll meet you out the alley."

Andy finished his pie and gulped his coffee, then went out the back door and walked through the alley and cranked up the roadster.

Sigler looked around for Louise and found her in the kitchen. "I'm going to Saxon to pick up some chickens and then I'm going to Pence. I'm going to get some working girls. Don't tell Emma where I'm going."

"You're not going to take your new car, are you?"

"No, a guy is driving me."

"Okay, love. Get some nice young ones. They get us a lot of dough."

"Ya, I'll do that."

Sigler walked out the back and got into the car with Andy.

"Andy, let's go to Saxon first and get those chickens, then we'll go to Pence on the way back. There's a couple of girls there who I want to talk to about working at the hotel. Know what I mean?"

"There's some real nice looking girls in Pence," Andy replied absentmindedly.

There was more on Andy's mind than a quick fling with a young girl. He was planning out how he would kill Sigler. *There's the abandoned mine shaft at Germania. I could shoot him and dump his body down the shaft. Nobody will ever find him. There's lots of bodies down there people have told me, but there's the insurance. She won't get any insurance if they don't find his body. Maybe I'll just dump him on the shore of Lake Lavina. Jesus, I don't want to do this.*

He put his hand in his pocket and felt the cold steel of the .38 Colt revolver. It was just over nine inches long with a four inch barrel. There were six bullets in the chamber. At the full cocked position, the revolver was ready to fire with a light squeeze on the trigger. Andy and Sigler drove south past Lake Lavina where he planned to shoot Sigler. He stopped the car.

"Something wrong, Andy?" Sigler asked.

"Naw, I gotta pee," Andy replied. He got out of the car and walked to the passenger side.

Andy began to have second thoughts about killing Sigler. They were not the best of friends, but Andy really had no grudge against Sigler, and even though he was cruel to Emma and the kids, he had never done wrong to Andy except once when Sigler threw rocks at him after Andy had to drag him off Junior. Andy decided to wait.

He walked to the side of the road and peed in the bushes. Then he got back in the car, and the two of them drove to a farm near Saxon. Sigler bought the chickens, put them in a crate and tied the crate to the back seat of the Ford roadster.

Andy and Sigler made their way from Saxon to Pence, a distance of about five miles. They stopped in a saloon, and Sigler talked to a couple of 16-year-old flappers. Bobbed hair, short skirts, smoking cigarettes. *These little ones sure are pretty.*

"You girls want to make some big money?" he asked them.

"Sure do, mister. And what might you have in mind?" one of them inquired.

"Come to Hurley with me and live in my hotel. I need girls for maid service and sure could use some kitchen help. I have four little children who need mothering. My wife died a few months ago, and I need some help," he lied. Once they got there, he would break them in quickly, he reasoned.

"Uh, mister, we have to think it over," the girl said. "Come back here again tomorrow night and we'll give you an answer, okay?"

"Ya, I will do that," Sigler told them. He didn't keep that appointment.

* * * *

9:30 pm

Andy dropped Sigler and the chickens off in the alley behind the Gogebic Hotel, drove the roadster to the New Central, got in his new coupe and drove home to Ironwood.

Sigler put the chickens in the coop just outside the back door and walked down the hall past the rooms and kitchen. Louise was having a drink at the bar.

"So, did you get everything done?" she asked.

"Ya. Got the chickens and talked to some little girls in Pence. I'm going to meet them tomorrow night and bring them here."

"Good. Come sit with me and have a drink or two."

"Is Ray Rice still here?"

"Yes, she is," Louise told him.

"Just a minute," Sigler replied. He went to the bar, took a medicine bottle out of his pocket and poured several drops of croton oil into a bottle of wine, then poured himself a glass of moonshine.

"What are you doing, Andrew?" asked Louise as she went to the bar.

"I'm gonna take care of that sow, Ray Rice. Don't tell, but I put some croton oil in this wine, and I will give it to her to drink."

Louise laughed. "Hey, you dirty old son-of-a-bitch, don't you know that croton oil gives a person the shits," Louise said. "I've heard people get the trots for days after taking just a little bit. She's gonna be running to the crapper all night."

Sigler laughed, too, when she described Ray's pending discomfort.

Louise walked behind the bar and knocked loudly on Ray's bedroom door.

"Hey, Ray!" she shouted. "C'mon out and have some wine with us before you fall asleep."

Ray was lying in bed fumbling with a crossword puzzle.

"In a minute," she called back. "Hang on. All I have on is my slip. I need to put on some clothes."

Ray, never one to say no to a free drink, put on her robe and joined them. Sigler poured her a glass of the spiked wine and Ray sipped it. "Good stuff. Thanks for inviting me," Ray said.

"Here, have another, Ray."

Sigler poured another glass, and Ray sipped it.

"Ya know, Andrew, you ain't such a bad egg after all," Ray said. "You either, Louise. I didn't think you guys liked me very much."

"Not so, Ray," Louise said. "You're a swell lady. Know something else, Ray? You've been holed up in this place too long. You should take a trip somewhere."

"Where would I go? St. Paul? Take the chance of meeting my husband? No, I think I'll...."

Before Ray could get the rest of the words out of her mouth, she got up and ran for the bathroom at the end of the hallway.

"Jesus, Andrew, now I feel sorry for her," Louise confessed.

"Never mind sorry. She's nothing but a pig. Be sure to tell anybody who asks that you had some of that wine, too, but don't tell them that I put croton oil in it."

"For Heaven's sake, no. I wouldn't tell anybody."

They drank alone until eleven when they went to bed.

Emma had been upstairs putting the children to bed, and afterward, she went to her own bedroom. At 1:00 am, she heard Junior whimpering and went to tend to him. On the way past Sigler's bedroom, she glanced in and saw him asleep.

Friday, May 2, 1924
5:30 am

Sigler got out of bed quietly to avoid waking the children. He crept down the stairs and grinned when he thought about Ray and the croton oil. When he got downstairs, Emma was in the kitchen starting her morning routine. She heard him moving about in the hallway.

"I thought I told you to leave last night and take that bitch Ray Rice with you," Sigler said when he saw her.

"If anybody ought to leave, it should be you! And take your whore with you," Emma shouted.

"Don't talk that way to me!" he shouted back at her. "And what is this about you applying for a driver's license and putting the car in your name?"

"I wanted one. I know how to drive and I had to get a driver's license."

"I told you that you were not allowed to drive," he shouted.

Sigler was about 10 feet from her. He picked up a bottle and threw it at her, hitting her in the chest. Just as he was reaching for another bottle to throw at her, Emma picked up a wooden clothes pole and smacked him in the side of the head as hard as she could.

"I told you never to hit me back," Sigler yelled. "I told you if you ever hit me back I'd kill you. You're done for now. I'll kill you. I'll kill you! Right now!"

He ran over to the old stove and fumbled around for the gun. Emma was quicker, running down the hall to the laundry room. From the kitchen, Sigler couldn't see her take the gun from the baby buggy. He looked around the kitchen for a weapon, grabbed a meat cleaver from the counter and ran from the kitchen toward the laundry room. Emma ran across the hall to Room Seven and locked the door. She leaped up on the bed and aimed the revolver at the door and waited for Sigler to come at her.

He easily broke open the door to the room.

"I'm gonna kill you, you son-of-a-bitch" Sigler yelled. He raised the meat cleaver and ran toward Emma. She grazed him on the left hand with the first shot. He dropped the cleaver and yelled. Then Emma shot him in the side. He fell to the ground, writhing in pain. She jumped off the bed.

"You're never gonna hit me again, Andrew," she said, and as she pointed the pistol at him, Sigler's eyes were open wide. He was bleeding hard from the wound to his side. He tried to grab her, but she moved away.

"No! No! Please you do not kill me. Have mercy! I will be good to you. I do not want to die," Sigler pleaded. "You are my wife. Our children. What becomes of them?"

"Shut up! Shut up!" Emma yelled and kicked him in the side, pointed the pistol at him, and shot him in the head.

There was blood on Emma and all over the room, blood on the bed, on the floor and on the walls. Emma panicked, dropped the gun, tore the sheets from the bed and threw them on the linoleum floor.

"Now what in hell am I supposed to do with you," she said to the lifeless Sigler. She looked at Sigler's body and suddenly realized what she had done.

Oh, my God! Oh, my God! I killed him! What am I gonna do! Think, Emma, think. The cops. I must find a cop. No, got to protect the children from this. Andy. Andy. I must call Andy. He'll know what to do. I have to get the babies up. I have to clean up this mess. Oh, my God. Oh, my God. Look at all the blood. I hope nobody heard the shots. I'm all covered with blood. Oh, my God. I've got to wash this blood off me.

She ran to the laundry room and washed the blood off her hands and face, then went through the kitchen to the front door of the dining room looking up and down Silver Street. There was no sign of commotion, just the normal seven o'clock comings and goings. There was no one gathering in front of the hotel. She was safe.

She ran to the phone and called the New Central saloon. Andy answered.

"New Central, Anderson here."

"Andy, this is Emma. I need a favor done."

"Okay. What?"

"There are some jugs that need moving from the back," she lied. "They're too heavy for me to lift. Could you come over and do that for me? I don't want to bother Sigler."

"I really can't leave just now."

"Please, Andy. It won't take but a few minutes."

"Aw, but I shouldn't leave the place alone. Just for a few minutes then, okay, Emma. I'll be right over."

I better take the old car. There's more room, and Emma didn't tell me if she wants me to take those jugs someplace. Andy drove the short block from the New Central to the rear of the hotel. He found Emma in the kitchen, crying.

"What's the matter?" Andy asked her.

"Something terrible has happened."

"What is it?" Andy asked.

"I just shot Sigler."

"Where is he?"

"In the back. In Room Seven," she told him.

"Where's Room Seven?"

"In the back across from the laundry room."

Andy went to the rear of the hall and saw Sigler lying on the floor, blood oozing out of his head and side, pooling beneath him on the linoleum floor. He went back to the kitchen.

"It's Sigler all right. He looks dead," he said to Emma. "How'd it happen?"

"He tried to kill me with a meat cleaver."

Andy went back to Room Seven and saw the cleaver on the edge of the bed. He also found the .32 Colt automatic and three spent cartridges on the floor. He left them there and walked back to the kitchen.

"What's to be done with his body? What arrangements will you make?" he asked.

"I want you to take it out and get rid of it."

"I can't do that, Emma."

"Yes, you can. Now help me with this. Please?"

Andy thought about this for a moment, realizing that he might be already implicated in Sigler's murder, since Emma and Ray Rice knew that he had agreed to kill him. But that was just boasting because he wanted to sound tough and manly to impress the women. *Aw, but she's been such a nice lady to me, and I feel so sorry for her and her kids.* Reluctantly, he gave in to her request and told Emma he'd help her.

"Where should I get rid of him?"

"Hell, Andy, I don't know. Use your imagination. Christ, dump him down a mine shaft or something. Just get rid of it so I can clean up in here before people start snooping around."

"Can't dump him down a mine shaft. You won't get the insurance for seven years if they don't find him."

"Right now, I don't give a tinker's dam where you dump it. Just get it out of here."

Andy went back to Room Seven and picked up the corpse. Then he and Emma managed to get Sigler's coat on the body. He dragged the corpse to the alley door and propped it up next to his roadster, struggling to get it in the passenger side, and set it up as best as he could so it would look like a normal passenger. He went back to Room Seven, picked up the gun and three cartridges and put them in Sigler's pocket.

"Emma, I will take the body and dump it off someplace. I don't know where, but I don't want to chance doing it at the mine. Too many people around during the day."

"Whatever you think, Andy. And take this money."

"I don't want any money."

"It's the least I can do for you for helping me out like this. Here, take it."

"No, I don't want it."

Emma slipped $40 into the pocket of Andy's coat and went back to Room Seven. She spotted Sigler's hat on the floor, picked it up and rushed to the alley.

"Wait a minute, Andy," she yelled, "you forgot his hat."

Andy drove up the hill and south on Highway 10 toward Mercer. The dirt road snaked through the woods, wet and muddy from melting snow. Pot holes and large, water-filled ruts kept the drive to barely a crawl. The body kept falling over and Andy had to adjust it frequently. He met several cars on the way. Thirty minutes later when he was near Layman's Creek, Andy stopped the car, opened the passenger door and dragged Sigler's body out to the ground. He picked it up and threw it as far as he could into the grass on the side of the road. On the way back, he slowed near the water plant and threw the .32 caliber that Emma had used to shoot Sigler into the Montreal River. Then he went back to work as if nothing had happened.

* * * *

8:00 am

Emma finished cleaning up the bloody mess in Room Seven and went upstairs to wake her children.

"Robert," she asked her oldest, "did you hear anything like firecrackers going off this morning?"

"No, Ma, I didn't," the boy replied. "Why?"

"Well, I thought I might have, but I guess I dreamt it," Emma answered. "Now wash up and get ready for school. I've a nice breakfast waiting."

"Yes, Ma."

After Robert had eaten and she had seen him off to school, Emma woke and dressed Junior and the twins and brought them downstairs to play and knocked on Ray's bedroom door.

"Come in," Ray said as she awoke, still feeling the effect of the croton oil.

"Sigler's dead," she said, and sat on the bed next to Ray.

"How?"

"Did you hear a gunshot this morning?"

"No, I didn't," Ray replied.

"Good, because I shot him back in Room Seven."

"What in the world were you doing in Room Seven?"

"I was in the kitchen and he came after me with a meat cleaver, so I grabbed the gun that I hid in the buggy. He came after me so I ran into Room Seven. He broke the door, and I shot him."

"What happened to his body?"

"It was a mess in that room. Blood all over the place. I called Andy and he came over and took him away, and then I burned the linoleum and bedding in the coal furnace."

"Oh, Christ," Emma said, "I think I hear Louise coming down. She'll be asking questions. I better go. I'll tell you more later."

* * * *

8:55 am

Louise came downstairs to the dining room where Emma sat after leaving Ray.

"Where's Sigler?" Louise asked.

"There was a man came looking for him earlier this morning. He said the man was taking him to Ashland."

"Funny, he didn't say anything to me."

"I guess he doesn't tell you everything, then, does he?" Emma scowled.

"Seems like he'd have said something, anyhow," Louise said, and left the dining room.

Emma said nothing.

After Louise left, Emma went across the street to the Iron Exchange Bank where she withdrew money to make the payment on the car Sigler had recently bought. She paid the bill at Norman's Auto just down the block on Third Avenue and arranged for Harold Norman to teach her how to drive the car later that morning. Although Emma had driven a Model T with a magneto and hand crank, she had no idea what to do with a key, a gearshift lever or a clutch.

* * * *

Iron County Sheriff Joseph Volant, age 36, was beginning the second year of his two-year term of office when the murder of Andrew Sigler took place. He had served as the undersheriff during the term of the past sheriff and learned a lot about saloon busting during that time. Fights, an occasional stabbing or a gunshot wound were common, but he knew very little about murder. Volant owned a butcher and confectionary shop on Copper Street. He lived with his wife, Katherine, in the sheriff's residence at the Iron County Jail.

The undersheriff was Richard Kalliomaa, a short, stocky, fireplug of a man of Finnish heritage who was raised on a farm in Oma Township, less than a mile from Layman's Creek where La Fave was guarding Sigler's body. Kalliomaa had grown up in the fields and woods where hunting and trapping were a way of life and had a keen sense of observation. He had been a member of the Hurley police department before being chosen for the undersheriff's job.

* * * *

3:15 pm

Joe Volant and Dick Kalliomaa were sitting in the jail office chatting with the prisoners in the bullpen. Volant had just bitten off a hunk of plug tobacco and was relaxing with his feet on his desk when the phone rang. He lifted the bell-shaped receiver from its hanger.

"Sheriff's office," he answered.

The voice at the other end yelled through the phone, "Joe! This is Eddie, the guy who drives the taxi. Sigler's been killed down by Layman's Creek. Harry La Fave is down there now!"

Volant lowered his feet to the floor, aimed a stream of tobacco juice at the spittoon, and pulled the receiver away from his ear.

"Hold on, fella, slow down. And quit shouting, Eddie, I ain't deaf. It's you that's deaf. Now tell me what happened."

"I was going back to Hurley and Harry La Fave stopped me. He found Sigler's body lying on the side of the road. Somebody blew a hole through his head. Harry said that I should tell you to get down there. He's down about a quarter mile this side of Layman's Creek on the Mercer Road."

Volant reached for his gun belt. "I guess you heard, Dick."

"Couldn't help it. Man's mighty noisy. Can't hear worth a damn."

"Lock the bullpen and let's go." Then he spoke into the telephone. "Eddie, run over to Charbonneau's store and tell him where to meet us."

Volant and Kalliomaa got into the sheriff's car, and Kalliomaa turned the crank on the siren. They headed south on the winding dirt road past the bluffs, Lake Lavina and through the woods in Oma Township. Twenty-five minutes after Eddie's call, they approached La Fave's car parked along side the road and pulled over.

"What have we got, Harry? Eddie says it's Sigler."

"It's Sigler all right. Look over here, Joe." La Fave motioned to the place where Sigler's body lay. Volant and Kalliomaa got out of the sheriff's car and went to where LaFave was standing.

The sheriff glanced at the ditch and jumped over it. He walked over to the body, stared down for a few seconds and shook his head in disbelief. "Jesus, Mary and Joseph, would you look at that. There's a hole clean through the head. He probably didn't even feel it. Mean as sin to his wife and kids." He sighed and turned toward La Fave. "Guess Emma's problems with him are over and done with." He squatted down and felt for a pulse on Sigler's neck before searching the dead man's pockets. Slowly, he stood up and scanned the area.

When Kalliomaa joined them he said, "there are footprints all around here. Harry, they yours?" La Fave assured him that he had looked all over and his were the only ones.

"See anything up there, Dick?" asked Volant as he looked toward the road.

"Nope. Not a thing."

Kalliomaa bent down over the body and turned Sigler's head so it was out of the shadow of the log.

"Look at this. Powder burns on the left side of his head. I'd say the gun was fired from a pretty close distance, about a foot or so. If it wasn't point blank, I don't think we'd see any powder burns. I read that stuff in a book."

Kalliomaa checked the immediate area around Sigler's body. "You know what's funny, Joe? I don't see any blood. Just a drop or two here on this rock where his head hit. None in the grass or the ditch and none on the road, either. Probably killed someplace else."

He stood up and looked around. "Know something else? I don't see any tracks where the body was dragged from the road. With all this muddy ground, you'd think we'd find something. And that's strange. Sigler wasn't a big fellow, ya know, five feet six or seven. Weighed less than me. Still, I'd think it'd take a couple of men to throw that body, uh, maybe eight, ten feet across that there ditch."

He walked around the body and scanned the woods and the gravel pit to the right of them. Snow was scattered here and there. He saw nothing unusual. "Did you find anything, Harry?" Volant asked as he jumped back over the ditch to the side of the road.

La Fave fished the cap, three buttons and the cartridge out of his pocket. "Found these on the road up there and this cap by that log." He handed the items to the sheriff.

"Looks like a .32 caliber. Buttons are probably from his mackinaw," Volant said to Kalliomaa who had jumped the ditch to join the pair. "See that? It's missing some buttons."

Just then, Joseph Charbonneau, the local coroner, furniture dealer and undertaker, arrived on the scene with Carl Silvoli, who helped him from time to time. After conversing with the coroner for a few minutes, Volant, Kalliomaa and La Fave drove back to Hurley. Charbonneau and Silvoli moved the body into the rear of the furniture delivery truck that doubled as a temporary hearse and took Sigler's body back to Hurley.

They had no sooner arrived in front of Charbonneau's furniture store than a small crowd began to gather and ask questions. The news spread like a forest fire that Sigler was dead and his body was being moved to the morgue.

After they locked the front door, the coroner and his assistant carried Sigler's body to a back room and placed it on a table where they undressed it.

Dr. C.C. Urquhart, the county medical examiner, noticed the activity from his second-floor office overlooking Silver Street. When he saw the crowd and a body being removed from Charbonneau's truck, he put on his coat, grabbed his medical bag, rushed down the stairs and ran to the alley in back of the furniture store. He rapped on the back door and Silvoli opened it. The medical examiner followed him to the back room and asked Charbonneau whose body he had recovered.

When the mortician told Urquhart that it was Sigler, the medical examiner raised his eyebrows and said, "Guess it had to happen sooner or later. Do we know who killed him?"

Urquhart glanced down at Sigler's body and saw the small bullet hole beneath Sigler's ear.

"Nope. Or at least Volant didn't say anything," Charbonneau answered. "Could have been anybody. Sigler only had a couple of friends, but plenty of enemies. Remember what he did to that guy's arm last year? Broke it bad. Smacked it with a chunk of wood."

"How could I forget?" said Dr. Urquhart. "Took me a couple of hours to piece the bones back together and set it."

The doctor took off his coat and tie and unbuttoned his stiff collar.

"I'm going to use your telephone to call Dr. Hambley," he said to Charbonneau as he walked to the office.

"Central, this is Dr. Urquhart. Will you ring Dr. Hambley? I'm not certain if he's in his office or at the hospital."

After a minute, he heard the operator answer. "I'll connect Dr. Hambley now, Dr. Urquhart."

Urquhart reached into his vest pocket and pulled out a pocket watch, checking the time. When Hambley answered, Urquhart told him what had occurred.

"I'll need some help with this. How soon can you be here?" he asked.

"In less than an hour," came the reply. "I'm just finishing up."

"I'll get an okay for the autopsy and wait here at Charbonneau's for you. See you shortly."

Dr. Urquhart returned to the morgue area and sat down. Charbonneau had not budged. The doctor was an impatient man, however, and he had no sooner sat down than he got up, reached into his medical bag, took out a scalpel and a bone saw and placed the tools on the metal table next to Sigler's body. He looked at the body on the table and noted the powder burns around the wound in Sigler's head. His eyes slowly scanned the upper torso. There was an abrasion on Sigler's right hand and what appeared to be another bullet entry wound under the left armpit with no sign of an exit wound. He inspected the lower abdomen.

Glancing up at the coroner, he said, "Sigler has had gonorrhea for about six months. He was getting treatment in Ashland off and on. I don't think the doctor there could do much. Look here."

Reluctantly, Charbonneau took a quick glance at Sigler's groin. Although he was a licensed mortician and the coroner, there were some things he found hard to stomach. The short, slim furniture dealer had been a boxer before becoming an undertaker and he still looked the part. A religious believer in fitness, he neither smoked nor drank and could be found jogging every day at dawn and after sunset. He found it hard to believe that a man could abuse his body as Sigler had done.

Dr. Hambley arrived and looked closely at Sigler's body.

"Gunshots? How'd this happen?"

"I have no idea. Harry La Fave found him down by Layman's Creek when they were coming back from Mercer."

"Sheriff been there?" Hambley asked.

"Yep. Didn't tell me anything, though."

"I'd hate to be the one who has to tell his wife."

"Yes. I agree with that statement, Doctor. Shall we proceed?"

"Why not, Doctor?"

Urquhart took notes. They did an external examination first.

"Body weight?" Urquhart asked.

"About 135 pounds, give or take a couple of pounds."

"Height?"

"Five foot six or seven."

"Cause of death was by gunshot. Do we agree?"

"Yes."

"The bullet wound to the head was probably the one that killed him. It's a perforating wound to the skull with entry about an inch in from the opening of the left ear. The exit wound is about at the same place on the right side. There's also a superficial non-puncture wound on the back of right hand extending from little finger across to the thumb about quarter inch. Here, help me turn him over."

The two medical men turned Sigler's body on the stomach.

"There's another wound," Hambley said. "It begins at about 4th intercostal position on an axillary line about six or seven inches below the armpit. The bullet entered the left side, extended downward, and went transversely through Sigler. The bullet is lodged here under skin. I'll dig for it." Hambley poked around with his scalpel. "There, I have it. It's about two inches above the wing of the ileum. About two inches back of an imaginary line dropped from the middle of the armpit down."

Charbonneau dug the bullet from Sigler's side and tossed it on a table.

"I don't see any bruises on the corpse, but there is the presence of gonorrhea under this bandage. Do you see anything else, Dr. Hambley?"

"No, I sure don't. I think that's it."

They turned the body over to Charbonneau to prepare it for burial.

* * * *

4:30 pm

Sheriff Volant arrived back at the Iron County Jail and immediately telephoned the district attorney's office. While

Volant was giving details to the district attorney, Kalliomaa poured them both a cup of coffee. It would be a long night.

* * * *

4:45 pm

District Attorney Warren B. Foster left his office at the Iron County courthouse and drove down the hill and across Silver Street to the city jail. An ambitious man who worked endless hours, the handsome, 37-year-old district attorney appeared full of pep that afternoon. His wife, the former Mildred Meade, put up with his having to be away from home often. His daughter, Mary Patricia, had turned three that past June. Today, his mind was on other than family matters. He was building a murder case against a man named Santini who had smacked Oscar Nordby with his cane and then jabbed the barrel of his revolver into Nordby's eye and shot him. That murder case was nothing like this one, though. Hurley had many homicides, but most were the result of a drunken brawl between lumberjacks or miners. He had yet to experience one like the Sigler murder, and his excitement was evident. Sheriff Volant opened the door, standing on the top step to wait for Foster. Foster entered the jail ahead of the sheriff.

"I'll need all the details you have on Sigler, Joe." He didn't give Volant a chance to reply. "Did you find the murder weapon or anything else that can lead us to the killer?"

"Nope. No gun. Not much to find, really. Harry picked up this .32 caliber shell and these three buttons that probably came off his mackinaw. That's all there was. Oh, and this cap that I believe belonged to Sigler. We couldn't even spot a footprint except for Harry's. No sign of a struggle. Didn't see any blood except on a rock where his head was at, and that was only a small spot. Harry and his wife were coming back from Mercer when she saw the body about 10 feet off the side of the road.

Whoever put him there must have been in a hurry because they didn't try to cover him up with brush. At least that's what I'd have done. Kalliomaa and I think there were a couple of men because the body was thrown so far from the side of the road, and there were no signs that it had been dragged. There were powder burns on his head, too. Shot at short range. About a foot we guess."

"Any idea who it was might have killed him?"

"Sigler sure wasn't liked around town. He treated his wife badly and beat his kids. She was always over at the Hurley police station complaining about the guy. I think she sure had a good motive. He kept whores, too, you know. Could've been one of them, or a woman who got pissed off at her husband for shacking up at Sigler's place, or a husband trying to find his wayward wife. We've had a few of them in the past. I'd say Emma had the best reason, though."

"I can vouch for that because Emma came to me a couple of times last year complaining that Sigler was smacking her around. Last April she went to the mayor and Judge Shimondle, and they told her to see me because she wanted to know what she could do about Sigler. She wanted him committed or jailed. I told her to divorce the guy because there was nothing the law could do to help her. She got real worried, and I remember her telling me that Sigler would kill her if she ever even tried to divorce him. I called him in, read him the riot act, and told him to leave town for about six months. He stuck around until September or October and then went to Superior for a while. Even though she had good reason to see him dead, let's not make that conclusion, yet."

Volant stroked his chin. "Well, the way I see it," he said, "she killed him or hired someone to do it. Either way, somebody other than Emma had to lug the body away if he was killed in Hurley. She's a small lady and sure wouldn't have had the strength to drag that body around, much less toss it 10 feet over a ditch. I'm inclined to believe she has something to do with it simply because I can't think of anyone else with as strong a motive."

Foster looked up from the pad where he had been taking notes. "There's that fellow whose arm Sigler broke last year. He sued, got his $800 in circuit court and left town. Far as I know, Sigler didn't have any good friends because of the way he treated his wife and kids. His folks still live here, don't they?"

"Yep, they live on Poplar Street," Volant replied. "I haven't told them yet. Guess it's up to me to do that, too. Anyhow, the way gossip travels around here, they probably already know he's dead. His brother Joe is still here, but I think his sister moved to Milwaukee. Not sure."

"Well," said Foster, "maybe it's time you two visited Emma. Bring her here, and I'll talk to her. Maybe Dick can stay back and search the hotel. I don't know, maybe she'll be willing to shed some light on all of this."

* * * *

5:15 pm

"Goofy" Nelson, a local cook and part-time lumberjack who often frequented Sigler's bar, rushed through the door into the Gogebic Restaurant about five minutes after he heard that it was Sigler at Charbonneau's morgue. Waving his arms over his head frantically, he shouted, "Hey, Emma! Did you know they found Sigler's body down by Layman's Creek? They got him over at Charbonneau's place."

The three patrons sitting at the bar raced out the door, along with the cook, Soo Ling.

Emma and Louise were in the kitchen washing and drying the dishes. Emma came out to the restaurant when she heard the commotion, wiping her wet hands on her apron.

"What are you yelling about, Goofy? Sounds like another screw came loose."

"They found your old man down by Layman's Creek. He's dead. They got him over in Charbonneau's morgue."

"What did you say, Goofy? Andrew? Dead? I don't understand."

Just then, Volant and Kalliomaa came through the door. Emma looked back and forth between the sheriff and Nelson.

Volant lowered his head. "Emma, best you sit down. Andrew's body was found this afternoon down near Layman's Creek. He'd been shot." said Volant.

Emma stared at them, a blank look on her face. She turned toward the sheriff.

"My God, I know. Sigler's dead. I just heard it from Goofy not a second before you two walked in."

Seeing that Volant and Foster were waiting for her to do or say something, she sat down at a table and motioned for them to sit, too. She looked at Nelson.

"Thanks for letting me know, Goofy. You can leave now. Go back to the excitement. The sheriff wants to talk to me."

She appeared too relaxed and composed for someone who just learned of the violent death of a spouse, the sheriff observed.

When Goofy was out the door, Volant stared at Emma for a minute. "Where were you last night, Emma?"

"I was here with my children and taking care of the hotel. Why? Where else would I be?"

"You were out, weren't you?"

"No, I was not," she snapped back. "I was right here at the hotel tending to my children and working like I do every night.

Why? You don't think I had anything to do with Andrew's death, do you? Just what the hell do you think?"

Volant was taken aback and got a puzzled expression on his face. *Why does Emma look so calm? The woman just found out her husband has been killed. Something's not right. She's not crying and looks far too calm under the circumstances.*

Volant and Kalliomaa looked at each other with open mouths and waited for some indication of grief, but none came. Volant turned to Emma.

"We can't talk here, Emma. Foster would like to see you over at the jail," Volant said gently.

"Why?"

"Aw, you're not charged with anything, Emma. He'd just like to ask you some questions about your husband's comings and goings last night. Better get your wraps."

"Maybe I can get one of the girls to watch the restaurant for me. Wait here. My coat and hat are in the kitchen."

Louise was wiping the last of the dishes when Emma entered the kitchen. She scowled and made a motion with her head toward the front of the building.

"What's the matter out there? What's going on?"

"Andrew's been killed."

Louise opened her mouth in amazement and gasped. Then, glaring at Emma and clenching her teeth, she replied in a voice barely audible, "You bitch! You stinking bitch! I told you there'd be trouble. He went to Pence to get girls last night just like I told you and those people did it. Those...those damn Dagos over there killed him. And I wouldn't be surprised if you had something to do with it, either! You two have been trying to kill each other since I got here. Maybe you finally got the chance."

Emma snatched up her coat and hat and said, "Louise, why don't you just get the hell out of here. I've thought you were a pain in the ass ever since Andrew hired you. You've been walking around here like you own the place...like...like some damn queen of the Nile and you've sucked up to Andrew since the minute you got here. I don't like you, and I especially don't like whores."

"Temper, temper, Emma. I just can't imagine why you don't like me," Louise replied sweetly. "I thought we were friends."

"Bitch!" Emma fired back.

Louise was laughing when Emma stamped out of the kitchen to the restaurant where Volant and Kalliomaa waited for her. They heard the commotion, but didn't really want to get in the middle of a fight between two ladies.

"Lordy, lordy, just listen to them. Sounds like a cat fight coming up," Kalliomaa said.

"Don't want to get those two riled up. Did you hear that remark about Dagos in Pence? I wonder if one of them fellas killed him." Volant asked.

"Could be. There's some real hotheads over there."

Just then Emma came out of the kitchen.

"All set, Emma?" asked the sheriff.

"How long do you think this will take? I have to get back here to take care of my children, and the supper crowd will be here soon," she asked.

"I really don't know. Probably will take some time. Dick is going to stay here and ask a few questions. But didn't you say you had someone to take charge while you're away," asked Volant. "How about Louise? Can't she watch the kids?"

"Louise? Ha! I wouldn't let her take care of my dog much less the children. She's about as reliable as a cheap wristwatch.

I guess the children will be okay by themselves for a short while, but I'd feel a lot better if somebody could watch out for them, though. Hold on just a minute. Let me speak to another one of the other girls."

"Well, hurry up. Foster's a busy man and can't be kept waiting forever."

When Emma disappeared, Foster suggested to Kalliomaa that he stay behind and search the hotel for anything at all that might be relevant, promising to send some deputies over to help.

Emma went across the hallway to the second bedroom. She knocked softly at the door and a weak voice answered, "Come in."

Ray Rice was lying on her bed like she had been doing for the past three days and nights, ever since Sigler spiked her wine with croton oil, a strong cathartic. It had taken a hold on Ray.

The shade was drawn on the single window and Ray was doing a crossword puzzle from the light of a bed lamp. Ray looked up from her puzzle and tried to smile.

"Hi, sweetie. Whatcha need?"

Emma put her finger to her lips.

"Shhhhh. Keep it to a whisper, Ray. Just listen to me. I don't want anyone to hear us. I have to go with the sheriff for a little while. They found Andrew's body and want me to go talk with the district attorney at the jail. Could you kind of keep an eye on things while I'm gone? The kids and the customers? I know you don't feel well, but just keep an ear open, okay? Tell the kids I had to go out and that I'll be back soon."

"Sure I will, honey," Ray answered. She sat on the edge of the bed and put on her bathrobe and slid into a pair of slippers. "God, I hope Louise doesn't get in my way. Start asking dumb questions and making comments about Sigler, I mean. I sure wish she'd leave now that he's gone. It would be just like her to try and take over the joint."

"I've already asked her to leave," replied Emma.

"Today, I hope."

"No, I guess I'll give her a few days to get herself together and find a place to go. But, if she's not out of here in couple of days, I'll get the sheriff and the mayor if I have to. They'll make her move out. You'll be okay for a while, won't you?"

"Yeah, I guess," said Ray.

"Listen, when I get back, why don't you get a taxi and go to the St. James for a few days until all this blows over. You'll be better off there than in this noisy place. Get a room with a flush toilet and a bathtub in it."

"I'd like that, Emma. I don't have much money, though. Can you spare me some?"

"I can loan you $30. That's all I can give you for now. I'll get some more later."

"I really appreciate that, Emma. I'll watch the kids and the restaurant until you get back. How long do you think it'll be?"

"Volant says not too long. Foster wants to ask me some questions. I just hope I don't tell him anything stupid."

"Stay calm and remember that the kids are just fine here with me."

"Are you okay alone with Louise?"

"I'll be fine. Now don't you worry."

"And if the cops come around asking questions, you don't know anything. Mum's the word, okay?"

"Mum's the word," Ray answered.

Emma said goodbye to Ray and went across the hallway and opened the door to the restaurant where Volant and Kalliomaa had just finished a third cup of help-yourself-it's-free coffee.

"Are you ready this time, Emma?" asked Sheriff Volant impatiently.

Emma didn't speak, but she nodded her head and left by the front door with the sheriff tagging behind, and the two of them got into the police car and rode to the jail.

Foster was waiting for them on the jail porch when they arrived. Volant held the door open and motioned for Emma to go in first.

"Sit here, Emma." Foster pointed to a wooden chair and then sat down himself. Volant grabbed a chair and placed it next to the district attorney.

"Emma, I have to..."

"Hold on just a minute, Warren. I need to send Dick some help over at the Sigler place."

He went to a back room of the jailhouse and told two deputies to meet Dick Kalliomaa at the Gogebic Hotel. When Volant got back to his office, Foster began questioning Emma.

"Where was your husband last night, Emma?"

"He was in his bed sleeping."

"What time did you see him last night?"

"I got up to check on the children, and he was in bed at one o'clock."

"And this morning? Where was he this morning?"

"After he got up, he went to Ashland to keep an appointment."

"About what time was that?"

"I think it was six o'clock or so."

"That's a little early for him to take the train. How did he get there?"

"A man came to the restaurant and drove him there."

"A man, you say?"

"Yes."

"What time was this, did you say?"

"Oh, I'd judge it to be six o'clock. The clock is off a little. It runs fast, so it could have been before that. Maybe quarter to the hour."

"Do you know who this man was? Had you ever seen him before?"

"No, I never saw him before."

"Sure about that?"

"I wonder....On second thought he may have been in the restaurant yesterday. I seem to remember Andrew talking to a man in one of the booths."

"What did this man look like?"

"I can't remember what he looked like. I know he had on a coat and cap. I didn't pay much attention."

"What happened, then, after your husband left?"

"I got the children up, got my older boy off to school and dressed the three little ones. Then I went to the Iron Exchange bank and withdrew some money to make a payment on the car. I took the money to Mr. Norman and later on he taught me how to drive it. The car, I mean. Then I came back to the restaurant. I was there until Goofy and Joe Volant came in and told me that Andrew was dead."

"And you didn't see or hear from your husband after he left this morning?" asked Foster.

"No, I didn't," replied Emma.

The two deputies joined Kalliomaa at the Gogebic Hotel where they questioned Ray Rice and Louise Mason. Neither of the two women offered the officers any information. Louise told them that she was upstairs sleeping that morning and the previous night. Ray told them a similar story. Neither woman had been feeling well.

The officers had just started to search the restaurant when young Robert Sigler slammed in through the side entrance. His schoolbooks were tied up with an old belt. Kalliomaa poked his head out of the kitchen door into the hallway.

"Hi, there, young fellow? Just getting home from school?"

"Yes, sir."

"Kinda late, ain't it?"

"No, sir, I was playing with my friends after school. My ma lets me. What you doing here? Where's my ma?"

"She had to go away for a little while. She'll be back soon."

Robert took off his coat, hung it up on a hook in the laundry room, and walked over to Kalliomaa. Dick saw that the boy had been crying.

"Come here, son," Kalliomaa said.

"You're the sheriff, ain't you?"

"I'm the undersheriff. I guess that's about the same thing. My name is Dick Kalliomaa, and this is Deputy Neimi, and this guy here is Deputy Sullivan."

The deputies said hello to Robert and then went upstairs to look around.

Robert looked at Kalliomaa and said meekly, "I think I know why you are here."

"Why do you think I'm here?"

"It's about my dad, right?"

"Yes. Do you know about your dad?"

"Yes, sir. Somebody shot him."

"How is it that you know somebody shot your dad?" asked Kalliomaa.

"Some kids at school told me that somebody shot him."

Robert's face screwed up as though he wanted to cry, but he didn't. Instead he walked over to a cooler filled with ice and fished out a bottle of strawberry soda pop. He opened it, and took a long swig. He wiped his mouth on his shirtsleeve and looked up at Kalliomaa.

"Do you mind if I ask you some questions about your pa?" Kalliomaa asked.

"No, sir. You can ask me questions."

"Your name is Robert, right?"

"Yes, sir. Robert Andrew Sigler."

"How old are you, son?"

"I'm eight."

"How was your pa to you, Robert? I mean how did he treat you?"

"He was mean and he beat me and was always hollering at me all the time. He never was nice to me at all."

"Did you like your pa?"

"I don't know. I liked him some, I guess."

"When was the last time you seen your pa, Robert?"

"When he went out last night."

"Where did he go?"

"I think when he went to buy some chickens."

"Do you know where he went to buy those chickens?"

"Saxon or Pence. I'm not sure."

"Did he go by himself?"

"I don't know. I don't think so."

"Had he ever gone to buy chickens before?"

"Yes, sir. Lots of times."

"Did he go by himself those times?"

"Sometimes he went by himself and sometimes he went with somebody else."

"What other people would he go with? Do you know their names?"

"Sometimes he went with my Uncle Bill, and sometimes he went with Andy."

"Do you remember who was in the restaurant last night?"

"Yes, sir. There was some lumberjacks here. Andy was here. And me and my ma."

Kalliomaa's eyebrows rose when he heard Robert mention Andy's name.

"Didja talk to him?"

"Who?"

"Andy."

"Yes, I did talk to him."

"What is Andy's last name? Do you know it?"

"No, his name is just Andy."

"What didja talk about with Andy, Robert?"

"Oh, nothing much, I guess. We just talked."

"Was there anybody else in the restaurant besides those lumberjacks and Andy and you and your ma?" Kalliomaa asked.

"I think there was a couple of Finlanders, too."

Kalliomaa noticed the two deputies had returned from their search of the hotel rooms.

"Did you find anything?"

"Nope. We looked upstairs. Didn't go into Lennon's office, though, because it was locked. Saw three little kids playing up there in one of the bedrooms. One of the hired help named Ray Rice was with them. She don't know anything. Said she was up all night with the runs. Didn't see or hear a thing. Talked to a working girl named Louise. No help there, either."

"I was just asking Robert, here, some questions. He says that his pa maybe went to buy some chickens last night with a man named Andy."

"Is there anything else you can tell us, Robert?"

"No, sir."

"Then, I guess you better get to your studying. We want you to grow up smart, you know," said Kalliomaa as he gave the boy a pat on the shoulder.

After Robert went up the stairs, Kalliomaa said to the deputies, "Guess we better get back to the jailhouse then. Not much more we can do here."

It was about 6:30 when Kalliomaa and the two deputies met Foster, Volant and Emma back at the Iron County jail. After taking Emma back to the hotel, they continued to put their heads together to see what information they had managed to gather.

"Did you find anything," Volant asked.

"Not much of anything. Young Robert Sigler said that his dad went to Saxon to buy some chickens. Said he went there with a guy named Andy."

"Guy named Andy, huh? Lotsa guys named Andy, but only one that comes to mind is Andy Anderson."

"Bet that's him. What do you think Joe?"

"Yep. Bet my socks on it. I bet he's the only friend Sigler had in town. Name is really Gudleski. Nice kid. Spent time in Green Bay but hasn't been in any trouble since he got out three or four years ago."

"That's what the young fella said. He told me Sigler and Andy went to buy chickens more than a few times," Kalliomaa told them.

"Think we ought to talk to Anderson, Warren?"

"Let's bring him in and ask him some questions. Doesn't he work at the New Central, Joe?"

"Yep, that's him. I'll ring them up."

Volant placed a phone call to the New Central and asked if Anderson was there. Bill Allen, the owner told him that Andy had been there most of the day, but had left.

"Do you know where he went?"

"Home, I suppose."

"Where does Anderson live?" Volant asked.

"Ironwood. Up the Norrie Location. Was living on Oak Street last I know for sure, but I think they moved a month or two ago."

"Any idea where?"

"Far as I know he still lives up Norrie. Someplace on the top of the hill."

"Shouldn't be hard to find him. Anybody know where they moved to?"

"His in-laws still live in the place he moved from. Ask them, I guess."

"They speak English?"

New Central where Andy worked.

"No, I don't think so. They're Finlanders. I know they have kids who talk English, though. They come in from time to time. I think the girls names are Inga and Bertha. Come in with Anderson's wife, Lily."

"Thanks for the information, Bill."

After he hung up the telephone, Foster and Volant agreed that they would question Andy the following day. It was a delay they would regret.

Saturday, May 3, 1924

It had rained Friday night, with the temperature hovering in the mid 30's, and it was still raining on Saturday. The sound of the alarm woke Emma from a sound sleep at 5:30. She felt very refreshed in spite of the events of the previous day. She was happy and calm. Sigler was dead. She could breathe again.

She jumped out of bed, dressed quickly and ran down the stairs to the kitchen. After lighting the huge, black cook stove, she made the coffee and put water on to boil. It was a routine she had done every day since they bought the hotel.

Louise Mason was sleeping soundly in one of the bedrooms across the hall from the kitchen when the sound of clanking pans and running water awakened her. She was hung over from drinking too much and smoking too many cigarettes the night before. She tried to shut the noise out by covering her head with her pillow, but after tossing and turning for a minute, decided to get out of bed and go to the second floor to sleep. Emma could not help but hear her.

"Louise, is that you?" Emma called out angrily. "I thought I told you to leave." She said it more to agitate Louise than anything. It worked.

"Aw, shut up! Do you have to make all that noise?" Louise yelled. She felt that her head was ready to burst any minute. "I'm going upstairs to sleep. Damn racket you make down here. I suppose I'll have to listen to those brats of yours screech and holler up there, too. Can't you keep those little shits quiet? I'm not feeling well this morning", she slurred.

"Louise, I've got some errands to run. If you're not gone by the time I get back, I'll have the sheriff see you on the next train out of town."

"Why don't you take your kids and leave yourself, Emma. I have no intention of leaving. Andrew meant for me to have this place. And you killed him, didn't you!"

"Louise, I have news for you. This is my restaurant and my hotel that Sigler had put in my name. I think you better be the one to leave," Emma shouted. "I'm going to see Volant right now. He'll get you out of here."

"Sure! Okay! I'll leave. And, believe me, I'll have a lot to tell Volant, myself!" Louise turned quickly and stomped up the stairs to a bedroom at the front of the second floor where she plopped down on the bed and promptly fell asleep.

After finishing up in the kitchen, Emma went upstairs to help her children get dressed. When he had finished his breakfast, Robert got himself off to play with his friends, and Emma arranged for one of the hired girls to babysit Junior and the twins. Then Emma walked to the St. James Hotel in Ironwood and went to Ray's room. Ray was awake and feeling much better.

Emma knocked quietly on the door to Ray's room.

"Ray? You awake?"

Ray opened the safety catch on the hotel door.

"Emma. Am I glad to see you."

"You sure look a lot better than you did yesterday, Ray. How ya feeling?"

"Pretty good. Got a good night's sleep. Took a bath when I got here and just plunked down on that nice soft bed there. I slept all night."

"Have you eaten yet?"

"No. I was thinking about doing that."

"C'mon, Ray. Let's get a cup of coffee or something," Emma said. "We've got to sort this mess out. I need you to help me figure out what to do next."

They walked out of the St. James to Suffolk Street and turned down Aurora to Reed's Restaurant in the new Masonic Temple building.

"What are you going to do?" Ray asked on the way to the restaurant.

"I wish I knew. The cops were asking me all kind of questions last night."

"They talked to me, too, when you were at Volant's office. I was too sick to even make sense. I told them that I had to watch the kids and the restaurant, and they didn't bother me anymore."

"The heat is on. I think the best thing to do is get rid of Andy somehow."

"Right. I agree. He's the only one besides you and me that knows anything about the murder."

"I'll ring him at the New Central and tell him to get out of town before the cops discover anything."

"Good idea," said Ray.

Arriving at the restaurant, they sat at a table where they couldn't be overheard and ordered a cup of coffee and some toast. They ate their toast and sipped at the coffee. After smoking a cigarette and drinking her coffee, Emma got up and called Andy from a phone booth in the restaurant.

"New Central," Andy answered.

"Listen, Andy, this is Emma. The cops have been here to see me and they're asking a lot of questions. They found Sigler's body."

"I heard that. It's all over the streets and in the morning newspaper."

"I think you had better burn your overcoat and beat it out of town."

"Why should I burn my overcoat?"

"Because you probably have Sigler's blood all over it. You don't want to let the cops see you or ask any questions. They'll probably think you killed Sigler."

"I didn't do anything except move the body."

"And that makes you just as guilty as me. I think its called accessory after the fact. It implicates you in the murder. And I think you should do nothing with your new car. Just leave it where it is. Take the old one," Emma advised.

"Why the old one? Why not the new car?"

"The cops will be looking for the new one. They won't be looking for your old Model T. Besides, it looks like every other car around here."

"What are you gonna do, Emma?"

"Don't worry about me. I'll be all right. And thanks for all you've done, Andy. Don't worry, I'll tell the cops what happened. They won't arrest you."

"If you say so, Emma. I'll leave town and lay low for awhile until the heat's off. Bye."

"Bye, Andy. Take it easy."

Emma hung up the phone and smiled to herself. *Well, that takes care of that until I can figure out what to do next.*

Emma and Ray went back to the St. James and checked out, then took the streetcar back to Hurley.

Meanwhile, Andy gathered up a few cigars, poured himself a shot of whiskey and belted it down. He forgot that he had put his overcoat, the old blood splattered shoes and the rags that he used to wipe Sigler's blood from the car seat under the bar. It didn't take him very long to leave town after Emma phoned him at work. He didn't even let his wife know that he was leaving, and he drove his new car even though Emma had warned him against it. He was wearing his best light gray suit. *Guess I'll drive on south and see what there is to see. Hide out for awhile. Maybe find a place of my own down there. Tomahawk maybe.*

He filled the gas tank and checked the water and oil in Ironwood then drove east along the county highway through Bessemer and Wakefield, maneuvering around the water-filled holes on the dirt and gravel road. When he got to Marenisco, about 30 miles from Ironwood, he turned south and traveled the back roads through the woods, past the tiny logging communities of Winchester and Tomahawk Lake, until he got to Rhinelander, Wisconsin. There he bought gas and stopped at a hotel, signing his brother-in-law's name to the guest register.

Meanwhile, the Hurley and Ironwood police spent much of the day asking questions and trying to locate Andy for questioning. Volant went back to the Gogebic Hotel and talked again to Emma.

"Have you seen Andy Anderson today?" Volant asked her.

"Who?"

"Andy Anderson. You know who he is, don't you?"

"Yes, I know him a little. Comes in for lunch sometimes."

"Have you seen him today?"

"No, I haven't. Why?"

"We're trying to find him. Do you mind if I look around?"

"No, be my guest. You won't find him here, though."

Volant searched all the rooms, but there was no indication that Andy had been there. Volant and the Ironwood Sheriff

Tom Jeffery located Andy's wife at home after they went to her in-laws and talked to one of the girls. She saw the two officers when they drove up and stopped at the house on Beech Street. *Oh, no. Not Andy. Please, God, don't let him be in any trouble or worse.* She opened the door and invited them in. There was a little boy sitting in the middle of the kitchen floor playing with a toy truck.

"Yes, what can I do for you?" she asked.

"Have you seen your husband today, Mrs. Anderson?" Volant asked her.

"Not since he left for work this morning," Lily replied. "Why? What's wrong?"

"We want to question him about a robbery in Hurley."

"Andy isn't in any trouble, is he? He's been straight since we got married."

"No, he's not in any trouble that we know of. All we want to do is ask him some questions."

"I'll let him know the minute he comes home."

"Thanks. By the way, where was your husband last night?"

"He was in bed when I got home around 9 or 9:30. Did you ask for him at work?"

"Not yet, but we'll be sure to do that. Thank you, Mrs. Anderson," Volant said.

Volant and Sheriff Jeffery got back in the squad car. After dropping Jeffery at the Ironwood City Hall, he drove back to Hurley.

Later that evening, Volant and Foster continued their search for Anderson. They went to the New Central saloon and asked if anyone had heard from him yet. Looking in the alley in the back of the saloon, they found an old Ford roadster parked next to the side of the barn. They shined their lights on the inside and saw something that looked like blood.

"Whose Ford is that next to the barn outside?" Volant demanded from the bartender.

"Probably Anderson's. He leaves his car in the back usually. Hey, come here a minute. I think these are his clothes under the bar. Do you want them?" They checked and found some bloody rags, Andy's overcoat and bloody shoes.

"You sure these are his?"

"Sure. I recognized them right off."

Volant bundled the clothes and shoes and took them with.

Then they went out, opened the car door and found dried blood on the seat and a bloodstained cartridge. They cut out the bloodstained part out of the back of the seat and took possession of the car. It was driven to the Hurley police station along with Andy's bloodstained clothes.

Meanwhile, having ignored Emma's advice to take his old car, Andy left the hotel at Rhinelander in his new coupe and drove to Antigo, then to Oshkosh, Fond du Lac, and Neenah-Menasha. He slept in his car overnight, not wanting to risk getting caught. While he was in Antigo, he chatted with a policeman to see what he could find out. The cop knew nothing about a murder in Hurley.

I had best ditch this suit. It's all wrinkled. Maybe I'll buy a new one. Andy went to a clothing store and purchased a brown suit. He looked in the mirror and admired himself. *Dapper. Yep, pretty dapper. I feel like a million bucks.*

It wasn't until he got to Green Bay on May 6 that he noticed a newspaper with his name in the headlines. Andy read the newspaper and, in a panic, drove to Sturgeon Bay on the Door

Peninsula. Broke, tired, and wanted for questioning for Sigler's murder, Andy sat on a park bench overlooking Lake Michigan.

A man came over and sat down next to him.

"Hi, Buddy, you look like you could use some help," the man said.

"Well, I could," he replied.

"Anything I can do?"

"Naw. Nothing anybody can do for me now."

"What's wrong, friend?" the man asked.

"Guess I have a little problem back home," Andy replied.

"We've all got problems and troubles. By the way, my name is John Gross." He thrust his hand to Andy.

"Pleased to meetcha. Andy Anderson's the name." He shook Gross's hand.

"I'm a book salesman. Sell religious books. Bibles. Inspirational books. That kind of books."

"No book can help me with the troubles I got. Hey, when I was in the Pen I read the Bible almost every day. The only book they let us read."

"You were in prison?"

"Yep. First reform school, then Green Bay. Right over there." Andy pointed to the general direction of the Green Bay Reformatory.

"You're not an escapee, are you?"

"Naw. I'm from Ironwood. The cops are looking for me cuz they probably think I killed a guy."

"Did you?"

"No. But I know who did."

"Andy, you should go back there and clear your name."

"I can't do that."

"Why not? If you're innocent of the crime, you'll be exonerated."

"It's not that. I'm flat busted. I ain't got no dough."

"If I give you five bucks, do you think you can make it on that?"

"Mister, I can make it with five bucks. I want to thank you."

"Have you had anything to eat, Andy?"

"Not for two days."

"C'mon. Let's have a sandwich."

"Aw, I couldn't do that to you." But Andy's stomach told him a different story.

Gross took Andy to a diner where they had breakfast of bacon, eggs and toast. They sat there drinking coffee for awhile. Andy really wanted a cigar but he dare not ask Gross for the money to buy some. Instead, he bummed a cigarette from the waitress.

After Gross paid the bill and left a quarter tip, he and Andy walked to Andy's car.

"I sure want to thank you," Andy told Gross for the hundredth time. "And, believe me, I'll high-tail it back to Hurley and make things straight with the cops."

"Andy, the Lord will look after you. Take care," Gross said.

Andy drove back to Ironwood and arrived before midnight, taking the old road toward Wakefield and turning left just before town to the County Road to Ironwood. He ran out of gas just beyond Puritan Location between Bessemer and Ironwood and moved his car off to the side of the road and ran. *Shit, but these hills are steep. Good thing I stay in shape.*

Andy stopped to rest near Jessieville and took off his jacket, then lit up a cigar. *There. That's better. I'll just stay here for a few minutes and take off again. Don't want any cops to see me. Makes no difference, though. Almost halfway there. It'll be a lot easier up ahead. Not as many hills to climb.*

Five minutes later, Andy got up, hooked his jacket over his shoulder and took off to cover the five miles to the Scott and Howe lumber yard in Ironwood where he rested in the roundhouse.

Monday, May 5, 1924

The Hurley Presbyterian Church on Copper Street was somber at 1:00 in the afternoon when Sigler's funeral service took place. Emma and the children were there along with Sigler's mother, father, sister and brother. Rev. Chester Harries delivered the message that in death there is no sorrow. There were few tears shed that day.

Emma was dressed in black, sporting a new black hat with an ostrich feather. Six Hurley merchants who had known Sigler acted as pall bearers. There was a short procession to the Hurley Cemetery, where Andrew Sigler was laid to rest beneath a modest grave marker.

Everyone except Emma and the children left. Emma sat quietly next to Sigler's open grave with her children until two men with shovels came to fill the hole with dirt.

"Come on, kids. It's time to go."

"Ma, where's Pa now?" Robert asked.

"He's in Heaven, Robert."

"Where's Heaven?" Junior piped in.

Emma pointed to the sky and said, "Up there. Way past where we can see."

"But Pa was mean to us and they told us in Sunday School that only good people go to Heaven. Pa wasn't good to you or us kids," Robert said.

"I guess sometimes God forgives. Your Pa didn't mean to do all those things he did to us. He was sick inside," Emma told him.

"There was times when I wished I had a gun so I could shoot him," Robert told her.

"I know. I know, Robert," Emma answered.

Thursday, May 8, 1924

Emma watched Silver Street from the window of the restaurant. When she saw Mayor Lennon coming down the street toward his office next door, she went out and met him.

"Morning, Mayor. Can I talk to you?"

"Sure, Emma. Come on up."

They climbed the stairs to Lennon's office and sat down.

"How's it going, Emma? My goodness, I haven't seen much of you since,..since..."

"You mean since Andrew was killed?"

"Yes."

"I've had plenty to do. Foster and Volant have kept me busy answering questions. And there's the kids to care for. The funeral and all that."

Emma took $50 from her purse.

"Mayor, I would like you to find Andrew's killer. Here's a $50 reward for the capture of the man who killed him. I just wish it could be more. Maybe this will bring some answers."

Lennon took the money. "Rest assured that I'll see what I can do. This should loosen some tongues. I'll be sure and let everyone know about the reward on the killer's head."

Satisfied that by giving the mayor the reward money she may have convinced him that she had nothing to do with her husband's murder, Emma returned to the restaurant. Louise met her at the door.

"Louise, I see you have your bags packed. Are you ready to leave?"

"Yes. And not a minute too soon, either."

"Where's those damn dogs of yours?" Emma asked her.

"I already took them to the station. I'm off. Toodles, deary. Don't do anything I'd do," Louise said with a smirk. "By the way, I'll see you in court."

"Oh, no, you won't."

With that said, Louise, carrying her hatbox, made her way to the railroad station, dragging her trunk. When she got there, Sheriff Volant was waiting.

"Where do you think you're going, Louise?" he asked her.

"Home," she said.

"Where might that be? We'll probably need you up here to testify if there's a trial."

"Chicago," Louise said. "4714 Kenwood Avenue. Whenever you want me for anything, just send me a telegram, Sheriff. You can get in touch with me there."

After seeing Louise off, Volant filed a formal arrest warrant: "Case Number 690, for Andrew Gudleski, aka Anderson, aka A.J. Anderson, on the first day of May, A.D. 1924 at the Town of Oma, in said county did willfully, feloniously, and of his malice aforethought, kill and murder Andrew Sigler."

Friday, May 9, 1924

Andy woke up early and decided that he'd better spend the day in the roundhouse. He was very tired and was having second thoughts about turning himself in. He just lay there, thinking about it all.

Meanwhile, Sheriff Tom Jeffrey and Undersheriff George Basket of the Ironwood Police Department located Andy's car on the old county road. They looked around Puritan Location for him, visited the home of his in-laws in Ironwood, and talked to his wife. They thoroughly searched each residence that early morning but found nothing.

Jeffrey and Basket drove Andy's car to Hurley and parked it next to the Hurley courthouse. Volant soon joined them.

"This is his new car, I guess," Volant said.

"Looks like he went through a lot of mud. Wonder where he took it?"

"Don't know for sure. At first we thought he was heading to Sault St. Marie. Folks around Negaunee thought they seen him there. We even figured he'd head to the Minnesota Iron Range," Volant told them.

"How about south into Wisconsin?"

"Pretty sure that's where he was. We got a report from Antigo just yesterday afternoon that he talked to an Antigo cop. Cop didn't realize it was Andy until he got off his shift at four o'clock. That's when they got the telegraph message."

"Think you'll catch him?"

"He's around here someplace. Got his car. We'll find him. He can't be holed up forever. Not many places to hide. Besides, everybody's looking for him. He'll get found."

"Well, we'll keep our eyes opened for him over our way."

"He's got family in Ironwood."

"Right. We've talked to his wife and her family; they haven't seen him. We've been keeping a lookout in case he shows his face."

"Thanks," Volant said. "Just hope he didn't steal another car and take off."

"We'd probably have heard something by this time."

"Guess you're right," Volant said. "Oh, by the way, Mrs. Sigler gave Lennon $50 yesterday to be used for a reward. Word's out on the street. Lot of folks around here that'd sell their grandmother for fifty bucks."

"You can say that again," Jeffrey said. "Just look at Basket here. A good example of somebody who'd do that. Anything for a buck, hey George?"

"Don't make anything as a cop in these parts. Gotta get it from someplace." Basket said, and the three men laughed.

Saturday, May 10, 1924
4:00 am

Andy woke after a cold, miserable and sleepless night in the Scott and Howe roundhouse. He had decided to turn himself in and take whatever happened. But first, there were a couple of things that he had to do. He walked up Norrie hill to his sister-in-law's house in Ironwood and banged on the back door.

"Andy, what're you doing here," Sigrid asked. "The cops have been all over here looking for you. They want you for Sigler's murder."

"I know. I know. Where's Dale? I need to talk to him. Get him quick. I'm in a hurry."

She ran upstairs to the bedroom where her husband was getting dressed.

"Dale! Andy's here and needs you quick," she said. Dale raced down the stairs.

"Andy! You're in some kind of trouble. Hurley cops are looking for you. What do you need?"

"Dale, I know we haven't had much to do with each other, but you're a straight shooter, and I need your help just now. I'm gonna give myself up to Volant. I need you to take this and keep it or get rid of it." Andy gave him the .38 that he'd been carrying since Ray taught him how to shoot it back in April.

"I don't want to get caught with it. It ain't registered to me, or anybody else," Andy told him.

"I hope this isn't the gun that killed Sigler," his brother-in-law asked him.

"No, it isn't. I've had this for a couple of months."

Dale took the gun, and Andy left.

* * * *

5:30 am

Andy walked slowly down Norrie Hill, went through the Ashland caves and took the bridge to Hurley, and turned north on First Avenue until he came to the Iron County Jail. He banged loudly on the jailhouse door. Volant was there to greet him.

"Hi, Andy. C'mon in," Volant said.

"Hi, Joe, I heard you're looking for me."

"I've been expecting you. I knew you'd show up in due time. There's an arrest warrant out for you, you know."

"I know. I heard. You ain't got nothing on me, Joe."

"Hold on. Don't say another word. I need to get the D.A. here before you say anything more, Andy."

Volant phoned Foster at home and told him that Anderson had turned himself in. Foster was at the jailhouse in minutes.

"Hi, Andy," Foster said.

"Hi, back to you. What'd you do, Foster, fly down here in an airplane?"

"Ha. You still can crack a joke, Andy."

"What I want to know is what this is all about."

"We found your car."

"So what?"

"We found blood in it, Andy."

"That was chicken blood."

"No, it wasn't, Andy. Sigler's kid told us that he saw you leave with Sigler the night he was killed."

"Right. Me and Sigler drove out to Saxon and bought some chickens."

"We think Sigler was murdered that night." Volant showed Andy the box that held his shoes and coat. "These clothes have blood all over them, and they're yours. Got anything to say about that?"

Andy turned pale as a ghost. He thought it over for a few minutes. *They think I killed Sigler. They're setting me up for something. Emma? Wonder how much she told them? They don't have the goods on me, but I don't want to get Emma in any trouble. Aw, hell. Might as well play along with them. See what they got cooked up.*

"I don't know nothing about it," Andy said. "Why don't you just go ahead and lock me up and be done with it. Sounds like you've already pinned the rap on me anyhow."

"Lock him up, Joe," Foster said.

"What charge?" asked Volant "

"Murder. Filed the warrant yesterday."

"Wait a minute. Murder? You really do have pinned it on me," Andy said.

"We do, Andy. Tell us what happened," Foster said.

"Nothing," Andy replied. "Nothing."

They took Andy to the bullpen and locked him up. He stayed there about an hour with several drunks before he was moved to a cell upstairs to the women's empty cellblock.

* * * *

7:30 am

Andy was wakened by the turnkey.

"Get up, Anderson. They want you at the courthouse in an hour."

"What for?"

"Dunno. I was told to get you out of the sack. That's all I know."

Andy got up and washed his face. "I don't guess I can have a bath or get some clean clothes," he asked.

"Nope. Got some breakfast for you, though. C'mon."

The jailer opened the door to Andy's cell and took him to Volant's office where he had a bowl of oatmeal and a cup of coffee. Volant watched him as he ate.

"Anything you want to tell me, Andy?" Volant asked.

"Nope."

"How did it happen?"

"Dunno what you're talking about."

"Sigler. Did you kill him?"

"Nope. Of course not."

"We think you did."

"Can't help you. I didn't kill him."

Volant showed Andy the bloody clothes, and Andy' face turned pale.

"How'd the blood get on your clothes and in your car, Andy?"

"Chickens, I told you. Had to kill some because they were fighting. Got blood all over the car."

"What time did you see Sigler last Thursday night?"

"After eight o'clock. I took him to Saxon to get them chickens."

"And you dropped him off at the Gogebic right after that?"

"Yep."

"Then what did you do?" Volant asked.

"I went home."

"What time was that?"

"About 9:30 I guess."

"Was your wife there when you got home?"

"She got home just after I went to bed."

"I'll be sure to check on that."

"Why'd you leave town?"

"I wanted to take a ride."

"How's that?"

"Got a new car."

"Where'd you get money for that new car?"

"Won it playing poker. I ain't answering any more questions, Sheriff. Hey, what's going on now? Jailer said I need to go to the courthouse."

"You'll see when we get there." Volant put handcuffs on Andy.

"What are these for?"

"What do you think they're for?"

Andy kept his silence. Volant told the jailer that they were leaving and drove Andy in the police car up the hill to the courthouse. They stopped in the rear of the courthouse and went in the back door to Judge Shemondle's chambers. Volant removed the handcuffs before he and Andy entered the judge's room.

"Morning, Sheriff, good to see you."

"Morning, Your Honor. I've brought Andrew Gudleski with me. He had his name changed to Andy Anderson, so that's what he goes by. He skipped town after Sigler was killed, there was blood in his car that he says came from chickens. I've been holding him at the jailhouse under suspicion of murder one pending your decision."

Shemondle cleared his throat. "Mr. Anderson, I've read about you in the papers and I've been briefed by Sheriff Volant and District Attorney Foster. Do you have anything to say?"

"Nothing."

"Nothing in your defense?" the judge responded.

"Nothing."

"In that case, Mr. Anderson, I order that you to be taken to the Iron County jail by the sheriff for the crime of murder and placed in custody until your hearing before the circuit court. The hearing is set for May 22, 1924. You will be held without the option of bail." He turned to Volant. "Take him away, Sheriff."

Volant put the cuffs back on Andy and led him to the squad car. When they were heading back to the jail, Volant said "You sure got yourself in a mess of trouble, boy."

"Not the first time."

"Do your wife and family know you've been arrested?"

"Dunno."

"Want me to say something to them?"

"Nope. Not necessary," Andy answered curtly.

"Guess most folks know already, anyhow," Volant said.

As a matter of fact, everybody who read the Ironwood Daily Globe knew. Headlines screamed that Gudleski was wanted for the murder. The newspaper rumors had him heading to Canada via Sault St. Marie, they had him going to Minnesota, and they carried an interview with the Antigo police officer who Andy was alleged to have had a conversation with on May 4.

* * * *

Volant sent the bloodstained upholstery he had cut from Andy's roadster to Dr. R.L. Hilman at Ashland for examination. Dr. Hilman wired the sheriff that the stains were human blood and not from chickens, and he would send the seatcover pieces to Madison for verification of his results.

* * * *

8:00 pm

The only way Andy and his wife could converse was through the bars of his cell when she came to visit.

"Oh, Andy, I don't believe this has happened. I don't believe you did this terrible thing," she wailed.

"C'mon, Lily. Quit your crying. I ain't going anywhere."

"Did you do what they said, Andy?"

"No. I did not," Andy replied.

"How long will you stay in this place, Andy?"

"Until I get to clear myself," he replied.

"Everybody is for you, Andy. Nobody believes you did this thing."

"I didn't."

"Andy, why did you leave town?" Lily asked.

"I got a new car and decided to take a ride. I guess I got carried away and drove too far."

"Where did you get money to buy a car?"

"I won it gambling," Andy told her.

"Gambling! You bought a different car with money you got gambling?"

"Yep."

"But, Andy, we haven't paid this month's rent yet. We will have to move back in with my mother and father."

"Probably. Now listen, Lily, I don't want you coming here and asking me any questions. And don't cry. I'll get out of this mess," Andy promised.

Lily visited Andy every day, and he had friends who brought him cigars and magazines. He played poker with the jailers and, in general, kept busy cleaning the cellblock.

Wednesday, May 21, 1924

Emma called the Ironwood Taxi Service and said she was in a hurry and had to go to Superior.

"Superior?" the dispatcher asked. "Why don't you take the train, Mrs. Sigler? It'd sure be a lot cheaper."

"Why? Don't you think I have the money? I'll hire the taxi."

"Okay, then. Wait outside the building and a driver will be there in a few minutes."

Emma was driven to Ashland where she told the driver to stop at a restaurant.

"Wait here," Emma told him, "I'll be right back."

Emma went into the restaurant and asked for a cup of coffee. While she was waiting, she used the pay phone to call the law office of Cadigan and Cadigan in Superior and made an appointment to see one of the attorneys, drank her coffee and went back to the waiting cab.

"Let's go. Off to Superior," she said.

Three hours later, at the law firm of Cadigan and Cadigan, she told the receptionist that she had an appointment to see one of the attorneys and was ushered into the office of Peter Cadigan.

"My name is Emma Sigler from Hurley," she started out. "My husband, Andrew, was murdered on May 1 or 2. A friend of mine named Andy Anderson is being held in the Hurley jail for killing him, but I think he is innocent, and I'd like to hire you to defend him."

"Yes, we know about the case. Is Mr. Anderson available or is he in jail?" Cadigan asked.

"He's in jail."

"Did the judge allow bail?"

"No, sir. He is being held without bail."

"Our fees are high, Mrs. Sigler."

"How much?"

"If you decide to retain us, I'll let you know later. We won't know the amount until we look into the case further. For the present, we'll need a retainer of $600 to defend Mr. Anderson.

Emma paid the $600 and took the taxi back to Hurley.

* * * *

Thursday, May 22, 1924

Andy's case was postponed to June 2 at the request of the district attorney. No explanation was given.

* * * *

Monday, June 2, 1924

Andy's case was once again postponed to June 12. There was still no reason given for the postponement.

Saturday evening, June 7, 1924

Ray Rice put the children to bed and came downstairs to the deserted restaurant where she saw Emma sitting quietly by herself.

"Hi, Emma," Ray said.

Emma looked up and saw her. "Oh, Ray. It's you. Hi, yourself."

"Whatcha up to?"

"Nothing. Just sitting here thinking."

"Bothering you, ain't it," Ray said.

"Yeah."

"Me, too. You know, Emma, I wonder if you shouldn't turn yourself in."

"I've been thinking about doing that, but I'm scared. It'd mean I'd lose my kids. I don't want that to happen."

"But it was self defense, Emma. Surely they'll believe you."

"Not the way this town operates. Nobody would believe that I didn't kill him on purpose. Volant and Foster would do anything to get me for Sigler's murder."

"I'd be happy to testify on your behalf. As a matter of fact, Emma, I think I'll talk to the sheriff on Monday. If you aren't gonna tell him, then I will, because I can't stand to see you this way. And they have Andy in jail for the crime; that's got to bother you. C'mon, Emma, the only way to get it off your chest is to tell the cops all about it."

"Okay, okay. On Monday I'll talk to Volant but only if you come with me."

Ray took a cigarette from her pack. "Want one, Emma?"

"Sure."

Ray passed the pack to Emma, lit a match and reached to light Emma's. "Let's have a drink," Ray suggested. "I sure could use one."

"That might be a good idea. I'll get us one."

Emma walked over to the back of the bar and planned to pour a glass of wine for each of them, but when she opened the cabinet she saw the bottle of wood alcohol that Sigler used to spike drinks for himself and the staff, preferring to save the good stuff for the paying customers. *This is potent stuff. Causes blindness. Ray's been pretty sick. Maybe I should use the good stuff. Naw, if there's one thing Ray can do it's handle her liquor. It'll be okay if I give her some, I suppose. She's had plenty of it before.*

She took it out from the cabinet and poured a large glass of the alcohol for Ray, mixed it with gin and just a splash of grenadine to tint it and took the concoction and her glass of wine to where Ray was sitting in the restaurant.

"Here ya go, Ray. Down the hatch."

"Hey, not bad. Tastes pretty good," Ray told her. She finished the drink in a couple of gulps and asked for another. Emma was still sipping her wine but she got up and made her another one.

They chatted for a few minutes and decided to call it a night. When they stood, Ray admitted to feeling a little dizzy so Emma helped her to her room and into bed. Ray immediately fell asleep.

Sunday afternoon, June 8, 1924

Ray had not stirred out of bed, so Emma knocked on her door.

"Ray? You okay?" No answer.

"Ray?" Emma walked into the room and found Ray still lying in her bed in the same position as Emma had left her the night before. She felt Ray's forehead and it was cold. There was no pulse. Ray was dead.

"My God. Oh, Ray," Emma said sadly. "You're okay now. No more misery for you, Hon. You're with the angels."

Emma sat on the side of the bed next to Ray and cried.

I might just as well have killed her. Why did this have to happen? If only I had given her the good stuff last night. The only friend I had is gone. The only person I could talk to. Dear God, take Ray into your heart. She was such a kind soul who saw nothing but misery. I'll miss you, Ray.

Emma phoned the sheriff's office and reported that Ray was dead. Her body was taken to Charbonneau's morgue.

* * * *

Foster and Volant showed up at the Gogebic Hotel to question Emma soon after she called.

"Tell us what happened to Mrs. Rice, Emma." asked Foster.

"We had a drink together last night, and she was complaining about not feeling well so I helped her to bed. In the morning I didn't hear from her so I knocked on the door to her room. I didn't hear any answer, so I went in and found her dead. That's all I know. Oh, poor Ray. She was so good to me. I'll miss her," Emma cried.

"I'm sorry, Emma. I know she was a friend," Volant told her. "Guess that's all we need to know. Will you be okay?"

"I'm fine. I've got things to do around here."

Volant and Foster left the Gogebic Hotel and walked across the street to Dr. Urquhart's office.

"Morning, Doc," Foster said. "Emma found Rachel Rice dead this afternoon. I want a complete examination of Ray

Rice's body. Need to find the cause of death. Can you do that in a hurry?"

"Sure. I'll get Dr. Hambley to help. We should have the results of the post mortem to you tomorrow morning. Is that soon enough?"

"That will do," replied Foster.

Monday, June 9, 1924

"Hi, Warren," Dr. Urquhart said as he sat in the chair in Foster's office. "Got the results of the post mortem here."

"What did you find out?"

"She died of alcohol poisoning. Found wood alcohol, methyl alcohol in her stomach and blood stream. I sent some internal organs to Madison for further examination. We won't know anything conclusive until I get the report from the state crime lab. But I'm darn near positive that the alcohol is what killed her. My preliminary tests show well over twenty percent alcohol in her blood. Enough to kill a horse."

Town gossip speculated that Ray was poisoned because she knew about the murder and it was feared that she might tell more than she had already revealed to the district attorney and the sheriff. According to the Daily Globe, "wild rumors circulated from time to time for officers to watch certain persons because of the belief that they might be poisoned if they told 'too much' of the murder case."

A coroner's jury was called to investigate the cause of death. They were dismissed pending results from the crime lab in Madison, and Ray's body was shipped to the home of her sister, Mrs. H.J. Gow, 163 Isabel Street, St. Paul.

PART TWO

Saturday, June 14, 1924

The morning train from Milwaukee arrived at the Ironwood Depot on time, and as usual, a crowd had gathered, some to meet someone, but most just to see who was traveling. Nobody paid much attention to the tall, thin man wearing a suit, tie and starched collar who stepped down from the coach. Just another salesman. He walked to the baggage claim area and lit a cigarette, then pretended to watch the suitcases and trunks being loaded on a baggage cart. His eyes moved back and forth from one person to another on the platform. He flicked his cigarette butt on the tracks under the train and gave the baggage master his claim stub. With the bustling crowd, no one noticed as he walked toward the Ironwood police car waiting in the parking lot.

"Mr. Halpin?" asked the officer who took his baggage. "Welcome to Ironwood, sir. How was the train trip?"

"Uncomfortable. Hot as blazes in that coach. I sure could use a bath." he answered. "Where are we off to?"

"Iron County has registered you at the St. James Hotel. It's only a few blocks away. They have nice rooms with hot and cold running water. Bathtub, flush toilets. Pretty good food, too. We've arranged for room service to bring you breakfast. Let them know what you want when you check in. Iron County is footing the bill, of course. In the meantime, while you're in Ironwood, our police department is at your disposal. Hop in and I'll drive you," the cop said.

"No thanks, I'd just as soon walk. Need to stretch my legs. How do I get to the St. James?"

The cop pointed to the south. "Head down Suffolk Street for a block," he said as he gestured with his hand, "then cross Aurora Street, and you can't miss it on the right."

Hayes nodded thanks but didn't speak. He retrieved his bag from the officer and walked to the St. James Hotel, where he registered under the name of Joe Halpin from Minneapolis. There were only three people on the Gogebic Range who knew that "Joe Halpin from Minneapolis" was really Joseph P. Hayes, a private detective from Milwaukee: the Iron County district attorney, Warren Foster; the Iron County Sheriff, Joseph Volant; and the undersheriff, Richard Kalliomaa.

Joe Hayes was the senior private investigator for the Russell Detective Agency. He had worked for them since August, 1915, and except for two years overseas during World War I, had been employed by the firm since then. Hayes was married and lived with his wife in an apartment on Wisconsin Avenue. He had a reputation for getting at the truth, and Iron County had hired Hayes specifically to see if he could get information out of Andy.

After eating his breakfast and taking a bath, Hayes rested until noon, and then went downstairs to the dining room of the St. James. He sat down at a table against the wall where he was sure to see anyone who entered, and ordered a bowl of soup, a ham on rye, and a cup of coffee. Just when he lit a Lucky Strike and started to sip a second cup of coffee, Sheriff Volant walked into the dining room and sat down across from Hayes. They shook hands. Hayes spoke first.

"I've been giving this case a lot of thought since your phone call, Sheriff. We have a tough nut to crack, I guess."

"It's the truth," replied Volant. "Anderson still sticks to his story that he didn't have anything to do with killing Sigler."

"Where's Anderson now?" asked Hayes.

"Lodged in the county jail."

"How long can you hold him?"

"Til the circuit court judge gets here in a few days. He's held without bail."

"Can he escape?"

"Not from my jail! Even if he could, he'd need some help. Anderson doesn't appear to have much up here, you know," Volant replied as he pointed to his head.

"We don't have a whole lot on him," Volant continued. "Lots of circumstantial stuff. So the guy leaves town for a few days. We can't hold him on that. Emma's kid says that his pa went out with Andy to get some chickens the night before we found Sigler dead. Nothing there, either. Found his car with blood splattered on the seat."

"What are you holding him on?"

"Suspicion of murder. Judge did issue a formal arrest warrant, so I guess we got plenty of time to get more of the facts of the case down." Volant paused. "Had to postpone his hearing at least twice."

"So what about the blood? Tell me more," said Hayes.

"He says its chicken blood, but it was human blood according to what Dr. Hilman told us. Hilman sent the seatcover pieces to Madison to be sure of it. That's about all we got."

"Didn't you fellows take any fingerprints?" asked Hayes in disbelief.

No, cuz nobody around here knows much about fingerprinting and besides, we don't have the equipment. I think the state can do that with their crime lab, but we don't have any of that new stuff you folks got in the city. I only read about that kind of thing in Police Gazette," he laughed.

"Ummm. Too bad," muttered Hayes. "What about the murder weapon?"

"Haven't found it yet. We combed the area where the murder took place. Nothing. Found a .32 caliber spent cartridge, a hat, and a few buttons from Sigler's mackinaw."

"And that's everything?" asked Hayes.

"Yep, that's it. Sorry. We done our best. Maybe Foster can shed some more light; if you're all set, we can go see him at the jail."

"Yeah, I'm all set here, Sheriff. Let's get the show on the road."

Hayes tossed a quarter on the table and signed the guest check. "Put it on my room tab," he told the waitress.

Volant and Hayes drove to Hurley to meet with the district attorney. On the way to Foster's office, they drove around Hurley where Volant pointed out the Gogebic Hotel, the Burton House, and City Hall before parking in back of Foster's office in the Paul Building and going in the back door. Foster's office was across from the Gogebic Hotel on the corner of Second Avenue and Silver Street, and they didn't want to take a chance on Emma seeing Hayes.

"Hi, Warren," Volant said when they entered the office. "Meet Joe Hayes."

Foster got up from his desk and put out his hand. Hayes shook it. "Good to meet you, Joe."

"Likewise, Mr. Foster."

"Call me Warren. Want a cup of coffee?"

"Okay, thanks. I think I will."

The district attorney got three cups of coffee.

"Thanks. What's the plan, Warren?" Hayes asked.

"We're open for any suggestions."

"Okay, here's what I'd like to do. I'd like to visit Emma Sigler and get close to her. I'll tell her that I'm from Milwaukee, and after I get on her good side, I'll let her know that I was involved with the Palmolive payroll robbery. Then you arrest me and put me in jail in the cell next to Anderson. I'll tell him the same thing. I'll tell Mrs. Sigler and Anderson that my name is 'Slim'. So if that sounds okay with you two, I'm now a bad guy. I'll get him to talk. Don't worry."

"Perfect!" Foster told him. "What do you think Sheriff?"

"Sounds like it might work."

"Course it'll work," Hayes said.

"Let's do it," Foster said.

Hayes left Foster's office through the back door and went immediately to the Gogebic hotel where he ordered a cup of coffee. Emma served him, and then began to pass the time of day with Hayes.

"Hi, I'm Emma. I'm the owner."

"Yeah?" Hayes sipped his coffee and nodded his head in greeting.

"New around here?" she asked.

"Yeah," Hayes replied.

"Where are you from?"

"Milwaukee. Say, you sure ask a lot of questions."

"Just like to meet and greet, especially handsome guys like you. I didn't get your name?"

"Joe Halpin. Just call me Slim."

"Okay, Slim it is then. So what brings you to town, Slim?"

"Just looking around."

"Where you staying?

"Ironwood. At the St. James."

"I was hoping you might stay here."

"The St. James is a nice joint, and I like it quiet sometimes. I like to read."

"We've got a nice place here, and it's a lot cheaper than the St. James. Usually quiet. Food's a lot better even. Give it a try."

"I must say that your coffee is better. Sure, why not. Hurley seems more lively than Ironwood. Never seen this many bars on one street ever. I think I'll take your offer, Emma. I'll stay here, then. You talked me into it."

"Mind if I sit down?" Emma asked.

"No, be my guest." Emma sat down in the booth across from Hayes.

"You say you like to read?" Emma asked. "I like to read myself. What kind of books do you read?"

"Oh, I like Thoreau, Oscar Wilde, Melville. You name it and I like to read it. I like philosophy the best. Psychology, too. Have you heard of a guy named Sigmund Freud?"

"Heard about him. Haven't read anything, though."

He writes about ego and id and all sorts of weird ideas. You read any good books lately?"

"The kids and I go to the library in Ironwood every so often. They have a good children's department. I borrow a lot of books for them. I got Heidi for them last month. Have you read it?"

Hayes chuckled. "No, I ain't into kids' books. But hey, I got to get going. I'm booked at the St. James tonight, but I think I'll register here tomorrow. You are open tomorrow, aren't you?"

"Mister, we're open seven days a week, 365 days a year. "

"How about breakfast in the morning?" Hayes asked.

"You got a deal. Ham and eggs? Fried spuds? Plenty of coffee?"

"That's the ticket. I'll be here. 8 o'clock okay?"

"Fine. I'll be waiting," Emma said.

Over the next few days, Hayes kept to his room, but when he came down for meals his eyes were moving constantly. When a stranger entered, he put his hand under his coat where one might have a shoulder holster. Soon, he gained Emma's confidence, and they had friendly chats about her children, Sigler, and reading. They worked crossword puzzles and played cards together and had a great time.

"What kind of work do you do, Slim?" Emma finally asked.

"I was in the Army in the Great War, but fell on hard times when I got out. Been drifting since. Made some money in the Palmolive payroll job.

"What do you mean?"

"I mean I pulled off the heist."

"That was you? Why, I had no idea that you were capable of that."

"Well, now you know. And I'd advise you not to tell anybody."

"I wouldn't dream of it," Emma assured Hayes. "There's a guy in jail who I paid two grand to bump off my old man. You can trust me."

"You had your old man bumped off? When was that?"

"Last month."

"No lie?"

"Yeah, I gave the guy $400 for the job, and I told him he'd get the rest soon as the insurance is paid."

"Jesus, you had your old man killed, huh? Couldn't you have just divorced him?

"Naw, it was him or me. My old man would have just as soon killed me first."

Emma hesitated for a bit and said "But I don't really believe the guy they're holding killed my husband. I think that somebody else got to him first. Maybe the cops got to him first. Know what I mean?"

"No, what?" Hayes asked.

"I mean that certain people in this town have been trying to nuzzle up to me for a long time. Maybe one of them did it, maybe not. Sigler had a lot of enemies and the son-of-a-bitch took it out on me. Beat me every chance he had. The kids, too. I hired some attorneys to defend Andy. That's how much I think he really didn't do the job."

"Who's Andy?"

"Andy Anderson. The guy in jail."

Thursday, June 19, 1924

Hayes left the Gogebic Hotel and reported in to the district attorney. He had everything under control, and it was time for him to be arrested and begin phase two.

"Did she say anything about the murder, Joe?" Foster asked.

"Well, this is one tough lady. At first she told me that she paid Anderson $2,000 to kill Sigler. Then she changed her story and said that Anderson didn't do it. Hinted that it might be a city official."

"What? Did she say who she thought it was?"

"No, except she told me that Anderson was innocent. Didn't say why. Just told me that Andy couldn't have killed Sigler. He was the best friend that Sigler had. She told me she hired some attorneys from Superior to defend him."

"Oh? I heard that somebody retained Cadigan, but I didn't know who it was. Good job, Joe."

"How we gonna pull off my arrest?"

"You go back to the Gogebic. Wait there and we'll be there sometime in the afternoon.

That afternoon about 4 o'clock, Hayes was sitting at the bar drinking coffee and smoking a cigarette when Volant and Kalliomaa entered and saw him at the bar chatting with Emma. They walked up to him, Volant on one side and Kalliomaa on the other. Hayes reached for the imaginary gun under his jacket, but Volant and Kalliomaa grabbed him.

"Your name Halpin?" Volant asked as he handcuffed Hayes.

"Yeah. Who wants to know."

Volant showed him his badge and the holstered gun at his side. "Sheriff. You're under arrest."

"What for?"

"The Palmolive heist."

Hayes got up and sneered, "You got nothing on me."

"Got a warrant for your arrest from Milwaukee. That's what we got on you, smart guy."

They took Hayes to the jail and put him in the cell next to Andy. Hayes and Andy eyed each other for the rest of the afternoon but didn't speak.

Not much transpired between the two on Friday or Saturday. They were required to mop the jailhouse floors and do general housekeeping around the jail. In the evening, Hayes read, and Andy just sat dejected on his cot waiting for a visit from his wife.

Friday, June 20, 1924

The afternoon mail arrived at the Gogebic Hotel. There were some bills and sympathy cards, and there was a letter addressed to Joe Halpin c/o Gogebic Hotel, Hurley.

Mmmm. Wonder what's in it. No return address. Postmarked Milwaukee. Emma turned the letter around and around in her hand. *I guess I'll steam it open. Could be important.* Emma took the letter over to the cook stove where she held it over the spout on the steaming tea kettle. The envelope opened easily after the glue began to melt. She opened the letter and read it. It was from a lady in Milwaukee.

> Dear Slim,
>
> I'm okay. Hope you are the same. Al and I are anxious to meet with you in Hurley. Things are getting hot down here if you know what I mean. The work you wrote about sounds easy. Nothing I haven't done before. Sounds like a great place to hide out. I sure hope that woman who runs the hotel will hire me. We'll be up on the train on Monday afternoon. Put in a good word for us. I'll bring the loot with like you asked me to. Well, take it easy, Slim. See you soon. Gracie.

"Well," Emma said aloud. "What do you think of that? Guess Mr. Halpin gets around. He sure could come in handy around here. I need a man to keep things in order. And he's got money."

Saturday, June 21, 1924

George Cooper from the Superior law firm of Cadigan and Cadigan visited Andy at the jail and questioned him about everything. Andy denied knowing anything about the murder except that a man named Miller killed Sigler. District Attorney Foster and Sheriff Volant came to see Andy that morning, too. They questioned him once again about the murder, but Andy stuck to his story that he heard a man named Miller did it. Foster knew he was lying.

"Andy, we got the lab results from Dr. Hilman and from Madison. That blood in your car was not chicken blood. It was human. Now come clean with us."

"It's from chickens I tell you."

"Listen, Andy, I can make a deal with you."

"Yeah, what kind of a deal?"

"If you confess to killing Sigler, I'll guarantee that you will only get from one to seven years. Maybe even get off. You'll probably just have to go back to Green Bay."

"One to seven, hey? And you'll guarantee that?"

"Yep. And at Green Bay, too. Not Waupun State Prison. One to seven, Andy."

"Let me think about it," Andy told them.

"Okay. We'll be waiting for your answer. But, remember, if you don't come clean with us, you'll probably get life at hard labor in Waupun."

"I'll let you know what I decide."

Late that night as Hayes was whistling a tune in his cell, Andy finally spoke. He got off his bunk and looked at Hayes through the bars of his cell. Hayes saw him and came nearer to Andy.

"So what are you in here for?" Andy whispered.

"Who wants to know?"

"Name is Andy Anderson."

"Call me Slim," Hayes replied.

"Okay, Slim."

"What are you in here for, Andy?"

"Murder. They say I killed a guy."

"They got me for the Palmolive heist in Milwaukee," said Hayes.

"Palmolive? I read about that in the papers. That was a 25 G job!"

"Yep. Big money."

"Was that your first time?" asked Andy.

"Naw. I pulled a bunch of jobs since getting out of the Army."

"Me, too. I spent a long time in the joint. Pulled my first heist when I was 11. Just nickel and dime stuff. Got out in 1918."

"Married?"

"Yeah. That's my wife who comes to see me every night."

"Nice lady. She thinks a lot of you."

"She does. She's a nice lady. Good wife and mother, too. Say, how long you in here for, Slim?"

"I'll be out Monday morning. They can't hold me in this joint. I got friends. How about you? You in here for long?"

"Dunno. I was supposed to go before the judge a couple weeks ago. Keep postponing it."

"Not good. Not good, Andy."

"Nope. Sure ain't good." Andy replied.

"Hey, anything I can do for you, just let me know."

"I appreciate that," Andy said.

"Hey, Andy, did you really kill that guy?"

"Naw, it was a guy name of Miller that killed Sigler," Andy lied. "Quiet, here comes the bull."

The jailhouse deputy came by and shot the breeze with them for awhile, then told them it was lights out. They slept.

Sunday, June 22, 1924

They were awakened at 7 am when the deputy came with a breakfast of oatmeal and coffee.

"How are you two this morning?" the deputy asked.

"Same as always," Andy replied. Hayes said nothing to the deputy.

After they ate their breakfast, they were told by the deputy on duty to clean up the jailhouse. They grabbed the mops and filled buckets with water, then proceeded with the daily chores. They were the only two prisoners in the jail area. The deputy was in Volant's office.

Hayes leaned on his mop. "Andy?"

"Yeah?"

"You say that you didn't kill Sigler."

"Right. A guy named Miller did."

"C'mon. I've been around a while, and I don't believe you. Miller, huh? You really killed him, right?" Hayes fumbled around for a bit with his mop. "Ya know, Andy, I really could use a guy like you. With my connections, I can make you a rich man."

"Yeah?" Andy stopped mopping.

"Right. So tell me what happened."

"Later, when we're back in our cages," Andy told him.

When they finished their housekeeping chores and were back in their cells, Andy sat down on the floor next to Hayes' cell. Hayes was lying on his cot reading. He dog-eared the page he was reading and sat on the floor across from Andy. "Wanna talk about it, Andy?" Hayes asked.

"Yeah."

"How'd it happen?"

Andy really wanted to impress Hayes. Hayes had already told him a lot about his past escapades, so Andy decided to embellish certain details.

"Well, it started a couple of months ago. This lady, Ray, told me that Emma Sigler would give me two grand to kill her husband. I says to her, 'That's a lot of dough. Lemme think about it.' I figured I could use the two thousand, so I told her I'd do it."

"Where did this Emma person get the money to pay you?"

"Said her old man had life insurance. Six, maybe seven grand. Emma said she would collect it and give me two thousand."

"Did she give you any money at that time?"

"She gave me 40 bucks."

"Did Ray or Emma tell you how it was to be done?" Hayes asked.

"Yeah. Ray told me that she had the gun to do it with. She and Emma bought it from a gun dealer in Ironwood. She gave him some money, five bucks, I think, so he wouldn't register it. Then Ray and I went out in the woods and practiced shooting."

"Then what happened?"

"Emma asked me to kill Sigler."

"What did she suggest you do?"

"Well, she says that I should shoot Sigler and dump his body in a mine shaft, but I told her that it wouldn't be a good idea. I told her that I thought there was a seven-year waiting period after a guy was missing before he was legally dead, so she couldn't get the insurance money until after seven years if he was just missing. I says to her that somebody needs to find that body."

"So what'd you do?"

"Well, one night I took Sigler out to kill him. Drove past Lake Lavina. I planned to shoot him there and dump his body there, but there was too many cars. I thought it best to wait until I had a better chance."

"I guess you got that chance," Hayes said.

"Yep, sure did. I bumped the guy off."

By this time, Andy was wound up in his fabrication of the killing of Sigler and Hayes played the role like an accomplished stage actor.

"Jesus, Andy. That really took guts to kill a guy. Closest I ever got was just carrying a gat. I ain't never killed no one."

"Ah, it was easy. I took the guy out on the Mercer Road and stopped by Layman's Creek and shot him."

"What happened?" asked Hayes.

"Well, like I was telling you, I drove down the Mercer Road, and when we were about to Layman's Creek, I was driving with my right hand on the wheel. I pulled out the gat and says to him, 'Now Andrew, if you got any message to send to your wife and kids, send it now.' Sigler says 'You're crazy.' I says, 'No, I mean it.' He tells me to stop the car, and I shot him and hit him in the side. Then Sigler threw a hand to his face, and I fired again. I think the bullet went through his hand and hit him in the head. I know I hit him in the head because blood spurted on the top of the seat and on the gat."

"What did you do then?"

"I pulled Sigler's body out of the car and threw him across the ditch about 10 feet into the woods."

"Do you think Sigler was still alive when you threw him into the woods?"

"Naw. He was dead as a doornail. But he grunted like a pig when he landed."

"What'd ya do after you dumped his body?"

"I tossed the gun in the woods and drove back to the New Central, parked in back and drove home to Ironwood in my new car. Then I went to bed."

"You went back home? Boy, you got real guts!" Hayes said. "How'd you end up getting pinched for the job?"

"Next morning I went to work, and Emma calls me and says I should leave town cuz the cops are asking questions. She gave me 40 bucks. I drove down to Green Bay and saw a newspaper article that the cops were looking for me. I drove back to about seven or eight miles from town and spent a couple of days in Hurley. I rolled around in some sawdust so they'd think I slept in the lumber yard. That's when they got me."

"Andy, you're a pretty savvy guy, and I hate to see you in this mess. Listen, they tell me that I'm getting out of this joint Monday morning because I'll fight extradition. Do you need money or anything? You'll need enough to get to Mexico at least."

"Money? Sure I need some. What I really want to do is somehow bust out of here and get lost someplace where nobody can find me. Mexico sounds good to me."

"I know how you can bust out."

"And how might that be, Slim?"

"Put a bar of soap in a sock, and when the jailer comes close to the bars, lay him out and grab the keys."

"Naw, I don't want to hurt anybody."

Hayes took off his left shoe. "Look here," he whispered.

Under the sole of his shoe, Hayes had placed a hacksaw blade. "Here, take this," he whispered as he passed the blade through the bars of the cell. Hide it in your shoe and use it at night to saw the bars off the window. When you cut the bars loose, tie the bedding to one of the window bars and lower yourself to the ground. I'll be there with a car to take you off."

"After I saw through the bars, how am I supposed to get that window open?" Andy asked. "There are all those glass blocks."

"It'll be a cinch. All you have to do is take the hacksaw blade and get it between those glass blocks and the glass blocks will drop down to the ground. Use the hacksaw to loosen the cement that's between those blocks, but do the bars first and then wait for me to give you a signal. Then do the glass blocks."

"How will you know when I'm ready to bust out?"

"I'll be by to see you."

"What about the money?"

"Listen, how about I see if I can arrange something with Emma. She still owes you for killing her old man. Write her a note."

"I don't know what to say."

"I'll tell you what to write," Hayes said.

Andy pulled out a sheet of Cadigan and Cadigan note paper the attorney had given him and wrote down what Hayes dictated to him with the stub of a pencil.

> Emma, I am OK in health only for my troubles I have as you see in papers and hear around town. I am not going to walk the streets in town any longer I guess. Cause they will not give me bail or a damn thing to say, or do. I sure thank you kid for your troubles and do not let Foster fill you up on stuff that I had lots to say cause I never said a word or mentioned your name in this at all. Now I met a friend of

mine in here and hes going to give me real aid in this place and wish you could help me in some money matters which you think is not sure, but this is my only chance I have to get out this place. So remember I still stick to my words. And you know it yourself. If I could only see you and talk to you I sure will someday. Now I must get down to business and make a getaway from here. Everybody not for me. Only against me. I need about $100 more or less if you can. The more I get the better on my side of story. This is know bunk which you might think cause me that is to suffer for this right through and your aid with Slims aid then I am all set for my ride far away. I do not think my lawyers are doing me very much only help me off in Hell all the time. You can come with Slim and see that he does as I say in this letter or note you could come and see me every night in the northwest corner of jail not talk but send me letters or notes of some kind. Get me. You sure done me good I must say. Now Emma please send me some cash through Slim and yourself you can see it go up on the string you can come in about 15 feet of jail after 12 o'clock in night, so paper getting short I must close and hope to hear from you and your aid also see you near the place. I will watch all the time. Goodbye, Andy

P.S. Do not be afraid of my wife not a word said only when she she comes asks dam fulish questions I hate to see her come and cry worry and other things like that I leave to Slim on that to see and say. See me through this thing as soon as possible. Do not waste your money on the lawyers and all they do is play with you and make me a damn fool of me. Remember do not say a word about Slim in this case because I know him well and know him a square guy. Slim can tell you what Foster said to me Saturday morning about me and I never said a word about you to him in any way. I mean every word I am thinking of in this note.[2]

Hayes grabbed the note from Andy. "I'll see to it this gets to Emma, okay?"

[2] Verbatim from trial transcript and Ironwood Daily Globe.

"I want to write it over again. I need to get some clean paper from the sheriff."

"It's fine, Andy. Just fine. If I can read it then Emma can."

"If you say so, Slim."

Andy sat for awhile on the floor and put his hands on his knees. There was something else on his mind.

"Listen, Slim," Andy said, "the coppers told me I'd get one to seven years if I confessed to killing Sigler. What do you think?"

"I wouldn't believe these small-town bulls if my life depended on it. I say bust out and stick with me. That's the only way you're gonna get out of this."

"Yeah, you're right I suppose."

"You bet I am. I've seen this happen before. They tell a guy something that'll get his hopes up, then they take it back and burn the guy anyhow."

Monday, June 23, 1924

The sheriff approached Hayes' cell. "Are you really going to fight extradition if Minneapolis authorities want you?" he asked.

"You bet your sweet life I am," Hayes told him.

"If that's the case, I'll turn you loose. That Minneapolis bunch have showed no intention of reimbursing us for our expense and trouble with you, so we're through with you. You're released to go, Halpin. I don't want to see your ugly face ever again in my jail." Volant unlocked the cell. "Now get out of here."

"You'll never see Slim Halpin in here, Sheriff, except as a visitor." He winked at Volant and smiled.

Volant left and Hayes turned to Andy. "Listen, Andy, you're as good as freed. Just keep to the plan."

Foster was waiting for Hayes in Volant's office.

"Let's get you registered at the Curry Hotel in Ironwood. You'll like it there. It's a nice place, Joe. Then you can visit with Emma. What did you get out of Anderson?"

"Got a full confession."

"You did? That's great! He told you that he killed Sigler, then?"

"Yep. Got everything. When I get to the hotel I'll write out my notes and give them to you."

The first thing Hayes did when he checked into his room was to phone Emma and arrange to meet with her that afternoon.

"Hi, Emma. This is Slim. I'm out of jail."

"Where are you?" she asked.

"At the Curry Hotel in Ironwood. Where can I meet you?"

"Do you know where Suffolk and Aurora intersect?"

"Yes, I do."

"Meet me there about 3 o'clock. I'll get my brother-in-law to drive me."

"Okay. Three o'clock. See you then," Hayes told her.

Hayes ordered room service, sat down, and wrote everything he could remember of the past few days. He took Andy's note and erased a period and penciled in another zero after the 100 that Andy had written.

"There," he said out loud. "That thousand bucks should be more money than Emma has lying around."

Then he lay down to rest. At 2:30, Hayes woke up and took a hot bath, then walked to the corner of Suffolk and Aurora. Emma was waiting for him.

"Slim!" Emma said. "God, am I glad to see you."

"Same here, Emma. Glad to see you." He gave her a kiss on the cheek.

"My brother-in-law is waiting for us at the end of the block," she told him.

Hayes followed Emma south on Suffolk Street to the corner of McLeod where there was a car waiting. Emma opened the back door of the car and invited Hayes to get in. She got in the back seat with him.

"Slim, this is my brother-in-law, Burton Day. Burt, meet Slim." Hayes reached over the seat and shook Day's hand.

Day drove them about three miles north of Ironwood before turning onto an old logging road. Day stayed in the car, and Emma and Hayes went up the road out of earshot of Day and sat down on the side of the road.

"Emma, did you have Sigler killed? I'm not real clear on that."

"Yes, I had him killed."

"Who was it that killed him?"

"No names, Slim. But I can tell you that Sigler should have been killed a long time ago. He was a sick man, and he was crazy. Did I tell you he got the clap and tried to give it to me? Beat the crap out of me and the kids if we looked cross-eyed at him."

"Why that rotten bastard, "Why didn't you kill him yourself?"

"I wish I would have, but I didn't think murdering him would solve my problems. It would only add to them."

"Why do you think the guy who killed him dumped his body in that place where it would be easily found?"

"I don't know. Not a bright idea I suppose. If it was me, I would have put his god-damn body in a shithouse."

"Here's something for you," Hayes said and handed her the letter that Andy had given him. "Andy told me to give this to you."

Emma read the letter. "How much did Andy tell you?"

"He told me the whole story about how he killed Sigler. He also told me that he understood that you had poisoned Ray, but this only made it worse for him."

"He what?" Emma turned white as a sheet. *Why would Andy lie to Slim about me? Why would he take the rap for me? And what's this about Ray? What does he know about me and Ray? He knows I wouldn't kill Ray. He knows she was my friend.*

Hayes must have deliberately lied that Andy had told him about Ray's death, hoping to get her to confess to murdering her. Andy had no knowledge of Ray's death. He was in jail on June 8, the day she died.

"I guess Andy told you how I had Sigler killed, but I'm telling the truth now. I didn't kill Ray," Emma said.

"You don't need to worry, Emma. Andy and I worked together at the Holbert Mill paper company in Green Bay. I know him well."

"What did he tell you about me?" she asked.

"Well, he told me in the first place about four months before he killed him, Ray suggested that Andy shoot Sigler and if he would do it, Ray would buy a gun for him. He said that you and Ray went to a hardware store in Ironwood in a cab and paid $32 for a .38 caliber pistol. And he said the clerk asked you to register it, and Ray gave the clerk a five buck tip so it didn't need to be registered."

"That's all hooey," Emma said.

"What I can't figure out is why you didn't hire a person wiser than Andy to do the job."

"I thought he was a pretty wise kid, but he bungled it and acted like a damn fool," Emma told Hayes. "I guess I have to do what he says now. I think he's foolish to want to break jail, though."

"Why's that?" Hayes asked. "Seems like that might be the only wise thing he can do."

"Naw. I think he can get off easy. Maybe go to Mexico."

"What about you? What will you do?"

"They haven't got anything on me, but Foster would like to prosecute me, anyway."

"What makes you think that?"

"I can tell by the way he talks."

"What about getting the money to Andy," Hayes asked.

"I've got a little money. What with all the bills Sigler left me, there isn't much."

"Can you come up with the grand that he wants?

"Not that much, but I can send some to him. I'll get him enough to get to Mexico. I've got to let Andy know that I didn't get the insurance money yet."

"Listen, bring some money in an envelope tonight, but first maybe we should drive to the cemetery and look for his signal. He says he's gonna hang a handkerchief from his cell window and hang a string down from the bars. Then we'll tie the money on the string and get it to him like he said in the note."

"Do you think there is any danger of my fingerprints on the money and the envelope?"

"Naw. I wouldn't worry too much about it," Hayes told her.

"Well, I don't want to take no chances."

"Suit yourself."

They drove to Riverside cemetery to see if they could spot the handkerchief signal that Andy said he'd hang out the window.

"I don't see anything," Emma said.

"I can't see it, either" Hayes answered. "Look there in the northwest corner of the second floor. That's where our cells were. Nothing there."

Emma scribbled a note and gave it to Hayes. "Is there a way you can get it to Andy?"

"Sure," Hayes answered and took the note. "I can get it to him in the morning. The cops told me I can visit him."

Day and Emma dropped Hayes off at the Chicago-Northwestern Depot in Ironwood.

"I'll give you a call later on. Plan to meet me at the library. I'll let you know what time to get there," Hayes told her.

Hayes got to his room at the Curry Hotel, read the note Emma had given him and phoned Foster.

"Hi, Warren, it's me, Joe Hayes. I've got the trap set up. Emma gave me a note for Anderson. Listen to this. It says 'Your add Ida Johnson, city, state. My add Miss Oscar Stack, Proctor, Minn. Personal. Will have much more in two weeks. Write to me in two weeks.' She's gonna put some money in an envelope for Anderson. I told her that I was going to visit Anderson tomorrow morning."

"Where are you supposed to meet her?"

"At the library in Ironwood."

"What time?"

"I told her I'd phone her with the time. Got any suggestions?"

"How's 8 o'clock this evening sound? That way Volant and I can do some snooping at the Gogebic without her there. Keep her busy for about an hour."

"Okay. I can do that. See you later, Warren."

Hayes got on the phone with Emma and told her to meet him at 8 o'clock. It was now just four. *Good. Plenty of time for a nap and supper.*

Meanwhile, Emma found a pair of white gloves, took $62 out of the cash register and dug around for an envelope. She washed the money and envelope. *I don't care what Slim told me, I don't want to take a chance.* She put on the gloves, took the money and envelope from the wash basin and found her iron.

Then she ironed the money and envelope dry. When she was done, she put the money in the envelope and sealed it.

Emma took the streetcar to Ironwood where Hayes was waiting for her on the corner of Norfolk and Aurora Streets just outside of the Ironwood Carnegie Library. Still wearing the gloves, Emma handed Hayes the blue envelope containing the money.

"Can they get my fingerprints off those bills?" Emma asked him again.

"Naw," Hayes told her. "Not a chance. This hick sheriff and that fool for a D.A. don't know nothing about fingerprinting."

"Well, I washed them just to be sure. Dried them with the iron."

"This is sure costing you a lot of money, Emma," Hayes said. "How much have you given Andy?"

"I've already paid Andy about $500," Emma told him.

"Andy told me you'd give him two grand if he bumped off Sigler."

"I'll give him the rest as soon as I get the insurance money."

"When will that be?"

"It should be in a few days. I hope to get it next week. Then I can send the rest to Andy. I mean if he can bust out and meet me in Proctor."

"Yeah. Know what you mean. Andy's a pretty savvy kid. I'd like to see him out of there. I think I know a way," Hayes told her.

"That'd be great, Slim. Get him to Mexico if you can."

While Hayes and Emma made their plan, sheriff's deputies were at the Gogebic Hotel looking for whatever they could find to incriminate Emma. They searched all the rooms, but found nothing significant.

Emma took the streetcar back to Hurley, and Hayes met with Foster again. Hayes and Foster opened the blue envelope and found the $62. That, along with the note that Emma had given Hayes was enough to involve Emma in Sigler's murder, they guessed.

Foster, Kalliomaa and two deputies went back to the Gogebic Hotel. Searching around in a dresser drawer, they found a package of blue envelopes similar to the one that she had given Hayes.

* * * *

A little after midnight, after an arrest warrant was issued, Volant and a deputy went to the Gogebic Hotel and arrested Emma as an accessory to Sigler's murder. She was led handcuffed to the Iron County Jail.

"Why am I being arrested?" Emma asked the district attorney.

"Do you know a man named Slim Halpin?"

Slim? He wouldn't have told them anything. I'm not telling Foster anything about Slim.

"No, I do not," Emma lied.

"Well, maybe this will refresh your memory." Foster showed her the note and the envelope with the money in it. "Where did this come from?" he asked.

"I have no idea where it came from."

Hayes entered Volant's office and Emma turned white.

"Wh..wh… What the hell is this? What are you doing here, Slim?"

"Meet Detective Joe Hayes from the Russell Detective Agency, Emma," Foster said.

"Hayes? Slim is a detective? You sons of bitches! You bastards! You set me up!" Emma shouted.

Emma was held in the sheriff's office for the time being to keep her as far away from Andy as possible.

About one o'clock that morning, Foster, Volant, Kaliomaa and Hayes visited Andy in his cell. Andy was snoring loudly when they woke him.

"Get up Andy. There's somebody here who wants to see you," Volant yelled.

Andy sat on the edge of his cot and rubbed his eyes. When he focused he saw the four men standing outside of his cell. The one who he paid the most attention to was Hayes.

"Slim!" Andy said when he saw Hayes. "They got you, I guess," he said drowsily.

"That's not the way it is. My real name is Joe Hayes. I'm a detective."

"What do you mean you're a detective?" Andy asked. Andy appeared very nervous. He just stood there in his cell and looked like he was about to cry.

"Just that. I'm a detective, and I want you to tell the district attorney and sheriff what you told me when I was locked up next to you."

"What are you talking about? I didn't tell you nothing. Are you crazy?

"Make it easy on yourself, Andy. Tell us what you told Detective Hayes."

"Nothing. That's what I told him. Nothing."

"Andy, like I told you before, if you confess I'll see to it that you get from one to seven, otherwise you'll get life in Waupun. The Big House. Hard labor. Talk to us, Andy."

I don't know nothing about it except that a guy named Miller was involved," Andy said.

Getting nothing from Andy, Volant went to get Emma from his residence on the main floor of the jail.

"Emma, get up. We're going to talk to Anderson," Volant told her.

"I'm sleeping. Dammit, can't you leave me alone?"

"This can't wait, Emma. Get up."

"Yeah, yeah, yeah. Get out of here then so I can get my robe on."

After she was dressed, Emma was led upstairs to Andy's cell.

"Emma," Foster said on the way to see Andy, "Ask Andy if he killed your husband."

"Okay. I'll do that, but I don't believe he did it."

"If he didn't do it, then who did, Emma?" Foster asked.

"I really don't know. There was a man who took my husband to Ashland that morning. I don't know any more than that."

"Who was this man?"

"I never saw him before. I don't know"

"What time was that?"

"Six or a quarter to six," Emma said.

"Remember to ask Anderson if he did the murder."

When they got to the cell, Emma looked at Andy and said "Andy, did you kill my husband?"

"I did nothing of the kind."

"Do you know who did then?" Emma asked.

"Somebody named Miller. All I know," Andy replied.

"Andy, I might be your last friend. Come straight with us," Foster said.

"Got nothing to say."

They could get nothing more out of Andy except denials. He claimed that he had not spoken to Hayes at the jail; he claimed that he had heard that a man named Miller had killed Sigler. He claimed that the blood in his car was from chickens. His story was the same as it had been since he walked into the sheriff's office on May 10.

About two in the morning, the sheriff locked Emma back in his residence.

Tuesday, June 24, 1924

Finally, it was Emma's turn in the court system. At 9 am, Volant took Emma to the Iron County municipal court, where the formal complaint was heard by Judge Flanagan.

The complaint read that "Andrew Gudleski, alias Andrew Anderson, and Emma Sigler, on May 1, 1924, did willfully and feloniously, and of malice aforethought, kill and murder Andrew Sigler, and that before the commission of said felony, Emma Sigler did, on and about May 1, 1924, feloniously and of her malice aforethought, counsel, hire and procure the said Andrew Anderson to commit in manner and form aforesaid, the said felony."

The case was adjourned to July 5, 1924, at 9 am in Judge Flanagan's office. No bail was allowed.

Emma arranged to have her sister and brother-in-law run the hotel and restaurant and take care of Robert. The twins were sent to live with her sister in Proctor, Minnesota, and Junior was sent to Emma's parents in Motley, Minnesota.

She was allowed to telephone Cadigan and Cadigan, the Superior, Wisconsin, attorneys and ask if they would represent her. The firm agreed to take on her defense; her hearing was scheduled for July 5, 1924. Emma had high hopes that she had a good defense and that she would be back running her restaurant in no time at all.

That afternoon, after she was told that she would be placed in a regular cell, Emma got sick. Dr. Urquhart was called but his examination was negative. He suggested that Emma was suffering from a case of the jitters. She was just nervous, he declared.

Junior, Robert, Lester and Leslie Sigler. Emma probably had this picture in her cell.

A reporter from the Ironwood Daily Globe was allowed to interview Emma in her cell:

"I was once a simple country maiden," she told the reporter, "but times changed me and I became hardened to the ways of the world, especially in the place of business that Sigler conducted in Hurley. I even endured the life of the place with prostitutes making their living in the building."

"He was too mean a man to live with," she told the reporter. "Two days before his death he beat me up so that I was hysterical, and that wasn't the only time."

She told of how that night a year ago last spring when Sigler chased her onto Silver Street while she was in her nightgown and beat her up. She was lying on the ground that was covered with snow, she said, and two Hurley men came to her rescue and pulled Sigler away.

"I was going to have him declared insane," she said, as she talked of Sigler and his actions over the past few years. "I was mad enough at times to shoot him myself."

"They think they've got the goods on me but they haven't. I don't believe Andy confessed," she said.

Over the next week, Emma kept busy in her cell and appeared quite contented and still confident that she would win her release, and then continued to deny that she had any connection with the plans for the slaying of her husband.

She was given a sewing machine during that first week in her cell to while away the time by sewing garments for needy children of Hurley and vicinity. "Better to do something for someone than to be idle," she maintained.

Wednesday, June 25, 1924

Andy was taken to Ashland by the district attorney where he appeared before Judge Risjord at the Circuit Court. Andy was in handcuffs, and a heavy chain was looped through them. Volant held the other end. Cadigan and Cadigan, Andy's attorneys, were not at the hearing.

"Mr. Gudleski, or is it Anderson?" the judge asked.

"Anderson."

"Is your name Gudleski or Anderson?"

"I had it changed to Anderson."

"Now, Mr. Anderson, you have pled guilty to the murder of Andrew Sigler in Hurley on or about May 2. You understand what this means, don't you?

"Yes."

"You understand that this is charging you with murder in the first degree? And you understand that upon a plea of guilty on this charge you will probably be sent to state prison for life? You understand that?"

"Yes."

"And you desire to plead guilty?

"I do."

"And you do that of your own free will and after consulting with your attorneys?"

"Yes."

"You know what your rights are?"

"Yes."

"And you know you have a right to a trial by jury on your plea of not guilty?"

"Yes."

"You know that?"

"Yes."

"You can have a trial by jury on a plea of not guilty. You know you have that right?"

"Yes, I do."

"I'm trying to tell you all your rights. You cannot afterwards say you didn't know what your rights were. At this time is there any question about your rights?"

"No, I have nothing I want to ask."

"You talked this over quite fully with the Cadigans I suppose at different times?"

"I have told them a different story entirely."

"You told your lawyers that you were not guilty? That you had nothing to do with it?"

"Yes, sir."

"They know, however, that you are pleading guilty at this time?"

"No, I didn't tell them."

"What induced you to plead guilty now instead of waiting for a trial?"

"I figured that their evidence was going to clear me up."

"On the statements that you made to them?"

"Yes. They thought they could help me out."

"What made you change your mind and make you come in and plead guilty now?"

"What Mr. Hayes talked to me in the cell."

Judge Risjord asked Hayes "You acted as investigator?"

"Yes."

Risjord turned back to Andy. "Did he he promise you any leniency if you agreed to plead guilty?"

"No, he didn't"

"He didn't make you any promises?"

"All the promises he made me was that he would try and bring Mrs. Sigler over."

"What do you mean?"

"I was to write her a note."

"So that you could see her?"

"Yes."

"At any rate, knowing all your rights in this matter and knowing you can have a trial by jury if you desire instead of pleading guilty and that the consequences of your plea of guilty probably will be life sentence and probably will be life sentence upon conviction upon a trial you still desire to plead guilty?"

"I desire to plead guilty."

"The plea is received and the judgment of the court is finding the defendant guilty of the offense charged. Do you care to make a statement of how this all happened?"

"I don't think it is necessary."

"That is not necessary so far as I am concerned."

"Four hundred dollars is all you got out of it?"

"Yes."

"She agreed originally to pay you $2,000?"

"She did."

"Was it that evening or next day she paid you $400?"

"The day after she paid $400 and was to pay $1,000 the next Saturday night which was never paid."

"Were you the only person involved in killing Sigler?"

"Yes."

"Do you understand that you will be sentenced to the state penitentiary, Mr. Anderson?"

"Yes."

"How do you feel about that?"

"Nothing. I feel nothing."

"Do you feel any remorse over killing Andrew Sigler?"

"Not a thing. A man who was so cruel and mean to his wife and children deserved to die."

"In that case, Mr. Anderson, I sentence you to spend the rest of your life at hard labor in the State Penitentiary at Waupun."

"You can't do that!" Andy shouted. He was crying.

"Why not, Mr. Anderson?"

"Foster told me I would get one to seven!"

"Mr. Foster is not here. Sheriff? Mr. Hayes? Do either of you know anything of this transaction that Mr. Anderson just spoke about?"

Neither man said a word.

"Do you have anything to say before the sheriff takes you to the state penitentiary, Mr. Anderson?"

"I sure do," Andy replied. "It isn't safe nowadays for young fellows to have anything to do with women. They'd better keep away from them."

Andy was immediately driven to the prison at Waupun by Sheriff Volant. On the way to Waupun, Andy and the sheriff talked about a number of things. Andy believed he would not be in the penitentiary for very long, he told Volant. Andy also told him there were a number of bodies in the Germania mine shaft.

"Guess we'll have to investigate those bodies," Volant told him.

"I'm pretty sure there is the body of a fella named Dvorak down there. I think he was was a cattle buyer."

"We'll look into that. Pretty dangerous down those shafts."

"Yeah," Andy replied. Other than a short conversation every now and then, he was silent for much of the trip.

"My wife made us some pasties, Andy. Would you like one?"

"What?"

"I said that my wife made us each a pasty. Want one?"

"No, I ain't hungry."

"Aw, c'mon, Andy. Least we can do is be friendly."

"I don't want to talk, Joe."

"Suit yourself. I'm going to eat one of these here pasties, though."

Volant reached in a paper bag and took one of the pasties wrapped up in wax paper and started to eat it. The aroma was too much for Andy.

"Maybe I will have one of them pasties, Joe."

"How about a cup of coffee to go with it? Bottle of pop, maybe?"

"Pop'll be fine, Joe. Can you take the cuffs off?"

"Promise you won't try to escape?"

"Naw, I can't. Got the leg irons on. Wouldn't do that anyhow. Got no money. Clothes on my back. If I tried that, it'd only be harder on me."

Volant stopped alongside the road and unlocked the cuffs. "I can't take you in the gates this way, Andy. I'll need to put 'em on again when we get to Waupun."

"Yeah. Suppose you do." They ate their pasties and drank their pop in silence. Six hours after leaving Hurley, they arrived at the huge limestone building known as the Wisconsin State Prison.

"Anything you'd like to tell me before I turn you over to the warden, Andy?"

"Yes, sir, Joe. I hope Emma Sigler will get the same as I did because she has been after me for a long time. If I did not do the job, she'd have somebody else do it."

"Who would she have got instead of you?"

"She did not tell me the name."

"Andy, we're pretty sure she killed Sigler, and it was not you that done it."

"Maybe you're right, Joe. Maybe you're right."

"Why, Andy?"

"Got nothing to say, Joe."

Volant snapped the cuffs back on Andy's wrists and drove to the guard shack. Joe showed the guard his credentials.

"Sheriff Joseph Volant. Iron County. Brought prisoner Andrew Anderson with me." He gave the guard the order for imprisonment. The guard took it and motioned Volant to drive into an enclosure where there was a second gate in front of them. The guard closed and locked the main gate.

"Well, Andy, this is it. Guess I'll see you from time to time."

"Yeah. So long, Joe. Do me a favor, okay?"

"Sure, Andy. If I can."

"Tell my wife not to worry about me, okay?"

"I'll do that, Andy."

A guard came out from the prison and took Andy inside. Volant's car was on a turnstile. He got out and turned the car in the opposite direction facing out of the prison. He heard the main door to the prison shut with a loud clang.

The guard took Andy to the processing center where a barber cut off his hair. Then he was issued prison clothes. Andy was given a set of striped pants and a jacket.

"When can I wash up?" Andy asked.

"No talking!" the guard snapped back. "You will speak when spoken to. You will address me as 'sir.' Now, the answer to your question is Saturday. Get into your stripes. Warden Lee will explain the rules of the prison."

Andy undressed and put on the striped prison clothes. He was led handcuffed to the warden's office.

"Take off the handcuffs," Warden Lee told the guard.

"Your name Anderson?" Warden Oscar Lee asked Andy.

"Yes, sir. Andrew Anderson."

"You are not Anderson anymore. You are number 16236. Is that clear, 16236?"

"Yes, sir. It is."

"What is your number?"

Andy looked at the number written in ink on his shirt. "16236," he said

"Sir!" the guard shouted at Andy. "You will address all guards and officers of this prison as 'sir.' And you will button your shirt using all buttons."

"Yes, sir. 16236, sir!" Andy shouted as he buttoned the top button of his striped shirt.

"Now then, 16236," Warden Oscar Lee continued, "825 inmates live here. There are 488 cells. This means that half of the inmates sleep on straw mattresses in the halls. You will be one of them. Eventually, you will be given a cell of your own.

Now about the rules. The rules of this prison are very simple. There will be no speaking to other inmates except on Sunday afternoon. And only quietly in the yard. Convicts walk in lockstep formation to and from the mess hall. Do you know what lockstep is, 16236?"

"Yes, sir. I am familiar with that term."

"I believe that all able-bodied inmates of this institution should be employed at regular labor of some kind. After a short time, you will be employed in the knitting factory along with 275 other prisoners. We also have a twine plant, a laundry, a tailor shop, an auto tag shop and a print shop. There are 50 inmates who work on our prison farm. On Saturday afternoon we hold a recreation period of athletics. A baseball game is usually scheduled with a visiting team from the outside. You are not, I repeat, not, allowed to talk to other inmates nor shout for your favorite team during this time. After the game, inmates are permitted to pitch horseshoes, box and engage in other forms of approved amusement. On Sunday afternoon you will be allowed to go out to the yard where you can mingle, play quiet games and visit quietly with the other inmates. Do you have any questions?"

"No, sir."

"You are dismissed. Mr. Linden, take prisoner 16236 and show him his sleeping area."

Linden, the guard, escorted Andy out of the warden's office to the main cellblock where Andy noticed each small, seven by four foot cell had a single prisoner. Each prisoner was handcuffed to his cell door watching Andy and Linden as they walked past. No one dared speak. Some prisoners made faces but most just stared straight ahead as if they were in a daze. This would be his home until his release, whenever that might be.

Monday, June 30 1924

The jailer came to Emma's cell and told her that the district attorney wanted to talk to her. She was crying.

"What does he want this time? Foster doesn't like me. All he does is ask questions. I don't want to see him."

"No choice, Emma. I was told to bring you to Volant's office so you have to go. This ain't the Ritz Hotel, you know."

Emma was led to the sheriff's office where Foster was waiting for her. He sat on Volant's chair in back of the desk. In front of the desk was a straight-backed wooden chair.

"Have a seat, Emma," Foster said pointing at the wooden chair. Emma was dressed in drab, loose-fitting jail work clothes.

Emma hung her head, and Foster could see that she was upset. Tears streamed down her face. She was shaking.

"What's wrong, Emma?"

"I got word last night that one of my twins is sick. I must see him and take care of him."

"Your attorney stopped by to see me yesterday after his visit with you. I know you want to see your kids, Emma, but that's not for me to say. The judge has to grant you a home visit. I'm afraid that Proctor is out of the question. Your kids will have to come here."

Emma stopped crying and mopped up her tears on the sleeve of her prison dress.

"Do you think that's possible?"

"Oh, I think it can be done. I've spoken to Judge Shemondle and he says he'll draw up the papers. It will happen, but I can't say when."

"That's a relief. I have some money to buy a train ticket for my sister and the twins."

"Uh...we can deal with that later, Emma. Right now I've got some more questions for you."

"I suppose you do," Emma answered. "Well, go ahead and ask, but I've told you everything I know already."

"In the first place, Emma, I'd like to know why you hired Cadigan and Cadigan to represent Anderson?"

"I felt sorry for him. I didn't think he did it then, and I still don't think he had anything to do with it."

"Twelve thousand is a lot of money for you to dish out."

"Who told you it was twelve grand? It was more like twelve hundred."

"Twelve thousand, Emma. You signed the papers."

"Well, they made a mistake."

"Yes, well.... Emma, you took a taxi to Superior and back?"

"No, I didn't."

"That's not what the Ironwood Taxi Service told me. They said they drove you to Superior and back. The taxi company has a record of it."

"Yes, I did take the taxi."

"Why did you lie about it?"

Emma didn't answer Foster's question. She just started to cry again.

"Who killed your husband, Emma?"

"I don't know. Christ, I'm so upset right now I don't know which way is up."

Saturday, July 5, 1924

Emma was up and about cleaning up her cell when the sheriff came by to take her to the courthouse where she would be formally told of the delay in the hearing.

"How are you this morning, Emma?"

"Pretty good. It's really cheerful here. I can actually hear birds singing. Ya know, Joe, I don't mind this little place. It ain't so bad."

"I'm glad to hear that. How's the food, by the way?"

"Not bad. Every couple of days my sister brings me a little something from the restaurant, ya know."

"I know about that, and I have no objection to it," Volant told her. "Well, we might as well get this done with. Your attorney should be there, too."

"I'm on my way as soon as you open the cage, Joe."

Volant started to put handcuffs on Emma, and then thought better of it.

"You don't need these, do you?"

"No, I sure ain't going to escape. I really appreciate that I don't have to wear them like the last time you took me over there."

The two of them got in the sheriff's car and drove up the hill to the courthouse, parked in the back parking lot and walked to the courtroom. Cooper was there along with Foster and Judge Shemondle.

"Mr. Cooper," Foster began. "I would like a postponement of the hearing until I've had time to contact some witnesses."

"Which witnesses," Cooper asked.

"Two material witnesses. I'm trying to subpoena Louise Mason from Chicago. And I can't locate the man they call Goofy Nelson anywhere in Hurley."

"I'd prefer a quick end to this. Mrs. Sigler is entitled to due process and a quick trial," Cooper retaliated.

"But, like I said, these witnesses are material to her case," Foster said. "I need to have them for the prosecution."

"All right, then. I will go along with the postponement," Cooper replied.

After making arrangements with the judge to hold the preliminary hearing on July 18, Cooper sat alone with Emma.

"Mrs. Sigler," he said.

"Please call me Emma. I really don't want to hear that name Sigler again. Never."

"Okay. I will call you Emma. Now then, Emma, I need to ask you some questions. I need straight answers, and I want you to tell me the truth. Without the truth there's no way I can defend you. You understand that, don't you?"

"Yes, I understand. I'll tell you all I know."

"Let's start at the beginning, Emma."

Emma began by telling him about Sigler's abuse of her and the boys. She told him that she wished many times that Sigler was dead. She told him about the prostitutes, but she denied knowing anything about Sigler's death.

"There's a man named Andy in the State Pen who said he did it, but I don't think he did," she told Cooper.

"Who do you think killed your husband?"

"I don't know. There was a man who took him to Ashland the morning he was shot, but I don't know his name. I had never seen him before."

"You are charged with being an accessory to your husband's murder. Why do you think that is?" asked Cooper.

"I think it's because somebody in this town has it in for me."

"Who's that?"

"Well, the sheriff, for one."

"Why do you think so?"

"He's been after me for a long time."

"Why?"

"I really have no idea."

"Mmmm. Is there anything else you'd like to tell me?" Cooper asked.

"Nothing I can think of."

"How well did you know Andy, the guy who is in Waupun for killing your husband?"

"I knew him. He'd stop by the restaurant now and then."

"He told the sheriff and district attorney that he killed Sigler and you put him up to it."

"That's not the truth. They're lying. I don't know why Andy would tell them that, anyhow."

"Why would they lie about it?"

"To get back at me."

"What for?"

"It's like I said. For not going along with Volant and Foster, I suppose. They want to pin this on me. Could be they didn't like Andy."

"Why do you suppose that is?"

"I understand that Andy was a jailbird. He did some hard time."

"Is that all you want to tell me, Emma?"

"That's all there is to tell."

"Your preliminary hearing has been re-scheduled for July 18, so that gives me time to..."

"Wait just a minute! Is that what all that talk was about? You mean to tell me they're going to keep me in that cell until July 18?"

"I'm afraid so. The district attorney needs more time to prepare the prosecution. And, to tell you the truth, it will give me more time to prepare a better defense."

"What are my chances of beating this rap?" Emma asked.

"I think you will get off if what you told me is the truth."

"It is the truth, Mr. Cooper." Emma answered. "I am not guilty of anything."

"All right, Emma. Is there anything else I can help you with before I leave?" Cooper asked.

"Well, I was hoping that I could see if everything is okay at my restaurant and talk to my son. Can you help me with that?"

"I'll talk to the district attorney. I can't promise you anything, however. Don't you talk to your family on the telephone?"

"Yes, but I sure would like to see them. It's been a long time."

"Like I say, I'll see what I can do then."

"Thank you very much, Mr. Cooper. You don't know how much I miss them all. I would like to see the twins and Junior, but I suppose that's out of the question."

"Not necessarily. I can check into that after the preliminary hearing."

* * * *

People in Hurley were getting tired of the Silver Street notoriety. They wanted to rid themselves of the bargirls and strippers. The last time an order to "clean house on wild women" was issued was on December 26, 1923, when Sheriff Volant reported finding 17 inmates of immoral places in Hurley. Since that time, however, Hurley had an exceptionally large list of "girls." In the past, women ordered out of Hurley moved to Ironwood until the order "blew over" and then returned to their familiar haunts.

On July 7, the Ironwood Daily Globe carried the following item that caused a reaction from its readers:

The order went out at noon for wild women to make a hasty departure from Hurley. District Attorney W.B. Foster issued the order to Sheriff Joseph Volant after he was informed by an inmate of one of the Hurley dives that the town is "chuck full of them". The complaint of Peter Sexton of Chicago that his wife had deserted him and had gone to Hurley in company of a man and another woman — the man being accustomed to the duties of bringing women to Hurley — brought out this order. Mae Sexton, the wife of the Chicago man, had been in one of the Hurley saloons for several days, she told the DA, and when she refused to return to her husband, she was given orders to be out of Hurley by 8 o'clock tonight. The man who introduced her to the ways of the Hurley underworld could not be found, however, said the officers who arrested Mrs. Sexton. Bobbed hair and blonde, the woman paced the floor in Hurley municipal court this morning and made so much noise with her French-heeled shoes that she was ordered to "sit down and stay there" until the court was ready to dispose of her case.

Friday, July 18, 1924

Once again, Emma was brought to the courthouse for her preliminary hearing, and once again it was postponed, this time to July 25. A writ of *habeas corpus* was served on the warden of Waupun State Prison ordering that Andy be brought to the court in Hurley so it could be determined whether or not he was imprisoned lawfully and whether or not he should be released from custody so he could testify at Emma's hearing.

This time, Emma understood what was being said between the attorneys, and she was very upset and stressed from the constant delays. She fainted and fell to the floor. Foster and Cooper raced over to her and picked her up, and Volant ran downstairs for a pitcher of water.

When he got back to the courtroom, Volant wiped Emma's forehead with a cold, wet rag and gave her some water.

"This isn't justice," Emma cried. "I should be home taking care of business and my children. Instead, you've got me locked up in that goddamn jail where it's either too hot or too cold."

"I understand your frustration, Emma, but we need to get Andy here to testify. It's the only snag we've come up against," Cooper told her.

"In another week I'll be free again, won't I?"

"Maybe, Emma," Cooper replied.

Emma was taken back to her hot cell at the County Jail accompanied by her attorney.

When they arrived at Volant's office, Emma beat her fists against Cooper. "Why? Why? Why?" she yelled. "Why am I being treated this way? I've done nothing wrong!" she screamed.

Volant came running into his office and grabbed Emma from behind. "Take it easy, Emma," he said. "I have some good news, too."

"What good news? There is no good news. I expected to be out of here this afternoon, and you have the gall to tell me there is good news?"

"Your twins are coming on the one o'clock train with your sister," Volant said.

"My babies will be here this afternoon?"

"Yes, they will, Emma."

"When can I see them?"

"You can meet them at the hotel this afternoon."

"Oh! This is the most wonderful thing that I can think of! Thank you! Thank you! I'm sorry I took off at you like that, Mr. Cooper."

"Under the circumstances, I fully can understand your frustration, Emma. It's been said that the wheels of justice turn slowly. Now why don't you eat and freshen up. Emma threw her arms around Cooper, gave him a big hug, and he turned a bright shade of crimson.

That afternoon, Sheriff Volant loaded Emma in his car and drove her to the Gogebic Hotel for the reunion with her sister and the twins. Emma was elated. They played games, they hugged and kissed, and it was over before she knew it. When it was time to go, Emma was reluctant to leave.

"Please, Joe, can't I stay just a little bit longer? They will be leaving tomorrow morning," she pleaded.

"Nope, I'm afraid not. But they can come to the jail and see you tonight."

"They can? That's wonderful!"

That night, Emma's sister brought the twins to visit her at the jail. Lester and Leslie played like typical kids who had just passed their toddler stage. They ransacked Volant's office and ran up and down the corridors, yelling and screaming all the while. They wanted candy and pop. Prisoners and jailers alike thought they were simply great little kids.

The next morning, Emma's sister took the twins back to Proctor, and Emma was alone again. Over the next week, Emma was visited several times by attorney George Cooper. He was not able to get more information from Emma, nor did she change her story.

Thursday, July 24, 1924

The evening before her preliminary hearing, Emma was understandably nervous. It was decided that she could wear her regular dress clothes to the courthouse rather than jail garb. She was taken to the Gogebic Hotel by the sheriff where she picked out a black dress, a black veil and a black vanity box, the same clothing she had worn at Sigler's funeral.

The preliminary hearing was to finally take place in the municipal court, Judge James Flandrena presiding. It was scheduled for 10 in the morning.

Bets were taken on the streets all around Hurley, Ironwood, Gile, Pence and Bessemer. Everyone talked about the crime. The odds favored that she would be held for trial rather than given her freedom. People placed bets that it was Anderson who killed Sigler, though, and not Emma.

"Emma, your attorney is here," the jailer said. "I'll take you down to Volant's office. He's waiting for you."

Emma was escorted downstairs and sat down opposite George Cooper.

"How's it been, Emma?"

"I'm a little nervous. I mean about the preliminary hearing tomorrow."

"You've got nothing to worry about. Be assured about that."

"What will happen? Who will be there?"

"Well, Louise..."

"Not Louise Mason! She'll tell nothing but lies."

"She must be there. If she lies on the witness stand, she'll be guilty of perjury."

"Yes, well, she's good at that."

"Andy Anderson will be there. There will be witnesses who will testify about your husband's attitude. It won't take long."

"What do you think will happen to me?"

"This isn't a formal trial, Emma. It's a preliminary hearing. Every person who is charged with a crime is entitled to a preliminary hearing. It is a test of the charge against you. The prosecutor must present evidence and witnesses that prove that it appears that an offense has been committed, and that there is probable cause to believe that the person accused committed it. If the judge does not find that it appears that an offense has been committed or that you are likely the person who committed the offense, you will be discharged and the charge is dismissed. It's that simple. Do you understand?"

"Ya, sure," Emma said as her eyes glazed over.

Friday, July 25, 1924

Crowds began to gather before dawn for the 10:00 hearing. Parking was at a premium, but most walked to the courthouse. The mob pushed their way up the cement steps to the massive door and waited. When the door was opened at 9:00, people rushed to the second floor of the courthouse to get a seat in the small municipal courtroom. When it became obvious that the municipal courtroom was too small to handle the crowd, everyone was moved to the circuit courtroom.

The courtroom had rows of bench seats that were quickly filled by people scrambling for seats. People stood in the back of the courtroom, in the aisles and in the hallway leading to the courtroom, in anticipation of hearing all the morbid details of the crime. It seemed as if all the non-working people of Iron County were there to see and hear Andy and Emma testify. Most of the spectators were women, some of them aged and feeble, some of them mothers like Emma, and scores of young, giggling flappers.

Andy had arrived early that morning accompanied by two guards from the prison and was taken immediately to the courtroom through the rear entrance.

Seated with Andy was a guard from the prison who kept an iron chain on the handcuffs that were attached to Andy's wrists. He was dressed in the same clothes he wore when he was sent to prison, but his hair was closely cropped and he puffed on the stub of a cigar until the hearing was opened.

The crowd stood and gawked as Emma was led in accompanied by the sheriff. She was not handcuffed. She was taken to the front table with her counsels Peter Cadigan and George Cooper, just an arm's length from where Andy was sitting. Emma glanced quickly at Andy, but the veil hid her gaze. He saw her and hung his head; he had made up his mind to protect Emma from more suffering.

Judge James Flandrena banged his gavel and asked for order at 10:15. Hayes was the first witness called. As he came to the front of the courtroom, Andy stood up, a wild look in his eyes. He sneered when he saw Hayes.

"You suckered me!" Andy shouted at Hayes. "Don't believe anything he tells you, Judge."

"Any more outbursts from you and I'll eject you from the courtroom," Flandrena warned.

Andy sat down defiantly. He tried to cross his arms in front of his chest but the handcuffs and chain prevented that.

Hayes told the Court all the details that Andy had told him in the cell and related his conversations with Emma. He presented the letter that Andy had written and the blue envelope with the money that Emma had given him to give to Andy.

Hayes quoted Emma as saying, "You can give this money to Andy and tell him I'll have the rest in a couple of days. Tell him I said for him not to break jail until after the hearing. If he does break, tell him to write me and I'll send him enough to take him to Mexico and send enough to live on for two years. He won't have to work for that time."

He also said that Mrs. Sigler was pressed by her creditors after Sigler was killed and didn't have much money on hand. "I'd just as soon be in jail," he said Mrs. Sigler told him. "I don't know what time the sheriff is coming to get me."

His testimony took only 20 minutes. Hayes was excused.

Then it was Andy's turn on the witness chair. He swaggered to the witness stand, the long chain attached to the handcuffs on his left wrist. His right hand was free. He rubbed the wrist to get the circulation flowing.

"Do you swear to tell the truth, the whole truth and nothing but the truth?" the judge asked Andy.

"No."

"Put your hand up," Judge Flandrena ordered.

"What for?" Andy answered.

"Mr. Anderson, you are a witness and are ordered to answer any and all questions put before you."

"I don't have to," Andy said.

The judge asked for a recess at 11:10 and told the guard to take Andy back to the jail.

"Why can't I stay here as well as the rest of them?" Andy yelled at the judge.

"We don't want you here, Mr. Anderson."

"I know why you and Foster don't want me here," Andy shouted as he was led in chains to the back door of the courtroom. Then he was hustled back to the Iron County Jail where he was kept overnight.

Emma was turned over to the sheriff to be held for trial on a date to be determined. She was denied bail and was lodged in a cell this time instead of staying in Volant's quarters.

* * * *

8:00 pm

Andy's wife brought him some cigars, clean undershirts and clean underwear. Emma was sitting in Volant's office.

"Come into my office, Mrs. Anderson." Lily followed Volant into his office.

"Please sit down." Volant motioned to a chair next to Emma.

"Have you two ever met?" the sheriff asked.

"No, I don't believe I know this lady," Emma answered, a puzzled look on her face.

"This is Mrs. Anderson, Andy's wife." Foster told her. "Mrs. Anderson, meet Emma Sigler."

Lily reached her hand out to Emma. "I'm so glad to meet you. I'm sorry about all of this. It can't be easy on you."

"Thank you," Emma replied. "The only hard thing is not being able to see my children more often. And it must be very hard on you, too, Mrs. Anderson."

"Please call me Lily."

"And you can call me Emma. I'm very sorry that Andy got caught up in this. It's not his fault, you know."

"What do you mean?"

"I don't believe that Andy had anything to do with my husband's death. I think someone else killed him."

"I don't think he did either. I pray that he'll be released. Our son and I miss him terribly."

"I can understand that."

"I've prayed for you, too, Emma."

"That was kind of you."

Emma and Lily sat uncomfortably, neither knowing what to say. Then Emma turned to Lily. "You know, when I was a little girl, I was brought up a Lutheran. I haven't been to church for years. I guess I've never been much for religion, and I really appreciate you telling me that. I didn't think anybody cared much what happened to me." She began to cry.

Lily went to her and held her hands in hers. "The church has been a big help to me over the years. I was raised a strict Finnish Lutheran, and I continue to go almost every Sunday. Oh, I've had some fun these past years, God knows." She looked Emma in the eyes and said in a whisper, "You know something, Emma? Andy is the best thing that has happened to me. I pray that you are right about him not being involved. I don't know what I'll do without him. I cry every night, thinking about how hard life is without him. I really understand your sorrows."

"I really don't miss my husband at all, Lily. He was a very mean, cruel man. He beat me and the children every day. I wanted to divorce him but he threatened to kill me if I filed papers. I wanted him committed to an insane asylum, but nobody would help me," Emma sobbed.

"Oh, my dear, I'm so sorry. I had no idea. Andy never talked about you at all, you know. But why, in heaven's name... why do people say that he killed your husband?"

With tears streaming down her face, Emma whispered, "It's this excuse for a town. It's the people who live here. Personally, I think that they couldn't find the person who did it, and Andy was a scapegoat. You know, there's a detective from Milwaukee who said that Andy confessed everything to him, but I believe Andy when he said that he didn't tell the detective anything."

"Andy may have had a bad break when he was just a kid and spent a long time in jail, but I know him well enough. He isn't a murderer."

"No, he's not," Emma told her.

Lily got up from her chair. "I have to see my husband now." Lily and Emma hugged.

"Everything will be okay. Now don't you worry none, Lily."

"Bye, Emma. If there's anything you need or if I can help in any way, let me know, okay?"

"Thanks, I will. Bye, Lily."

Lily asked Foster to take her to Andy. He led her up the stairs to his cell and stayed there while Lily talked to Andy through the bars of the cell door.

"Hi, Lily," Andy said. "I'm glad you came."

"Hi, Andy. Here, I brought you some clean drawers and underwear shirts." She stuffed them through the cell bars.

"Thanks. I smell pretty ripe," he laughed.

"I brought you some cigars, too."

"Thanks. Where's Randy?"

"Wilma and Ivy are taking care of him. They take pretty good care of him, you know. They adore him."

"So do I. I wish I was out of here so we could play again."

"Oh, Andy, I wish you could come home."

"I'll be back, Lily."

"Yes, but when?"

"Like the D.A. told me. One to seven years. Closer to one, I'd say. That life sentence won't hold."

"A year. Won't I see you before that?"

"Only in prison."

"Will you be back to testify at Emma's trial?"

"Naw, I don't think so."

"Oh, Andy. I wish you'd change your mind about that. You're so stubborn."

"I'll give it some thought."

"But, Andy. It...it would mean a lot to me."

"Yeah, mean a lot to me, too, I guess."

"Clear it all up, Andy. I know, and Mrs. Sigler knows, that you didn't kill her husband."

"Mrs. Sigler? You've talked to Emma?"

"I just met her for the first time in the sheriff's office. She's a nice lady, Andy. I feel real sorry for her. She's in this whole thing very deep."

"Yeah, well...."

"Do you understand, Andy?"

"Yeah, I do. You know, Lily? I think I will testify at her trial and tell everything."

"Everything?" Lily asked.

"Yeah, everything. I mean all that I know. It's the only way. I didn't do it, Lily."

"I know, Andy."

"Don't worry about it, Lily. I'll be here for the trial."

"When will they take you back to prison?"

"First thing in the morning."

Lily started to cry. "It's such a long time, Andy. Such a long time."

"Aw, it ain't such a bad place there. I get fed, a place to sleep, and I got friends. There's work during the day and...."

"Do you need any money? I can always borrow some from the family."

"Not right now. Send me some once in a while. I can buy things there if I need to. Tobacco, candy. That sort of stuff."

"I will, Andy. I promise to write often."

"Good bye, Lily. You better go now."

"Bye, Andy." They held hands for a bit, and Lily left the jail.

Saturday, July 26, 1924

The next morning, there were several of Andy's friends waiting for him outside the jailhouse to give him cigars and to say goodbye. He thanked all of them and was whisked into the state car and taken to Waupun.

When Andy arrived at the prison, he was processed, given his prison clothes and locked back in his cell to wait for the evening meal. The most difficult thing about prison life, he thought, was that the inmates could not speak unless spoken to by an officer or guard. The only time prisoners were allowed to speak was for 10 minutes during the evening meal. It hadn't been any different at the Green Bay Reformatory where Andy had spent his late teenaged years. In 1924, a typical day for a prisoner in Waupun consisted of five hours of labor, four and a half hours of technical and educational training, and one hour devoted to military drill.

Andy was assigned to work in the prison hosiery mill as a thread winder. As always, strict silence was maintained. If a prisoner broke the rules, corporal punishment or harsh discipline was meted out. Guards did not hesitate to smack a prisoner with an oak cane fitted with a heavy brass tip. Prisoners received punishment for routine offenses ranging from laziness to theft; the punishment ranging from small fines to solitary confinement with milk and bread. Laughing in the dining room resulted in a $5 fine; assaulting an officer resulted in reduced rations and a week handcuffed to the cell door.

Assistant Superintendent Norman Nuss was a boxer. Prisoners who consistently broke the rules earned the privilege of going a few rounds in the ring with Nuss. The prisoners always lost.

During Andy's stay in Waupun, he kept to himself for the most part. He wasn't classified as a model prisoner, but he didn't break any rules either.

Friday, September 19, 1924

It was Emma's 28th birthday. Her cell in the county jail was barely big enough to walk around in. There was a cot, a slop bucket and a small table attached to the wall. She had fitted the barred window with curtains. She managed to keep busy in her cell sewing, reading and writing poetry. She sat forlornly in her tiny cell wishing that it would be over, that it would all go away. She thought about her sickly mother and about Sigler. She jotted down a poem.

It's now just a short time before
My troubles and strife will be over.
Then homeward my thoughts I will bend
A few days with mother to spend.

Then soon she will be forgetting
The grief I have cost her this year.
'Twas a strain on me, also while waiting
The trial
But I know I have nothing to fear.

I stuck with him thru trouble & strife
In sickness I stayed by his side
I mean, the Dad of my children
God bless them all, and be my guide.

She cried until she could cry no more. She didn't know what to do, so she picked up a magazine and after paging through it, she put it on the table and lay down. She was lonely and getting more depressed every day. She could look out the window through an eight by eight space through the bars where there was a glass block taken out. Other than that small area, she had no view toward the west.

Emma thought a lot about her children. She remembered when she entered the twins in a baby contest two years before and how Sigler had got angry when she nursed them.

I wish I could see them and hold them. I wonder how they're doing? My poor babies. I want my mother.

Thursday, December 18, 1924

Winfred Zabel, the 46-year-old former Milwaukee County district attorney was in Hurley on a tax litigation case. People in the State of Wisconsin referred to him as the "Clarence Darrow of the North" because of his ability to prosecute criminals. In 1910, Zabel, a Social-Democrat, had practically single-handedly cleaned up prostitution in Milwaukee. Zabel produced a report showing Milwaukee was home to some 200 brothels with about 1,000 "residents." Each resident, the statistics showed, "entertained" about 15 visitors a day and each visitor spent at least $1. Some quick math showed that prostitution was a $5.5 million industry in Milwaukee.

While he was in the county clerk's office he was approached by Florence Noldeau who told him about Emma's case.

"Mrs. Sigler has been in jail since June and has always maintained that she is innocent of the murder of her husband. Won't you please go down and talk to her and see if there isn't anything you can do for the poor woman?"

"I'm thoroughly acquainted with the case, and there doesn't appear to be anything I can do for her," Zabel replied.

"She's innocent, Mr. Zabel."

"It looks like a clear-cut case against Mrs. Sigler and Anderson. Unless the jury can be convinced that she was justified in hiring Anderson to kill her husband, because of the brutal way he treated her, there doesn't seem to be anything anyone can do."

"I'm firmly convinced that Emma Sigler is innocent. Please see what you can do for her?" Miss Naldeau pleaded.

"I can do that, but Anderson's story is in perfect accord with the facts dug up during the murder investigation, his acceptance of a life sentence, and Mrs. Sigler's activities in aiding Anderson fit perfectly with the part Anderson said she played in instigating the murder. It sounds to me like a cut and dried case of murder."

"Please? This is a case for justifiable homicide if I ever heard of one."

"I will visit Mrs. Sigler. That's the least I can do."

Monday, December 22, 1924

Three days after her mother died, Emma was visited by Zabel. She was taken to the sheriff's office and offered a seat. She couldn't help but notice Zabel sitting in the office. There were not many men in Hurley who wore three-piece suits or ties. He stood when she entered.

"Mrs. Sigler?"

"Why, yes. Uh...."

Mrs. Sigler, my name is Winfred Zabel. I'll make this introduction brief. I'm in Hurley on other matters, but Miss Florence Nadeau suggested that I look into your case."

"Florence Nadeau? Why?"

"She believes that you are innocent of killing your husband."

"I am."

"Well, that's what I'm here to find out. If you're telling the truth about your innocence, then I may be willing to defend you."

"Why doesn't Mr. Cadigan's firm want to defend me?"

"I have no doubt that Cadigan and Cadigan would defend you, but if what Miss Nadeau tells me is true, then I will take on your case."

"I don't have any money for...."

"I will do it for free, Mrs. Sigler."

"I see," she replied.

Emma was quite suspicious of Zabel after her experience with Hayes. She was non-committal and sullen.

"Why would you want to do that?"

"I came to Hurley for another case having to do with taxes, but my heart is with defending the innocent."

"What do you mean?" Emma asked suspiciously.

"I was the district attorney of Milwaukee County, and I miss the courtroom. I want to defend you, Mrs. Sigler, but you and I have to trust each other. You must tell me what happened."

Emma mulled Zabel's comment over. "How much do you know about my case?"

"The only thing I know right now is that Miss Nadeau believes you to be innocent."

"What about Cadigan? What about them?"

"I know Peter Cadigan and will consult with him."

"All right, Mr. Zabel, I'll go along with you."

"Thank you. Now, there are certain points that I must clear up, Mrs. Sigler."

"Yes, go on."

"First of all, how are you being treated during your incarceration here?"

"Very well, I suppose. I have no grudge against anybody here."

"I trust that your health is adequate?"

"My health has been generally well, thank you. But I'm pregnant."

"What? How's that?"

"I said that I am a couple of months pregnant."

"I hesitate to ask you this personal question, Mrs. Sigler, but are you certain?"

"Mr. Zabel," Emma answered, "I've been pregnant at least five times and I know how I feel during pregnancy. I also have not had my monthly...uh...sickness for two months."

"Have you told anyone else?"

"I told the sheriff."

"Did he believe you?"

"I don't think so."

"But, you've been in this jail since July. Who might the father be?"

"I don't want to get anyone into any trouble."

"I understand. The name of the father can wait. Mrs. Sigler, you have brought a new light on your trial. Do you realize that? You have a new defense."

"How do you mean?"

"I mean that the possibility of your being pregnant means that the jury will not think kindly on the affairs of your jailers. I may be able to get your case thrown out of court."

"Do you mean that I may not have to have a trial?"

"It's possible. But you must promise me not mention your pregnancy to anyone again until I tell you to do it."

"Okay. I won't say anything more about it."

"Did you kill your husband, Mrs. Sigler?"

"No."

"Did you hire Anderson to kill him?"

"Well, I did at first, but Andy didn't kill my husband."

"What do you mean?"

"I mean just that. Andy lied himself into prison. He had nothing to do with the murder in the manner he told Hayes."

"What do you mean? He confessed to Hayes and he's serving life in prison because of it."

Emma looked at Zabel, but said nothing. *I think Zabel is being straight with me. Maybe I should tell him what happened.*

Zabel studied Emma for a few minutes. *I just don't understand by any stretch of the imagination what the purpose is for her to conceal the truth, if that was what they were doing. Anderson is in for life, so he's got nothing to lose by telling the truth. Unless a miracle happens, this woman also faces life when brought to trial, so there's no reason for her to remain silent.*

As if Emma could read his thoughts, she looked at Zabel. "Mr. Zabel?"

"Yes?"

"Are we alone? I mean can anybody hear us?"

"No. Why do you ask?"

"I have a confession to make."

"Tell me."

"I killed my husband. I asked Andy Anderson to take his body away."

Zabel waited for Emma to tell him more, but she said nothing.

"Who else knows about this?" Zabel finally asked.

"Just me and Andy. He shouldn't be in Waupun. I take full responsibility for my husband's death."

"Would you like to tell me what happened?"

"Well, Sigler threatened many times to kill me. He hated the kids. On the morning of May 2, he came downstairs, and I was in the kitchen getting ready for my morning duties. Make coffee, start the laundry. That sort of daily chores. He had bought a new car, and I wanted to drive it so I got a driver's license. He didn't like that so we started to quarrel. He picked up a bottle and threw it at me. I hit him with a clothes pole so he wouldn't get near me. He had hidden a gun a few days before, but I found it and hid it in a baby buggy. I grabbed the gun from the buggy and ran to one of the back rooms. He broke the door down, and he had a meat cleaver in his hands. I was terrified. He said that he would kill me. I shot at him three times. I know I hit him in the side and then in the head. Then I called Andy and asked him to take Sigler's body and get rid of it."

"Why didn't you tell this before? Why did you let Anderson go to prison?"

"I don't know. I was afraid. I didn't want to lose my children. I thought of the embarrassment it would cause to my parents."

"Why are you telling me now?"

"Mr. Zabel, my mother died three days ago. She and my father are the only people I trust in this world. And now my mother is dead." Emma started sobbing. "I've thought about Sigler's death all summer, and I'm truly sad about it. For a long time I was glad he was dead, but now...now.... I don't know Mr. Zabel," Emma said between sobs. "Oh, I'm all balled up inside. I'm glad I finally told someone about this."

"Where did your mother die?"

"She died at Deerwood. That's in Minnesota near Brainerd. They took her body to Washburn where she'll be buried."

"Where is your father?"

"In Washburn, I suppose, attending to Mother's funeral. I don't know. Why?"

"Emma, you just told me that your father is the one remaining person who you trust. What you need to do is write all of this down and tell your father everything that happened. We need your full confession in writing. And please, for your sake, don't tell anyone else what you just told me. It's very important that you tell no one about your pregnancy or the circumstances of your husband's death."

"I won't say a word. You said that I should write it all down and let my father see it?"

"Yes, he's the only one to know."

"Can you get my father here to visit me here?"

"Yes, I can do that. I can even try to get a court order for you to visit your father in Washburn and attend the funeral."

"Oh, Mr. Zabel.... If you could pull that off, it would be a miracle."

"I can try, but I don't guarantee any success. You are being held without bail, so I have to get to the judge, and the district attorney has to approve the order."

Tuesday, December 23, 1924

The first thing in the morning Zabel rushed to Foster's office on Silver Street and requested an order be issued for Emma to attend her mother's funeral and to visit with her father for a few days in Washburn. Foster was sitting with his feet up on his desk reading the morning newspaper and barely bothered to look up at Zabel.

"Good morning, Mr. Foster."

"Morning."

"A minute of your time, sir?"

Foster removed his feet from his desk and put the newspaper down. "Go ahead, Zabel."

"I would like that a temporary order be made so Mrs. Sigler can go to Washburn for a few days."

"I won't do that."

"Mr. Foster, you are not being fair to my client. Her mother just died and they were very close. It's nearly Christmas."

"Nothing I can do. I will not let that woman out of this jurisdiction, plain and simple, Mr. Zabel."

"All right, then. Do you have any objection to her father visiting her alone?"

"I can't stop him from visiting her. Her sister can see her and her children. And that's all."

"So be it. With your permission, I will make the arrangements, Mr. Foster. And by the way, please note my strong objection to your refusal to grant my client a temporary leave from the jail."

"So noted, Mr. Zabel." Foster put his feet back on his desk, leaned back in his chair and continued reading the newspaper.

"Mr. Foster, I was hoping that you and I would be able to get along amicably."

The district attorney gave Zabel a smug grin and furrowed his brow. "She is guilty, Zabel; she is as guilty as sin. I'll see you in court on January 2, when I will prove it. Have a good Christmas, Mr. Zabel, and a very pleasant New Year."

Zabel stomped out of Foster's office, drove to the jail and asked to see Emma. He was escorted upstairs to her cell where she was huddled up in a blanket while trimming a hat. The opening of her glass block window was stuffed with rags to keep out the cold.

"Good morning, Emma," Zabel said.

"Good morning."

"I see they finally gave you an electric heater."

"It's the only thing I've ever kicked about. Whenever I wanted more heat at the hotel I got it."

"Yes. Well I'm glad you are finally somewhat comfortable."

Emma brushed her hair back with her hand and scowled. "There isn't enough heat in this jail on cold days. It's not Volant's fault that it's cold in here. The County did a lousy job when they built this place."

"Uh...Emma, I have some bad news."

"Go ahead and tell me. I hear nothing but bad news it seems."

"Foster won't release you to attend your mother's funeral."

"What do you mean?"

"He won't approve the release."

"I need to go! My father..."

"Yes, I know, Emma. I'm sure your father would like you there, but there's nothing I can do."

"Is he afraid I'll escape? Why else? I don't understand Foster's attitude. Can't he send Volant and some guards along?"

"Washburn is out of his jurisdiction. That may have something to do with it."

"I'm even willing to hire the sheriff of Ashland County and any other officers needed for a bodyguard."

"It won't happen, Emma. Foster was very clear on that."

"I think I can break out of here."

"Don't even consider that, Emma."

"Why not? Last week they found a couple of files and a hacksaw in the beds of two prisoners downstairs. I overheard that Pete something-or-other and George Smoda stole the tools from a plumber who was working here. There's plenty of opportunity to make a break for it."

"No, Emma, don't. Your trial is only a month away. It will only be harder on you when you get caught, but I have some good news, too."

"Good news? What?"

"Foster said that your father can come to visit you here at the jail."

Emma jumped up and gave Zabel a hug. "That's wonderful! When? How can he get here? How soon?"

"Whenever he can make arrangements, Emma. I think your sister can arrange something."

"I can ask her when she gets here this afternoon."

"Fine. It's settled then. By the way, I may be leaving for Milwaukee tomorrow, so I may not see you until after the New Year. Will you be all right?"

"I'll be okay. I have some sewing I'll be working on. I started six winter coats. I'm sewing four for my children and two for the war orphans I've been supporting in Washburn."

"That's very noble of you to do that, Emma."

"It keeps my mind clear. I enjoy sewing."

"Well, then, goodbye, Emma. Stay occupied. It's the best medicine."

"Good bye, Mr. Zabel."

After Zabel left her, Emma wrote her confession. After she finished, she hid it under her pillow.

Wednesday, December 24, 1924

On a hunch that she might have something to tell him, and because he wanted to wish her a happy Christmas, Zabel went to the jail to see her, and she was very pleased to see him.

"Mr Zabel!" she shouted when she saw him approaching her cell. "I thought you were going home today."

"Good morning, Emma. It's Christmas Eve, and I wanted to see you one last time before the trial. Here, I brought you a present." Zabel gave her a package wrapped in colorful paper with a bow. "Go ahead, open it."

Emma unwrapped the package and found a thimble, some needles and thread and a red pincushion.

"It's lovely and very thoughtful of you to do that. And I have a present for you, too." Emma reached under her pillow and pulled out the 12-page written confession.

"What's this?" Zabel asked. "Emma, it's your confession! This could well be the nicest gift anyone has ever given me."

Zabel quickly read the confession and handed it back to Emma.

I've got to get to Waupun and see Andy Anderson and find out what he has to say about this.

"What should I do with it?" Emma asked.

"I want you to show it to your father, discuss it with him, and ask him to witness it."

"I will."

"Thank you, Emma. There are things I have to do, so I will leave now."

* * * *

Instead of driving to Milwaukee, and after he phoned his wife to tell her he'd be a little late, Zabel drove to Waupun and met with Andy to get his reaction to the confession Emma had given him.

Andy was taken to the office of Warden Lee where Zabel, Lee, Deputy Warden Taft and a legal reporter were present.

"Andy, I've been retained by Mrs. Sigler. We want you to tell us the truth about the Sigler murder."

"I can't remember it. I lost my mind in this place and everything else," he said as he eyed the officers.

"I just came from Hurley, and I'm on my way to Milwaukee. I came here to get your story. I want you to understand that we are shooting square with you," Zabel told him.

"I expect you are. I don't doubt it a bit," Andy sneered.

"You don't think for a moment I'm trying to double-cross you, do you?"

"I've already been double-crossed, so it don't make any difference."

"Let me ask you this, Andy, if you had absolutely nothing to do with the killing of Mrs. Sigler's husband, will you tell me so?"

"No, I didn't have nothing to do with the killing of her husband."

"That is exactly what I'm driving at. Did you take the body away after it was done?"

Andy's eyes opened wide in surprise. *This guy that's shooting questions at me has the true facts. No use keeping it from him anymore.*

"Now if you don't mind," Zabel went on, "I'd like to have you tell me just exactly how you got into this thing and to what extent. I want the truth because I don't want to go to court on a fictitious defense."

Then Andy opened up. He told a story that corroborated Emma's confession in every detail. Zabel was convinced that it was true. *How can it be otherwise? This man and Emma haven't seen each other for five months; they had no possible means of communication and couldn't tell the same story unless it was true.*

When Andy finished, Zabel asked, "Why were you willing to take a life sentence, to sacrifice your wife and baby just to keep your word to this woman?"

"The district attorney promised that I would only get a short term of one to seven years if I pleaded guilty and didn't cause any trouble."

"Even at that, seven years is a terrible price to pay, it seems to me."

"Well, I knew that Emma would do the right thing by my family and myself. She would see that I didn't lose by it if I didn't give her away. But I got double-crossed when I got the life sentence, and I was just waiting to see what she would do before I said anything more. I knew she'd play square as long as I did."

"In your confession to Hayes, why did you implicate her if you wanted to protect her?"

"That confession was a lie. He had been bragging so much about his crimes, and I never figured he was a detective. I thought if I got on good terms with him and make him think I was a bad guy, he would help me get out of jail. If I could make him think she had hired me to kill Sigler, he wouldn't be apt to try and come back and blackmail her, and he wouldn't wonder why she was willing to give me money or help me get out."

"Andy, you've told us the truth. Mrs. Sigler's trial is next month. I'll start the procedure to get you there so you can tell the jury all that you've told me."

"I'll be there, Mr. Zabel. I'll be there."

"That's a good decision, Andy. I'm very pleased."

"Uh, Mr. Zabel, could you do me a favor?"

"I could, Andy, what is it?"

"Bring me some cigars to the trial."

"I will be most happy to do that, sir."

Christmas Day, 1924

Emma spent Christmas in the Hurley jail. Her son, Robert was allowed to visit with her along with her sister, Maty. Robert was told that his mother was in the hospital, and that is what he wanted to believe. He really knew that his mother was locked up in the jail. Kids at school had been teasing him about it ever since she was locked up.

Nyah, nyah. Bobby's mom's a jailbird. She's a puh...puh...prisoner. Locked up cuz she killed your Pa. Nyah, nyah, nyah.

Shut up! Shut up! You don't know what you're talking about! She's not in jail. She's in the hospital!

"Maty? Did you go to Ma's funeral?"

"It was very beautiful, Emma. I wish you could have been there. Ma looked nice. They did a good job on her."

"They wouldn't let me go, you know. That damn Foster. Oh, how I wish I could have gone. I wanted to see Pa. Do you think you could get him here?"

"That won't be too hard to do; he's staying with us at the hotel. He came yesterday. He's still mourning Ma's death; otherwise he would have come with us. He's in a bad way, Emma."

"He's not sick is he?"

"I think everything has got to him. He's depressed. Christmas, Ma dying, you in jail. All that."

"Oh, poor Pa. I'm so sorry I've put all of you through this nightmare."

"It ain't your fault, Emma. Nothing you could do about any of it."

"I suppose you're right." Emma turned to Robert, finally. "And how are you getting along?"

"I'm fine, Ma. Look, Ma. I made you a Christmas present in school."

He proudly gave Emma the gift he had wrapped in paper and ribbon and she opened it.

"Oh, Robert! It's beautiful," she said as she held the small, clay ashtray in her hand. "Such a pretty color, too. You remembered that blue is my favorite."

"Thank you so very much, Robert. Now, then, is Maty taking good care of you?"

"Yes, she is." He hesitated and looked down at his feet.

"Ma?"

"What, Robert?"

"When can you get out of this place and come home?"

"It will be soon. Soon, Robert."

"Soon? When is soon?"

"After the new year."

"How long is that from now, Ma?"

"In a couple of weeks. I have to get well before I can come home."

"Yes, Ma."

"Come here, Robert and give your Ma a hug."

Robert, like most 10-year-olds, avoided hugging, kissing or anything that had to do with affection. Nonetheless, he threw his arms around Emma.

"Ma, I miss you."

"I miss you, too, Robert."

After a few boo-hoos and sniffles, Emma moved closer to her sister.

"How's things going at the hotel Maty?"

"Oh, so-so, I suppose. We still have the restaurant going and the soda fountain. The girls are all gone, thank goodness. I'll be very happy when you can take over the place again."

"So will I, Maty. So will I."

"We have to get going, Emma."

"Thanks for coming. And thanks for bringing Robert, Maty."

"I'll bring Pa by tomorrow. Will that be okay?"

"That will be just wonderful. Bye, Maty. And thanks. Bye, Robert. Be good."

"I will, Ma."

Emma was taken back to her cell where she she placed Robert's gift on the narrow window sill next to a picture of her children. She tried to read, but she couldn't concentrate. She paced around the cell, and her head was spinning with thoughts of her mother, her father, her children, Andrew, Andy and the trial. When she finished pacing, Emma hid under her blanket and fell asleep.

December 26, 1924

"Emma, you have a visitor," the jailer shouted as he came up the stairs. Emma's father followed him to her cell.

Robert Schroth was an old man with hunched shoulders that reflected years of labor and hardship. The jailer opened her cell, and Emma gave her father a hug.

"How ya doing, Pa?"

"Oh, I'm all right, I suppose. It's been tough."

"I know, Pa."

"Pa, I got something to tell you."

"What might that be?"

"I shot Sigler."

"What? How? Why?" Shroth stuttered.

"I wrote it all down. I killed him defending myself, and then I called Andy Anderson and asked him to take his body away."

"Why? Why, Emma? Why didn't you tell the police?"

"I thought it would be better for the children if I kept it quiet. I tried to get rid of any clues, and I thought of you and poor Ma. Guess I made the wrong choice."

"Oh, my God, Emma. This is terrible. I can't believe you did this thing."

Emma handed her father the confession[3] she had written. He read it slowly.

> Sigler left the place at 8 o'clock. No one knew at that time with who.
>
> That evening about 11 o'clock we heard footsteps upstairs & wondered who it could be. I closed the place at 12:30 &

[3] Verbatim.

Sigler was not home yet so at Louise's warning & request I slept downstairs but went upstairs to cover the babies.

I noticed Sigler in bed & hurried down again so I would not disturb him. I told Louise Sigler was in bed & she thot perhaps some one gave him a beating & he was ashamed to show himself so he went up the front way.

At 5:30 in the morning I went up to cover the twins before starting the washing & saw no one there.

I went down again & into the laundry & about 6:30 someone rapped at the back door.

I opened & a man asked for Sigler. I said he left before 6 this morning and he said, "well I promised I'd call for him & he was to drive to Ashland with me." The man said he was in Bessemer with Sigler the night before.

Later I heard someone in the kitchen & I looked & it was Sigler. I said "where were you? I was upstairs & you weren't in bed." He said he was in the bathroom. He put on his over coat muffler & hat & walked to the back door. After looking out he got cross & said that damn fool isn't comming either. I said who are you looking for. He said oh a man was going to Ashland & ask me to drive down with him instead of by train.

I said well the man was here & you weren't home. He Sigler said what did you do that for. Well, I said, I didn't know you were in the bathroom. Sigler said you done it for meanness & started an argument with me saying I had no business ordering the car license without asking him & a few other things & I told him I had no time to argue I had work to do. He said yes & your working days are over with in this shack & then thru a bottle at me stricking me in the chest. As he stooped for another bottle I hit him across the face with the wash pole. He said "I always told you that if you ever hit me back I'd kill you & I'll do it too." He entered the store room & went toward a stove where he kept his revolver. But I had hid it the previous day. I hid it in the baby carriage. Same room but near the door & I grabbed it & run & locked myself in the back bedroom (then no. 7). He soon followed me & started to pound on the door. I said if you break in I'll shoot. He said I don't give a damn. I'll kill you if you don't open this door. Your done for. Just as the door opened I shot down striking the bed. He approached me in spite of this with a meat cleaver in the left hand & as he did I shot again aiming at the hand & cleaver to disarm he raised both arms toward me & I shot again stricking him in the temple. He fell face down & I dropped the gat & run to the front. I was going to tell Louise but she had gone on 3rd floor for a more quieter room. There are 6 doors between this room in which I shot & Rachel's room & being sick she aparently hadn't heard anything.

I went to the front door to see if I could see someone I knew to call in. I seemed caged & every minute and hour. No one I knew in sight. I went upstairs again thinking of calling Louise & then went into the children's room instead.

Sigler had planned on opening up a bar room in the place & I opposed to this. He wanted Andy G. to take charge of it. This entered my mind just then so in my excitement I phoned the place where Andy worked. I asked him to come up & he said he couldn't & asked what for. I said Sigler had a jug he wanted taken down there & he should get it.

Then the thot came to me to ask Andy to move the body. I thot if the body was found & no clues it would be better for the children & my invalid mother. I knew if I were accused even in self defence the strain would be to much for her.

I paced the floor until Andy came wishing I could induce him to take the body away. I wouldn't have done it but I was hysterical & then for the sake of my boys and my parents. I feel justified in defending myself as I did. My consience don't bother me, only that I got Andy mixed into it.

Upon his arrival I told Andy as best I could & begged him to take the body away somewhere, where it would be found soon. He objected. Said he couldn't get mixed into it. Some one would see him. He peeked in the room & said,

"He's dead alright." I pleaded & told him if he was suspected I'd tell the truth. Andy evidently had a few drinks before he came & I offered him a big drink of good whisky I had saved for medicine purpose. Finally he decided he'd take the chance & I told him then, if he'd ever squell on me I'd implicate him. I told him to take gat & shells & throw them away. When he came back for the cap after putting body in car I gave him about 250.00 said in case he needed it & he put it back on the table but I took it again & put it in his pocket. But he insisted he'd return it in a short time if not suspected.

I didn't watch Andy pick up the body & dreaded to go in the room but finally picked up courage enough. I knew it had to be done. There was some old linoleum on the floor & I rolled it up and put it in the furnace.

When Andy gave himself up I waited from one date to another for his hearing & I would freely go on the stand & say just how I killed in order to defend myself but then the detective interfered. Andy thot it best to plead guilty for the time being & until my trial.

He was afraid to say that I shot because I told him that if he squelled I would go against him also. But I didn't mean that he should take life in prison for something he hadn't done.

"Is this the whole truth, Emma? Is this the way it happened?"

"Yes, Pa. I was hysterical at the time, but it is clear as a bell to me. The way it all happened, I mean."

"I will sign my name on the bottom. If you say this is the way it happened, I will believe you."

Shroth signed "Das ist gavislich var"[4] (This is the truth) Rob't Schroth

[4] The German words he wrote before his signature appear to read this way.

"Now what, Emma. Now what will you do? Will you turn this over to the police?"

"No, Pa. My attorney, Mr. Zabel, told me not to say anything to the district attorney or the sheriff."

"But why, Emma?"

"Because he told me that I will get off by pleading self defense. The district attorney only wants to see me go to prison."

The jailer came just then and told Emma that it was time for her father to leave. She held her father's hand for a moment.

"Don't worry, Pa. It will be okay."

"I will be at the trial, Emma. I will pray for you."

"Thanks, Pa. No matter what happens, I know you and the rest of the family are with me."

"It's in God's hands now, Emma."

December 27, 1924

Zabel returned to Hurley convinced that Emma had killed her husband in self defense, especially after hearing Andy tell about his part in the crime. He met with Emma in her cell.

"How was your Christmas, Emma?"

"It was wonderful. I got to see my son, Robert, and my father. Look at what Robert made me." Emma showed Zabel the ashtray.

"Very nice. Very nice, indeed," Zabel said as he examined it.

Emma reached under her pillow for the confession and handed it to Zabel. "Here, Mr. Zabel. My father read it, and after I told him all that happened, he signed it."

"Let me see if I can understand this German that he wrote. I believe it says 'this is certainly true.' Is that close to correct?"

"Something like that," Emma said.

"I only had a glance at it last week. I'll read it again."

"I hope everything is clear, Mr. Zabel. I wrote it as best as I could."

Zabel read Emma's confession, then looked at her and smiled. "This is exactly what I need, Emma. Oh, by the way, I visited Andy Anderson at Waupun on Christmas Eve."

"You saw Andy?"

"Yes, and he told me everything, and he corroborated your story to the letter."

"How is he?"

"He's as well as he can be, and he's going to testify at the trial."

"He will? That's wonderful! Oh, that poor man. For the life of me, I can't figure out why he didn't tell all."

"I believe he felt sorry for you, and he didn't want to see you suffer. He told me that you would have taken care of his wife and child."

"Is there a chance he can be released from prison?"

"I don't think so, Emma. He confessed to Sigler's murder, and he's already been convicted."

"Is there anything you can do?"

"I don't know. First I need to concentrate on your case."

"I understand. What are you going to do next?"

"I'll see if I can get you out on bail, and then I'll ask for a continuance."

"Bail? It would be nice to be able to walk out of here."

"I won't guarantee anything. The judge has to make that decision."

"But, still..."

"If the judge grants bail, then we have to raise the bail bond."

"There are plenty of people around here who'll do that."

"I'll do my best to find a bondsman, Emma. I must leave and draw up the affidavit."

Friday, January 2, 1925

Zabel filed an affidavit for the state to show just cause why Emma should not be released on bail and why the case should not be continued until the next term of the circuit court that opened on January 12. The reason for the continuance, Zabel told Judge Risjord, was to find out more facts about the slaying and plan Emma's defense. Circuit Court Judge G.N. Risjord told Zabel that he would give his decision on both points later.

Sheriff Volant picked up Emma from the courthouse. The two rode in silence down the hill, and when they got past Silver Street, Volant stopped the car.

"You told me a couple of months ago that you were pregnant."

"I did not. I told you no such thing."

"In any case, Emma, there's a rumor on the street that you are pregnant. Is this true or isn't it?"

"No, it isn't."

"Why is this story on the street then?"

"I have no idea sheriff, but it is not true."

"I think you told me this story and started the rumor so you could get the sympathy of the court. Maybe get you bail or a continuance?"

"No, I had nothing to do with spreading this rumor."

"Well, it won't do you any good. We're gonna lock you up for a long time."

"That remains to be seen, Joe. I'll be back in charge of the restaurant soon."

Tuesday, January 6, 1925

Judge Risjord appointed Clarence Lameroux, a 64-year-old Ashland attorney, to assist Foster in the prosecution's case. The next day, Lameroux arrived in Hurley and met with Foster in his office.

"How strong a case do we have, Warren? Do you think she's guilty?"

"She's guilty, all right, C.P. Problem is will the jury believe it?"

"There were no witnesses, correct?"

"No witnesses to the crime."

"Who are we bringing to the stand?"

"Just five. A lady name of Louise Mason, detective Hayes and a girl named Lempi, Emil Erickson and LaFave. Mason lives in Chicago. I subpoenaed her yesterday. Zabel will try to get Anderson here from Waupun. I doubt he'll be coming, though. Problem is, we don't know when the trial will take place. Zabel was granted a continuance until Monday the 12th. I just know he'll ask for another delay."

"It sounds like we have a strong circumstantial case against Mrs. Sigler."

"That's what we have. Zabel is going to try sympathy on the jury."

"How's that?"

"Play up the pregnancy and that she has four kids to care for."

"Is she really pregnant?"

"Dunno. One day she says she is and the next day she says she isn't. She told Volant that she was a couple of months ago, but denied it last Friday. Personally, I think Zabel would have a good insanity plea. She's nuts."

"How's this Mason lady gonna play up?"

"I don't know. She's not going to be very reliable as a witness. She was one of Sigler's prostitutes so I think Zabel will land on her pretty hard. This lady is tough and very poised, though. With a little coaching she should be able to hold her own"

"And the rest of our witnesses? How will they do?"

"Hayes will be our best witness. He got Anderson's confession and all the evidence we need to prove she's part of it. Got a little surprise coming up, too, if I can get her to cooperate."

"What? Who?"

"A kid by the name of Lempi Luoma. Works down the street. She was a prostitute or a waitress at the Gogebic for a very short time. She'll testify that Anderson took her for a ride and told her that Emma would do anything to get Sigler killed."

"What are the chances of nailing Mrs. Sigler for murder one?"

"Accessory before the fact, maybe. The evidence we have so far shows that she hired Anderson to do the job. Pretty safe bet that she's an accomplice. I just wish I could get evidence that she planned and carried out the murder, but that's a stretch. There's no doubt that she hired Anderson for the job, though.

"So we have Hayes, Mason and this Luoma girl. Anybody else?"

"Guy named Erickson owns an employment agency across from the Gogebic Hotel. He saw Anderson and Emma talking on the day Anderson skipped town. We'll bring him in. Volant will testify. La Fave about finding the body. That's about it. Pretty much rests on Hayes."

"Do we know who Zabel will bring in?"

"Anderson, if he can get him here from Waupun. People around town who knew Sigler was a son-of-a-bitch. Probably the boy, Robert, will be asked to take the stand."

Volant and Lameroux met several times over the course of the week to plan the prosecution's case.

Monday, January 12, 1925

As expected, Winfred Zabel filed for a continuance and bail with Judge Risjord. His argument contended that because he had been retained only a short time before to defend Emma, he had not had sufficient time to prepare a defense. In the motion Emma stated that she had been advised by counsel that she had a "good and meritorious defense" and that witnesses who cannot be located and whose whereabouts are unknown to the defendant are needed to prove her defense. The argument for releasing her on bail was based on the fact that she had four children to care for. The motion also stated that her hotel and restaurant business was being entirely neglected, and she was unable to meet taxes and interest payments on her property while confined in the county jail awaiting trial. She further contended that her health had been greatly impaired since her incarceration.

Judge Risjord denied a continuance of her case over the present term of circuit court but continued it to January 26. With consent of Volant, the court decided to admit Mrs. Sigler to bail of $20,000. Zabel was confident he could arrange for a bail bond. He was wrong. Nobody was willing to pay the price, so Emma stayed in the County lock-up.

Emma was interviewed by a reporter from the Daily Globe in her cell.

"Mrs. Sigler, your trial is scheduled to start a week from today. How do you feel about it?"

"I'm a little disturbed. The waiting is the worst thing."

"You aren't worried about your case, are you?

"Well, I don't seem to be, do I?"

"Seven months is a long time to spend in this jail. How have you been coping?"

"This seven months has been like a month. The time has gone by fast."

"How do you think the outcome of the trial will be?"

"I think I will be acquitted."

"So you believe you will be going home soon?"

"Yes, but some time back I read that the state was making a strenuous effort to convict me through the loopholes."

"What will you do if you are acquitted?"

"I'll run my business as I did before I was arrested. I've been keeping tabs on how things have been running. The whole place has been neglected. I haven't been able to pay the taxes. My sister and brother-in-law have been running it for the past seven months and they're doing the best they can, but they aren't business people."

"You have four children, don't you Mrs. Sigler?"

"Yes. Robert was ten last August, Junior is four and the twins Lester and Leslie are three. They will be four in March. The three little ones think I'm in the hospital. Robert told me that he doesn't like the idea of his mother staying away so long and insists I ought to return to him."

"Why don't you think you have been released on bail, Mrs. Sigler?"

"There's one man in Hurley who I blame for the whole thing. He's been poisoning the minds of people who might have wanted to see me free so I could tend to my personal affairs."

"How do you feel about the charges against you?"

"As an accomplice before the fact?"

"Yes."

"My conscience hasn't bothered me. I don't feel guilty of any wrongdoing. I have already done just what any level-headed woman would have done in my circumstance. Nevertheless, that is not saying that I'm guilty of the crime the state has against me."

"Do you have any regrets in helping out Andy Anderson?"

"No, I'm not sorry for that at all. I don't hold a grudge against him, either, for implicating me in his confession."

"What did you mean when you told me that the state is going to convict you through the loopholes?"

"Well, I've heard of persons being convicted on circumstantial evidence" she said, "or through self confession. But the state is going to bring up a new sort of conviction in my case. I wonder how it will feel to be convicted through loopholes. But the police can rest assured that before the state has the pleasure of cross examining the defendant, the loopholes will be automatically diminished. I'll be glad when I can spill my heart to the public. My conscience hasn't bothered me. I have not considered it a punishment that I have been kept behind bars and steel doors, securely locked for seven months. I am not sorry for making an attempt to help Andy. Neither do I hold a grudge against him if he implicated me in his confession. Have you ever heard this poem?

Stone walls do not a prison make
Nor iron bars a cage.
Mind's innocence and quiet take
That for a hermitage.
If I have freedom in my love
And in my soul am free,
Angels alone that soar above
Enjoy such liberty."

"That was a lovely piece of poetry, Mrs. Sigler. Did you write that yourself?"

"No. It was written a long time ago by a poet name of Richard Lovelace. I think he might have been in a prison somewhere when he wrote it."

The Globe reporter stood up and put on her hat, a tight-fitting cloche.

"I'm sorry to run out on you like this, but I have a deadline to meet, You sure are a wonderful person. Thank you for allowing me to interview you, Mrs. Sigler. Now, before I leave is there anything else you'd like to tell the readers?"

"Just write that I'm anxious to get back and to take charge of the hotel. I realize I have a big responsibility ahead of me managing the business and bringing up the four little hopefuls. It is a burden, but a pleasant one. I can prove it to the public that I am worthy of my freedom."

PART THREE

Monday, January 26, 1925

Zabel filed an affidavit of prejudice against Judge Risjord and called for a new judge to sit on the bench. Judge W.R. Foley of Superior was directed to hold court. The affidavit was filed by defense counsel, but in the absence of Zabel, Peter J. Zisch appeared in court. When Lameroux asked Zisch if he was an attorney he replied in the negative, saying he had been employed as a clerk in Mr. Zabel's office for the last two or three months. A jury panel had been summoned to appear but was dismissed until the trial the next day. The defense asked for an order to be given to the warden at Waupun State Prison to bring Andy to Hurley and appear as a witness. Judge Risjord granted the order and the phone call was made. Andy would be in Hurley on Wednesday morning. It would take all of Tuesday to select the jury.

Tuesday, January 27, 1925

Judge Foley arrived at the Hurley courthouse promptly at 9 am. A large crowd of spectators had been waiting for the doors to open. The order of the day was to empanel a jury.

For the first time since she had been in court, Emma's father, Robert Shroth, sat in attendance. He was the only member of her family there.

Zabel examined the jurors at length as to whether they believed in "the code of self-defense." He didn't reveal the nature of the defense and nothing was said to indicate what plan he would follow to free Emma. He referred repeatedly to "alleged interviews" and what were "purported to be interviews" with Mrs. Sigler and published recently in the Ironwood Daily Globe and tried hard to belittle the newspaper articles. He got several jurors to admit that sometimes the newspapers weren't always right. He also questioned each juror as to whether he or she was acquainted with Joseph P. Hayes.

Charles Parker, who served as a juror in the Santini case, was the first man called to the jury box. Later, however, he was disqualified because of the fact that he was a deputy sheriff in Iron County. Of the first 12 potential jurors called, five were women, and it was indicated that a number of women would be left on the jury. A number of jurors were challenged for cause and others were excused for various reasons. Not a few of the jurors said they had set opinions as to the guilt or innocence of the defendant, which resulted in their being excused from jury duty.

Mrs. Kate Saari was excused because she was the township treasurer of the Town of Oma and had to return to the town and proceed with the collection of taxes, she said. Mrs. Katie Cossette was excused because her baby required her attention, and she would be unable to remain away from home at night, she told the court. Only one challenge for cause was denied, and that was when Mr. Zabel challenged Alfred Erickson of Montreal. Mr. Erickson later was stricken from the list.

The jury had not been picked by the time of the noon recess, but by 2:15, the 12 jurors and alternates had been selected. The jury was made up of four women, all housewives and mothers, and eight men. Ernest Miller was picked as the foreman.

After a short recess, Judge Foley came into the courtroom, robes flowing, and sat down. He banged a gavel three times and shouted "Order! Order in the court!" The crowd quieted down, and Foley asked the clerk to read the charges.

"Has the defendant been arraigned, Mr. District Attorney?" Foley asked,

"She has not," Foster answered.

"Do you want me to arraign her?"

"Yes, your honor."

"Mrs. Sigler, how do you wish to plead?"

"My client will plead not guilty, your honor," Zabel answered.

"Is this your desire, Mrs. Sigler, to plead not guilty?"

"Yes."

Before the judge ordered the court to call the jury for trial, Foster requested a motion of *nolle prosequi* on the first count of murder. He was satisfied, for the time being, of dismissing the count of murder and trying her on the second charge of accessory before the fact. The motion was granted, and a reading of the charge was made. Zabel formally entered the plea of not guilty to the charge of having "counseled, hired and procured the services of Andy Anderson, alias Andrew Gudleski, to commit the said felony of murder."

Foster said that the prosecution would call only four or five witnesses: Harry La Fave, Charbonneau the undertaker, Dr. Urquhart, Joe Hayes, and Louise Mason.

The question of overnight housing of the jury was brought up. It was decided to take them to an Ironwood hotel since there was not enough room for them in Hurley.

Zabel reserved his opening address until the state rested. Foster asked for a brief recess to see if his witnesses were all present. He asked that all witnesses be excluded from the courtroom. Zabel objected to doing that, but Judge Foley granted the request, and all witnesses were taken to the smaller municipal courtroom.

After the transcript of Andy's appearance before Judge Risjord in Ashland was admitted as evidence, the first order of business was for La Fave to explain how he found the body. Then, Coroner Joseph Charbonneau testified that he and Carl Silvoli retrieved the body. Dr. Urquhart explained that he did the autopsy. Zabel asked Urquhart for the details, to verify the presence of gonorrhea and to explain the angle of the bullet wounds. Urquhart was unable to recall any bruises on Sigler's face, but he admitted that he didn't look for any.

Joseph Hayes was the next to testify for the prosecution. He verified his experience as a detective and related everything that Andy had told him in the jailhouse. Try as he might, when Zabel cross-examined him, he was unable to shake Hayes from his story.

The jury was told in detail about the killing of Sigler by Andy as told to the detective by Anderson when they occupied cells in the Iron County jail, Hayes posing as a "badman." He related how he made an appointment to meet Mrs. Sigler in Ironwood, posing as a go-between for Emma and Andy, and how they drove out on the Lake Superior Road, a distance of about four miles north of Ironwood, where he related the story to Mrs. Sigler in order to "wise her up" that he was acquainted with the facts of the murder.

"Three or four months before Sigler was killed, Mrs. Jack Rice, whose given name was Rachel and who was known as 'Ray,' suggested that Andy murder Sigler," said Hayes as he related the story as it was told him by Andy.

"Ray said 'If you murder him, I'll buy the gun.' He and Ray went to the hardware store in Ironwood, paid $32 for it and gave the clerk an $8 tip so as not to have to register."

Then Hayes related Anderson's story of how Mrs. Sigler said "I'll pay you for killing Sigler. I'll give you $2,000 if you kill him and leave no evidence for the officers."

According to Hayes, later on Mrs. Sigler called Anderson at the saloon where he was working and told him "For Christ's Sake, when are you going to do this job! If you don't do it pretty soon I'll do it." Andy said "No, women always bungle things."

"Andy had planned to kill Sigler before he did, taking his victim out for a ride one night when their automobile became stalled in the mud and Gudleski was afraid of being detected if they went through with the job at that time. Later, the night of the murder, he planned to take Sigler to Lake Lavina and there shoot him and throw his body into the lake, but an automobile appeared on the scene and he drove on, fearful lest he be detected."

According to Hayes's story, Mrs. Sigler called Andy at the saloon the day after the shooting and warned him that if he had any bloody clothes, to get rid of them. That day she gave Andy $400 according to Hayes. During their conversation on Lake Superior Road, Hayes told Mrs. Sigler that Anderson was of the impression Mrs. Sigler had done away with Mrs. Rice, who died shortly after Sigler's murder.

Wednesday, January 28, 1925

It was a cold, blustery morning with near-blizzard conditions. The temperature was -16, but it didn't prevent the curious from attending the trial. After all, this was Hurley, and a little blizzard never got in the way of something interesting happening in the Northwoods. It was rumored that Louise Mason and Emma would take the stand, and they would be able to see and hear Andy testify. An hour before the doors opened at 8 am., hundreds of people had already been allowed to enter the Hurley courthouse on Iron Street to escape the freezing temperatures. Deputies had to lock the doors early because the crush of spectators became too overwhelming for them. The crowd rushed up the stairs to the second floor where they tried in vain to enter the small municipal courtroom. It became evident very soon after the doors were opened that something had to be done to accommodate the spectators. The people were shuttled from the tiny municipal courtroom into the much larger circuit courtroom across the hall. Hordes of people dressed in heavy coats and rubber boots sat on long wooden benches. There was not enough space in that courtroom, either, and there was a standing-room-only crowd. More than 100 people were left outside the building in the cold, and they were told to come back after the noon recess. Several young boys made their way to the back of the building and broke into the basement through the coal chute.

"We could have sold tickets to this affair," Foster whispered to Lameroux.

"That's the truth." Lameroux turned around in his chair. "My God! Just look at all those people. Looks like everyone from Hurley is here."

Hundreds of people were all talking at the same time as they encountered friends and neighbors whom they had neither seen nor spoken to since the onset of winter.

A few minutes after Judge Foley entered the courtroom, Lameroux brought Louise Mason to the witness chair. Spectators commented on the way she strutted to the witness chair like a model. She appeared to be more intelligent than the average woman in the haunts of Hurley, and because of that, her admissions were all the more startling. Louise may have been a crowd-pleasing witness, but her answers lacked credibility. She was unable to keep her facts straight, and she told some flagrant lies, conveniently turning around the chicken story. Sigler, she said, told her that he was going to purchase the chickens, but he told Emma he was going to Pence to buy some girls. It was obvious that she had been coached by Foster and Lameroux, but in spite of the coaching, there were many holes in her testimony.

"Where do you live, Mrs. Mason?" Lameroux began.

"Beg pardon?"

"Where do you live? Where's your home?"

"Presently, in Chicago."

"Where were you living on or about the first of May a year ago?'

"Superior. 1705 Fourteenth Street."[5]

"Your home was at Superior at that time?

"Yes, sir."

"Where were you on the first of May?"

"I was in Hurley."

"Did you come to Hurley at that time?

[5] A search of the Superior city directory showed no such address, nor any person named Louise Mason.

"I came the night before the first of May."

"Did you know the defendant, Mrs. Emma Sigler?"

"Yes, sir."

"How long had you known her?"

"I met her in October before the murder for the first time, I suppose. October, 1923."

"Did you know Andrew Sigler, her husband?"

"Yes, sir."

"How long had you known them?"

"I met Mrs. Sigler at the same time."

"Where did you meet them"

"At their hotel."

"They were running a hotel at that time?"

"Yes, sir."

"Was that the Gogebic?"

"Yes, sir."

"Were you employed there for awhile?"

"Yes, sir."

"For how long were you there?"

"From the latter part of October, 1923 to the ninth of January, 1924."

"Did you know Andrew Anderson or Andrew Gudleski?"

"No, sir."

"Never saw him?"

"No, never saw him."

"What work were you doing there at the hotel?"

"I assisted Mrs. Sigler in taking care of the children and in doing general housework."

"How many children has she?"

"She has four."

"You came there at what time the day before?"

"I came there the day before on the evening train."

"On the evening of April 30?"

"Yes, sir."

"How long did you stay there?"

"After the murder, I stayed I think until the following Tuesday."

"That is after Mr. Sigler disappeared?"

"Yes, sir."

"How many days was it after that you went away?"

"I came Wednesday night and I think I left Tuesday."

"Did you see Andrew Sigler, the deceased at the hotel that night there? At that place of business?"

"The night I arrived you mean?"

"Well, I will say the night you arrived. Was he around there that night?"

"Yes, sir."

"The next day?"

"Yes, sir."

"Did you see him there the night of May 1?"

"Yes, sir."

"When did you see him last that evening of May 1?"

"Well, Mr. Sigler received a telephone call about eight o'clock and he went out after that. That was the last I ever saw of him."

"About eight o'clock on the night of May 1, you say? Where? How did he go out of the building?"

"After his telephone call, he came out into the kitchen and put on his coat, mackinaw and sweater, then he left from the side door."

"If you saw a diagram of the building, would you recognize it you think?"

"I think so."

Louise was asked by Lameroux to look at a diagram hanging from the wall. She stepped down to the sketch and attempted to explain the position of the various rooms, but her testimony was somewhat confusing. She didn't know north from south, east from west, or left from right. Exasperated, Zabel objected, and Louise was excused. Volant was called to explain the location of the various rooms on the sketch that he had made of the layout of the first floor of the Gogebic Hotel.

Louise was recalled to the stand and Lameroux continued his direct examination of her.

"State, Mrs. Mason, whether or not you were present when Mr. Sigler left on the evening of May 1?"

"Yes, I was in the kitchen."

"And where did he go?"

"He went out the side door of what they call the sewing room."

"What did you do with reference to the door?"

"He went out and I locked it."

"Do you know when that door was unlocked again?"

"No, I couldn't say."

"Where was Mrs. Sigler at this time?"

"Well, I thought she was upstairs with the children."

"Where did they keep the children?"

"The children slept upstairs in her apartment. That and the nursery were upstairs over the kitchen."

"Who else was there that evening?"

"There was no one else there in that place that evening but Mrs. Sigler and Mrs. Rice who was very ill."

"Where was Mrs. Rice?"

"Confined to her room. In the room next to the sewing room."

"How late was the place kept open that night?"

"I think between twelve and one. I think around one o'clock Mrs. Sigler decided to close."

"Who had been there from eight o'clock up until one in charge of the place?"

"Well, during the time shortly after Mr. Sigler left, the little boy.... I heard her little boy she calls Junior crying and I went upstairs."

"Let me ask this question. After Mr. Sigler left the building and went out the side door, when did you next see Mrs. Sigler after that?"

"When Mrs. Sigler came through Mrs. Rice's room and asked me where her husband was."

"How long had she left?"

"I'd say about five minutes or more."

"And she asked you what?"

"She asked me where her husband went. I said he told me he was going into the country to buy chickens."

"Now then, from what time on after you had this talk with Mrs. Sigler what were you doing around there? You and Mrs. Sigler."

"Mrs. Sigler was taking care of the children and I was in the kitchen doing kitchen work because the help had left."

"There was no there help there at that time?"

"No, sir."

"Well, did anything take place with you and Mrs. Sigler relative to her husband not coming back?"

"Well, she asked me where her husband went I told her that he went out in the country to buy chickens. 'No', she said. 'You are mistaken. He's going out to Pence to get some women to come here.'"

"What else?"

"Well, I said, 'I don't know. Only what he told me.' Because the week before he had gone out on the same errand but he didn't get any."

Zabel objected to the chicken testimony as "incompetent, irrelevant, and immaterial." His objection was noted and the part that read "Because the week before he had gone out on the same errand but he didn't get any" was stricken out. Lameroux continued.

"Did Mrs. Sigler say anything to you about her husband going to Pence?"

"She told me she knew he was going to Pence and if he went out there he was going to have some trouble and I would hear about him having a bullet hole through his body. That he would have trouble with those people out there."

"Now, when was it that you had that conversation with her?"

"Right after her husband left a little while."

"That is, the time you spoke to her of that, she came into the kitchen?"

"Yes, sir."

"Following that, what did you do?"

"I went upstairs to the nursery and stayed with the little boy until he went to sleep."

"How long were you there probably?"

"I don't know exactly. Maybe a half hour. I'm not quite sure."

"Where was Mrs. Sigler during that period?"

"Mrs. Sigler was looking after the restaurant downstairs."

"After this half hour, what did she do then?"

"I came downstairs, and she told me that she knew that her husband had gone to Pence because the man who was supposed to go in the country with him to get those chickens had just left. She had served him a cup of coffee."

"What hour was that?"

"I don't know when it was exactly, but it was a little while before her husband left."

"Now go on and relate what further conversation you had with her that evening relative to anything that could have any bearing on the question."

"Well, after about 10:30 we remarked that it was strange he didn't come home."

"Who remarked?"

"Mrs. Rice and I. We were talking about him being out at 10:30."

"What did you say to Mrs. Sigler if anything?"

"I remarked about it later to her. I said 'What do you suppose is keeping him out so late?' She didn't know. She decided she would close around twelve or one o'clock. Finally she did.

She closed, I think, about one and in the meantime she went upstairs."

"Where were you at that time?"

"Downstairs with Mrs. Rice. Mrs. Sigler told me that her husband was upstairs and in bed."

"You say you were downstairs with Mrs. Rice?"

"Yes,"

"She went upstairs?"

"Yes, she went upstairs."

"Where did you see her again?"

"She came right downstairs again."

"How long was she up there?"

"Not more than a few minutes. She rushed downstairs again and said her husband was upstairs and in bed. She said she didn't seem to be so worried. The place was closed. She asked if she could sleep with me. She was nervous. I said I didn't care. She and I occupied a room together that night. Mrs. Rice slept in the adjoining room."

"What room did you occupy? One of those lower rooms?"

"No, Mrs. Sigler and I occupied one of the larger rooms that was used by the waitresses. There was two beds in it. We used just one bed."

"Where is that located?"

"Across the hall from the room that I occupied. It was right near the stairway,"

Lameroux pointed to the diagram on the wall and picked out Louise's and Ray's rooms. "Do you have to pass through those two rooms in order to pass down the stairway to get out?"

"No, I don't just understand your question."

"You stayed downstairs? You and Mrs. Sigler?"

"Yes. Mrs. Sigler and I occupied the same room. In the room they used for the waitresses. The room had two beds in it, but we only used one."

"What next happened between you and Mrs. Sigler relative to the disappearance of Mr. Sigler?"

"I don't think we commented any more about it. She seemed satisfied that he was there."

Zabel raised an objection. "It calls for a conclusion," he said. The objection was sustained.

"Just say what happened without how she seemed," Lameroux continued.

"Well, I think we retired and went to sleep and I don't remember anything that was said or any more about it or her affairs of any kind until a little before five o'clock. She got up and went upstairs and came downstairs again and she said to me 'Andrew has left. Gone out.' And she supposed he had taken the train for Ashland."

Judge Foley interrupted. "Is that what she said? 'she supposed'?"

"Yes, 'she supposed.'"

"What did you say to her if anything?"

"I said, 'I don't see why he should leave so early because the train doesn't leave 'til near seven o'clock.' It was five o'clock."

"What did you say to her?"

"I said I thought that was funny that he would get up so early to take the train to Ashland because the railroad station is not open at that hour."

"What did she say to that?"

"She said she knew he went to Ashland. Seemed satisfied."

"Were you around the Gogebic Hotel the next day?"

"I was there all day."

"Were you there when word came of Sigler's death?"

"Yes, sir."

"Did you see Mrs. Sigler at that time?"

"Yes, sir."

"Who brought the message?"

"I think a fella by the name of Nelson"

"What did she say when this word came?"

"Well, she was call...."

Zabel interrupted. "Wait. Who?"

"It was around evening. Mrs Sigler. She was called out of the kitchen, I think, by the sheriff, and later I was called out of the kitchen. And they asked what time he had left. They questioned Mrs. Sigler, and they also questioned me."

"Did you hear the report that was made? The report from this man that came back?"

"Yes."

"Where were you when Nelson made the report?"

"Mrs. Sigler and I were at the sink. I think that she washed the dishes, and I was wiping them. Nelson came in and said, 'Did you know Andrew's body was found out near Mercer?'"

"What did she say?"

"She said no, she didn't."

"Anything else said by her? What was her appearance or talk? How did she appear?"

"Very cool and unconcerned."

"About what time did you get that word?"

"Shortly after lunch. An hour or so. Possibly around two o'clock."

"What was Mrs. Sigler doing in the forenoon?"

"Well, as I said before, we had no help and she and I were doing the work together. She was taking care of her business."

"Do you remember of her going out at all?"

"Yes. She was waiting for the bank to open at nine o'clock. She went over to the bank and came back."

Zabel objected. "Wait a minute. Tell us what you know yourself."

"Well, I intended to do that. She came over to the bank. Came home from the bank. Showed me a large roll of bills and said she was going to pay the car that day. Made a payment on her car."

"After that, did she go away again during the day?"

"No, sir, she didn't."

"Did you have any financial deal with her that day?"

"With Mrs. Sigler?"

" Yes, on the second."

"Well, no I didn't have. Well, I had in regard to twenty dollars."

"Tell us what deal you had with her."

Zabel objected to the question as immaterial. Judge Foley overruled him.

"Tell us what it was."

"Mrs. Rice was leaving for St. Paul and Mrs. Sigler owed her $20 and she came and asked...Mrs. Sigler asked me if I would loan her $20 to give to Mrs. Rice as she was going away. I told her I would. She said she didn't have any money."

"Did you say anything to her about not having any money?"

"I said to Mrs. Rice...."

"Not to Mrs. Rice. Did you say anything to Mrs. Sigler about it?"

"No, I didn't. But I thought it it was strange."

Judge Foley interrupted. "No, wait a minute. Not what you thought."

"I said, 'why don't you pay it?' She says 'I haven't any money.'"

Lameroux continued. "Well, you say you let her have $20 that day."

"That day. Yes, sir."

"What was it you say she said about paying her money up?"

"She said she had paid a bill that day."

"Did you say anything to her about the money she got from the bank?"

"No, when she got back from the bank she remarked that she was going to make a payment on the car."

"Well, I'm speaking now about the time Mrs. Rice went. What excuse, if any, did Mrs. Sigler make about not having any money?"

An objection was made by Zabel that Lamoreux was leading the witness. Foley agreed that the question was not material.

Louise asked for a glass of water. Her mouth was very dry because she had been told by Foster and Lameroux that Zabel would try to "rake her over the coals" as it were. It made her quite nervous, but she was determined to stay calm and maintain her poise. The tough cross examination by Zabel began.

She avoided answering many of his questions, and he was successful in catching her in several lies. He was out to discredit Louise's testimony and, for the most part, succeeded in doing just that.

"What was your business in Superior before you came to Hurley in October, Mrs. Mason?"

"Pardon me?"

"What was your business?"

"I was living with Mrs. Barrett."[6]

"What were you doing?"

"Sewing."

"How did you come to live in Hurley?"

"I stopped at the Gogebic Hotel."

"What business brought you to Hurley?"

"We came over on a motor trip and then I went into the hotel and stopped for the night and met Mr. and Mrs. Sigler."

"Who is we?"

"A lady friend of mine from Mellen."

"What became of her?"

"She went back."

"Siglers hadn't advertised for help, had they?

"I wasn't aware of any advertising."

"Did you apply for a job at the Gogebic Hotel at that time?"

"No, sir. Not at the time."

"Who spoke to you about employment there?"

"Mrs. Sigler and her husband. After I had my dinner."

"How did they know you were open for a job?"

---

[6] Superior city directory had no person named Barrett listed.

"Well, Mrs. Sigler asked me if I would care to stay there and we made arrangements that night."

"And you were a maid and were employed to take care of the children and do housework?"

"Yes, sir."

"As a matter of fact, didn't you engage in prostitution at that place?"

Louise hesitated.

"Answer me!" Zabel demanded.

Judge Foley told Louise to answer the question or not answer.

"Well, I refuse to answer!"

"Why do you refuse to answer?"

Lameroux objected to the question. He accused Zabel of badgering the witness. Foley overruled the objection and called for an answer.

"What, is your refusal to answer based upon the ground that your answer may tend to incriminate you? I didn't hear your answer."

"I didn't answer."

"What is your answer?"

"I haven't any answer to make."

"Is the reason you refuse to answer my question is because the answer might tend to incriminate you?"

"Well, it might."

"That is the reason you decline to answer it, is it?"

Louise did not answer the question. She glared at Zabel defiantly and wanted to stick her tongue out at him. She remained collected. He could not, would not, get her to lose face and explode. Zabel fired questions rapidly, and Louise answered them just as rapidly.

"And now. Are you living in Chicago?"

"Yes, sir."

"Where in Chicago?"

"4714 Kenwood Avenue."[7]

"What is your business in Chicago?"

"I'm not doing anything in Chicago. Living there with relatives."

"Are you engaged in prostitution in Chicago?"

"No, sir. I am not."

"You have reformed since you left Hurley, have you?"

"I refuse to answer."

"While you lived at Siglers, did you bring any baggage?"

"Hand baggage and a trunk."

"You had a trunk with you?"

"Yes, sir."

"Brought that along on your visit to Hurley?"

"Well, later on I sent for my trunk."

"I asked you if you if you brought the trunk with you when you came."

"No, we had hand baggage."

"Did you bring anything else besides hand baggage?"

"A hat box and a club bag. I think that is all."

"Did you bring four dogs or three?"

"No, sir. I had one."

[7] There was no one living at that address in 1923.

"Did you have three dogs sent to you later?"

"No, sir. I never owned three. I had two little dogs."

"Didn't you have three little dogs while you lived at the Gogebic Hotel?"

"One of the dogs belonged to Mrs. Sigler."

"You took care of the children?"

"I assisted her in taking care of them."

"You don't like Mrs. Sigler, do you?"

"I never showed any dislike for her."

"Ever call her names?"

"Well, not until after..."

"Did you?"

"Beg your pardon?"

"Did you call her names?"

"Well, we never had any argument or any quarrel."

"Won't you answer my question, please?"

"Yes, I called her names after the murder."

"Did you call her a damn bitch?"

"Yes, sir."

"Did you call her children damn little brats?"

"No, sir."

"Sure about that?"

"Pardon?"

"Did you call her children damnable brats?"

"In a letter, yes I did."

"Those are the children you claim you were hired to take care of, were they? Those are the children you refer to in that expression in a letter to Mrs. Rice? Those are the children you claim you were hired to take care of?"

"Yes, sir."

"How old were those children when you moved there?"

"Pardon?"

"How old?"

"I think the oldest child is ten and the other one is five and the twins, I believe are about two. Two and a half years."

"You referred to them in those letters, did you not, as being the worst demons this side of hell?"

"Yes, sir."

"Meaning those four little children. That right?"

"Yes, sir."

"What other names did you call Mrs. Sigler?"

"I don't recollect."

"Did you have any trouble with her while you were living there?"

"None whatsoever."

"Have any trouble with Mr. Sigler while you were living there?"

"Oh, occasionally we might have a cross word or something."

"Did you call Mr. Sigler any names?"

"No, sir. I never did."

"Did you call him a piss cutter?"

Louise just glared coldly at Zabel and said nothing. She got one of those if-looks-could-kill expressions on her face. Her eyes squinted, her forehead wrinkled, and her lips were pursed into a hard, thin line.

"Answer me!"

"Yes, sir!" Louise spit out. Zabel was beginning to shake Louise's poise.

"And why'd you call him that?"

"Well, uh.... We used to call one another names in a joking way."

"You thought it a joke to call a man that?"

"He considered it so."

"Did you?"

"We used to joke about different things."

"Did you consider it a joke when you called him those names?"

"I did. Yes."

"Weren't there another reason for calling him that?"

"Pardon?"

"Wasn't there another reason for calling him that?"

"No. I haven't."

"Did you ever refer to him by that name in letters to other people?"

"I believe one time I did to Mrs. Rice."

"Also in joke?"

"Yes, sir."

"And you sent that letter through the United States mail?"

"Yes, sir."

"Did you know that Mr. Sigler was diseased?"

"No, only from remarks that were made."

"He told you that, didn't he?"

"Pardon?"

"He told you he was."

"She told me he was."

"Didn't he tell you?"

"I heard them discuss it one night in the kitchen."

"Didn't he tell you he was diseased with gonorrhea?"

"He and she both were talking about it. I happened to be present at the time."

"Didn't you warn Mrs. Sigler about the danger of infection?"

"I did."

"Didn't Mrs. Sigler tell you that she thought it was bladder trouble and that you told her then?"

"No, it was gonorrhea," she blurted out. "I don't remember."

"Did you put her wise to his condition?"

"I don't remember."

"You will not say you didn't, will you?"

"Mrs. Sigler informed me that she thought he had disease."

"Didn't she tell you she thought it was bladder trouble?"

"She told me the doctor told her he had a venereal disease. Some doctor."

"Didn't you tell her it was not bladder trouble but gonorrhea trouble that her husband had told you?"

"Mrs. Sigler? Mr. Sigler?"

"Didn't you tell her it was gonorrhea?"

"No, sir."

"Wasn't that what you meant when you referred to him as a piss cutter?"

"No. No."

"Isn't that, among your class of associates, the usual term of men afflicted that way?"

"Oh, no."

"Is this letter your handwriting?"

"Yes, sir." Two letters written by Louise to Mrs. Rice were marked as Exhibits A and B.

"It consists of two sheets. Your handwriting?"

"Yes, sir."

"You wrote both of these letters?"

"Yes, sir."

"To a Mrs. Rice?"

"I did."

"Also a widow?"

"Mrs. Rice is not a widow."

"You wrote those letters after you left Sigler's?"

"I wrote one letter warning Mrs. Rice not to go back."

Lameroux said that the answer was not responsive and should be stricken from the record. The objection was granted by Judge Foley.

"Did you write both of these letters after you left the Gogebic Hotel?"

"I couldn't say. I have forgotten."

"You were at Ironwood when you wrote one of them, Letter B, were you not?"

"I don't know. One letter I wrote to Mrs. Rice warning her not to go back." Zabel moved to strike that answer. The motion was granted.

"Will you answer the questions?"

"I don't recollect the other."

"Now, just before May 1, 1924, you'd been in Superior, had you not?"

"Yes, sir."

"For about how long?"

"Over six weeks."

"Why did you go to Superior?"

"I was ill at the time from the effects of pleurisy."

"What was your business during those six weeks?"

"I was confined to my bed most of the time. I wasn't doing anything."

"Were you paid any wages while you were living at the Gogebic?"

"Pardon?"

"Answer that. Yes or no?"

"Mrs Sigler didn't pay me any wages. No."

"Will you answer the question, please? Were you paid any wages while at the Gogebic Hotel?"

"No I wasn't."

"How did you make your living during that time?"

"Well, I didn't make a living at the Gogebic Hotel."

"Just existed?"

"I wasn't there any length of time."

"Were you there from May... from October until about six weeks before May 1st, were you not?"

"No, I left shortly after the holidays. Went to Chicago."

"What was the longest continuous period you were there?"

"I worked from the later part of October until the ninth of January. After that I never worked there."

"What wages did you get from October until January?"

"I received no wages."

"You did receive money while there, did you not?"

"I did."

"From men?"

"Yes, sir."

"For sexual intercourse?"

"For drinks!"

"For sexual intercourse?"

"I sold liquor there!"

"Did you get money for anything else?"

"Yes, sir!"

"For sexual intercourse?" Zabel shouted.

"Yes, sir!" Louise shouted back.

There was a quiet stir as people shuffled in their seats and gasps from the old ladies in the audience. Foster and Lameroux glanced at each other. "Well, he finally got what he was fishing for," Lameroux whispered.

Zabel continued his cross examination of Louise. He questioned her at length about her comings and goings during the night of the night of the murder and the next morning.

"You slept quite late in the morning, didn't you?"

"No, sir. I did not."

"What time do you generally get up in the morning or did you at that time?"

"Next morning Mrs. Sigler awakened me before five o'clock."

"You remained in bed, didn't you?"

"No, I got up after that."

"Five o'clock?"

"It was a little before five when I got up. She was also up. I went out into the kitchen and built a fire and I stayed up the rest of the day."

"Didn't you go upstairs?"

"No, I didn't."

"Did you go back to sleep?"

"No, I didn't. I stayed up."

"Didn't you go upstairs and go back to sleep on account of the noise downstairs?"

"No, not on that day. No, sir. Mondays are washdays in that household. Mondays and Tuesdays."[8]

"When Mrs. Sigler did her washing herself?"

"She had help that assisted her."

"But she did most of it?"

"Yes, sir."

"And there was quite a good deal of work in that respect in the hotel. Lots of wash?"

"Yes, sir."

"Four children?"

"Yes, sir."

"Lots of grown-ups?"

"Yes, sir."

"Lots of boarders?"

"Yes, sir."

---

[8] Washdays were on Tuesday and Thursday, according to Emma.

"Isn't it a fact that you usually slept until about eight-thirty, nine o'clock?"

"No, sir. I never slept later than eight."

"How?"

"Hardly ever later than eight o'clock."

"Wasn't it nine o'clock when you got up that morning? Yes?"

"No. sir. Mrs. Sigler awakened me at five, and she was excited because her husband wasn't there. And I was quite awake, and I stayed up the rest of the morning."

"You were a witness at the preliminary examination on July 25?"

"Yes, sir."

"Weren't you asked this question: 'You went there about the first of October and you were there October, November and December and up to the tenth of January. What time did you get up during that time? Did you make this answer: 'eight thirty or nine o'clock.'"

"I may have."

"How?"

"I may have made that answer. Mrs. Sigler usually got up between five and six every morning. Around that time. About six o'clock."

"And on washdays to get started a little bit earlier?"

"Sometimes."

"When is the next time that you saw Mr. Sigler after he left on the evening of May 1?"

"I never saw him after that."

"You knew, did you not, that Mr. and Mrs. Sigler had purchased an automobile?"

"I wasn't sure. I heard them speak of it, but I didn't know."

"And that certain payments had to be made?"

"I heard Mrs. Sigler make the statement she had to pay $500 on a car the first of May."

"Well, you know they bought a car, didn't you."

"I heard them say so, but I never saw the car."

"Wasn't there a violent quarrel over the mere matter of in whose name the license was to be?"

"Yes, sir. But I was not there when it happened."

"Did you hear Mr. Sigler leave the house in the morning?"

"The morning after he left the night before?"

"Yes."

"No, sir. I never did."

"Did you see his profile or his picture in the mirror before he left?"

"I can't really say."

"Did you not say so in a letter to Ray Rice. Do you recollect, Madam?"

"I may have mentioned it in a letter to Ray."

"Didn't you write in your letter to Ray Rice that you saw a flash of him in a mirror?"

"Yes, sir."

"And referred to him as the poor piss cutter when you referred to Sigler?"

"Yes, sir."

"Now by that, of course, you mean the morning of May 2, 1924."

"Yes, sir."

Zabel asked Louise about lights burning in the house at night; there were several. She said they always kept the doors locked to the outside and to her room.

"Now, Mrs. Sigler objected frequently to your staying there?"

"Beg pardon?"

"Mrs. Sigler objected frequently to your staying in that place. In the hotel."

"Not to my knowledge."

"Didn't she insist upon your leaving?"

"She never said so to me."

"Did Sigler follow you to Superior?"

"Not to my knowledge."

"Did he call for you at Superior?"

"He called upon me while I was in Superior."

"Ask you to come back with him?"

"Well, he asked... Yes, he did."

"And didn't he tell you in these words 'That damn bitch', meaning his wife, 'hasn't anything to say'?"

"No."

"Didn't you tell... didn't you say you didn't care to come home because his wife objects?"

"Mrs. Sigler never objected to my knowledge."

"Didn't you say that to Mr. Sigler and didn't he say 'That damn bitch hasn't anything to say'?"

"Not to me."

"He did, though, in the Gogebic Hotel after calling her that name?"

"Yes."

"And son of a bitch?"

"Yes, sir."

"And other words that are equally as vile and appropious?"

"Yes, sir."

"And where did he find you at Superior?"

"He found me at 1705 Fourteenth Street[9] where I always lived. Been living two years."

"He took you to a theatre party?"

"Mr. Sigler took the lady that I lived with and her husband. There were five of us in the party. To the theatre."

"Do you know what he came to Superior for?"

"Well, he bought some clothes. He bought an overcoat."

"Did you pick the clothes out for him?"

"I went with him the day he bought his suit and his overcoat."

"Helped select them, didn't you?"

"Yes, sir. And then bought some birds."

"What kind of birds?"

"Pardon?"

"What kind of birds?"

"He bought some canaries and those Mexican lovebirds."

"That was a very appropriate place to coach them, wasn't it?"

Lameroux objected. It was sustained.

"How long did he stay there?"

---

[9] The Superior City Directory for that year lists no person named Louise; it is a private dwelling.

"Mr. Sigler stopped with Mrs. Sigler's parents."

"You helped pick out the lovebirds?"

"No, I knew nothing about the birds. He bought them."

"You don't consider yourself a judge of them?"

"I know nothing about birds."

"Dogs is your specialty, isn't it?"

"Yes, sir."

"Did you come back with him?"

"Yes, sir. That night."

"Drive back?"

"No, we came back on the train."

"Did he pay your fare?"

"No, I paid my own fare."

"Where did you get the money from?"

"Pardon?"

"Did you have any money?"

"I have a bank account in Superior."

"Had you not been working in Superior?"

"I have an account there for some little time."

Zabel consulted his notes for a minute or so, and then continued with his cross examination of Louise.

"Mrs. Sigler made no secret of the fact that she had to make a payment on the automobile?"

"No."

"How did Sigler treat his children?"

"I beg your pardon?"

"How did Sigler treat his children?"

"At times he was very kind to them and at times very violent."

"Very brutal, wasn't he?"

"Yes, sir. At times."

"And you and Mrs. Sigler had to protect them?"

"Yes, sir."

Zabel concluded his questioning and Lameroux redirected to see if he could salvage anything of Louise's testimony.

He questioned Louise about the flash of light she saw on Friday morning, May 2. Even though she had told Zabel that she thought it was Sigler, she told Lameroux it was not of any consequence and was probably meaningless. Lameroux asked her, in detail, where the mirror was in relationship to furniture and the windows. Again, she couldn't tell left from right or north from south. Her answers came off as quite confusing.

Following Louise's testimony, the jury was instructed by Judge Foley to refrain from talking about the day's events before being taken to the Curry Hotel in Ironwood and sequestered for the evening.

Thursday, January 29, 1925

Once again, the courtroom was packed. Today, folks were hoping that Andy Anderson would be on the stand to tell all. They got their wish, but first Lameroux brought Louise to the stand to clarify her relationship with Emma. Louise indicated throughout her testimony that it was good. She was also questioned about the relationship between Sigler and Emma, and she stated that there was constant fighting going on; Emma called Sigler "vile names" and vice-versa.

Zabel asked Louise if she had any conversations with Lameroux before the morning's session. She denied that, at first, but admitted that she spoke to Lameroux about things other than her testimony. She had no idea why she was presently on the stand.

Hayes was called by Lameroux to identify Andy as the man who was in the cell next to him in the county jail.

Then Andy was called as a witness for the defense. A prison guard held on to the end of the chain attached to the handcuffs. His ankles were shackled. He appeared nervous as Zabel questioned him.

"Your name is Andrew Anderson?"

"It is."

"Are you sometimes known by any other name?"

"Why, Gudleski. Yes."

"How old a man are you?'

"I am twenty-nine."[10]

---

[10] Andy was 28. I have found 3 birth dates for him: 3/12/1896, 11/13/1896 and 11/15/1896, depending on the source. Andy's son told me it was 11/15/1896, and that is the date of record.

"Married?"

"Yes, sir."

"Children?"

"I have one boy."

"How long have you been living in Hurley?"

"Why, I have been living in Ironwood but have been working in Hurley."

"At the present time since June or July you have been at Waupun?"

"I have."

"In the State's prison?"

"I have."

"What was your occupation here in Ironwood or in Hurley during the spring of 1924?"

"It was electrician."

"Who did you work for?"

"For Mr. Dominic Friola."

"Where is his place of business with reference to the Gogebic Hotel?"

"It is next door. It is in the next building right at the Gogebic."

"Did you know Andrew Sigler?"

"I did."

"Did you know this defendant?"

"I do."

"During the time you have known them have you been in a position to observe how he treated his wife?"

"I have."

"How did he treat her?"

"Mean. Brutal."

"Can you tell this court and jury some of the things you witnessed concerning the treatment of his wife?"

"I can. At one time Mrs. Sigler had come running out and hollered for help. I was working in the back of the shop cleaning a battery while the man was coming out carrying a cleaver or a knife. I don't know what you would call it, but it was something with a sharp edge. Came chasing after her. I had stopped him and told him to use his brains. Mr. Sigler had picked up a club and threw at me which hit me alongside my face and I went in back on my work. I closed the door and went in. Another time I was in the Gogebic Cafe when Mr. Sigler had attempted to throw boiling water in her face. Another time in the Gogebic Cafe where I did part the two from fighting. Mr. Sigler was mauling his wife or was beating her. That is all I can say."

"What if any other names did he use to her?"

"Why, he had used the words in vile as son-of-a-bitch. Called her a whore. Dirty sow."

"What was his treatment of the children?"

"They were mean for a father to his children."

"What did you observe in that respect?"

"Why, one of the little boys was playing out in the back one day and Mr. Sigler had told him to do something which the kid did not understand him or catch him at the time he was saying it and he had taken the little boy, Junior, and hit him so hard over the face with his fists. I went into the electric shop to get a glass of water to bring him to and took the child in."

"How old was that child?"

"I have no idea how old the child was. I have an idea he is about five years at the present time. At that time he was four."

"Where were you on the first day of May, 1924?"

"On the first day of May, 1924, I was working all day long at the New Central."

"Did you any time at that day did you go to the Gogebic Hotel?"

"During the noon hour."

"What did you do there?"

"I was in the barber shop and got a shave and a haircut and stopped in there."

"Was Sigler there then?"

"He was there."

"Did you come there again that day?"

"I did."

"What time?"

"That was about in the evening about nine o'clock or half past eight."

"And what did you come there for?"

"Why, I had a cup of coffee and a piece of pie and went home."

"Had you seen Sigler in that home or that house that evening?"

"I did not."

"When was the last time you had seen him alive?"

"The last time I had seen Sigler alive was May 1. At dinnertime."

"Where were you on the morning of May 2?"

"On the morning of May 2, I left home, went to my place of work, cleaned my place up and sat around."

“Where were you during the night between May 1 and May 2?”

“I was home in bed.”

‘What time did you go to bed?”

“I went home in bed at about quarter after nine.”

“Was your wife at home when you went to bed?”

“She was not at home.”

“Do you remember when she came home?”

“I have no idea when she came home.”

“Were you awakened by her?”

“I was awakened by her.”

“Who opened the door for her?”

“She opened it herself.”

“Did you know where she was?”

“Been down at her aunt’s place or her cousin’s place at trio practice. Choir practice.”

“What time did you get up on the morning of May 2?”

“Got up at five o’clock or five thirty the same as I’ve been getting up every morning.”

What was the first thing you did?”

“Got up and dressed, got my breakfast, took my car and went to work.”

“Where did you work?”

“New Central.”

“New Central? What is that?”

“That is a soft drink parlor nowadays.”

“It is supposed to be?”

“Supposed to be.”

"Where is that located?"

"Located on the corner of Silver Street and First Avenue South."

"What work were you performing that morning when you came there and started to work?"

"I started cleaning up the place. Mopping the floor, cleaning glasses, cleaning the bar. General housework."

"How long did you remain there?"

"Remained there about half an hour."

"Then what happened?"

"Mrs. Sigler had called me on the telephone."

"What did she say?"

"Told me to come up. She wanted to see me."

"Is that all she said?"

"No. I told her at first I could not leave the place. I refused to come up. She had then told me to come up. That she or Mr. Sigler, Andrew, had a jug for me to take down. Or a jar. And thinking that the jar was too heavy for me to carry I had taken my car and drove up to the back."

"What kind of car was it?"

"It was Ford roadster."

"What time did you get over to the Gogebic Hotel?"

"I presume it was quarter to seven."

"In the morning?"

"In the morning."

"Whereabouts with reference to that building did you park your Ford car?"

"In the back."

"Near what entrance?"

"In the side door entrance."

"Is that an alley?"

"Just a lot between two buildings."

"What is the first room you got into as you came into the building?"

"The first room I got into as I came into the building, as I understand the building, is a sort of washroom. Laundry room."

"Washing? Whom did you find in the building?"

"I found Mrs. Sigler in the kitchen."

"Anyone else?"

"I did not."

"What did you say and what did she say?"

"I didn't say anything when I entered."

"Did you take notice of her condition that morning?"

"I did. She was hysterical."

"What was the next thing that happened?"

"I asked her what was the matter? She said 'nothing.' I finally had coaxed her up and asked her to really tell me what was the matter, and she finally told me that had shot Andrew Sigler."

"What did you say?"

"I says 'where is he?' She told me in Room Seven. I says 'where is room seven?' She says 'downstairs in the back.' I went into Room Seven and found Mr. Sigler laying on the bed... not on the bed, pardon me. On the floor."

"In what position was he laying there?"

"He was laying, I would consider, in a scuffling manner."

"Was he dead or alive?"

"He was dead."

"What else did you see in the room?"

"Saw blood on the linoleum on the floor. Gun was laying there with three empty shells and on the side of the bed which I approximately have an idea it was just balancing was a cleaver or these meat cutters."

"What else was there in the room?"

"There was a table in there and bed and chair and cuspidor."

"What else did you do then?"

"I went back to her."

"What was the condition of the room when you saw it there?"

"The room at the time I entered it was messy. Mussy."

"What do you mean by mussy?"

"Everything was disarranged. Wasn't arranged right."

"How was the bed?"

"It was scuffled up. Mussed up."

"Where was Mrs. Sigler when you entered that room and saw this body?"

"Still in the kitchen."

"What did you do?"

"I went out and asked her what is to be done."

"What did she say?"

"She didn't say anything."

"What was the next thing that was said?"

"Then she told me to put that body in the car. I refused and she had then told me that she would put the body in the car herself and drive it out. I says no because it was going to get me in wrong. She says 'you take that body and put it in the car or if somebody comes in here some people will think you done it.' I have taken the body and put the body in my car."

"Was there anything said about money?"

"There wasn't anything mentioned about money at that time."

"What did you do with the body?"

"I took the body and put it in my car. Carried it out and put it in my car."

"How was the body dressed?"

"It had an overcoat on. That was all. Of course, suit and clothes."

"What kind of overcoat?"

"I have no idea of the color of the overcoat."

"Do you know anything about a muffler?"

"No, I do not."

"Was there a cap?"

"I went in for the cap after I took the body out to the car."

"What did you do with the body after you got it into the car?"

"I had a time to adjusting it to set it up right."

"Set it up?"

"I did and lifted it to the right side of the car."

"What did you intend doing with it?"

"I intended just putting it out on the road someplace where it would be found."

"Did you.... What became of the gun and shells?"

"The gun and shells? I went in for his cap. I had to have his cap. I went in for his cap and then I had taken the gun and shells off the floor and they were full of blood or they were lying in a mass of blood."

"What did you do with the gun and shells?"

"I took the gun and shells and put them in Mr. Sigler's lap."

"What kind of gun was it?"

".32 automatic. Colt."

"Was there anything then said between you and her?"

"Nothing said as to any arrangements for the body or anything of the kind but she had given me the sum of two hundred and some odd dollars. Ninety or fifty some odd dollars."

"Relate the circumstances under which this money made its appearance there."

"The way the money took appearance there was to give me help in case I should get in trouble."

"Did you accept the money?"

"I did refuse it."

"You refused it?"

"I refused it."

"Did you get it later?"

"She handed me the money and I put it back on the table and Mrs. Sigler slipped or put the money in my pocketbook."

"Then what did you do?"

"I drove off with the body on the road."

"What road?"

"On the Hurley-Mercer Road."

"Do you know the number of the highway?"

"Number 10."

"What happened on the way out?"

"I met a couple of cars and the body was leaning toward me. I shoved it back in place and went out there on the Mercer Road and threw the body in the ditch. Across the ditch."

"Across the ditch?"

"Across the ditch."

"How did you get the body out of the car?"

"I pulled it out."

"And do you know what became of the gun?"

"I had the gun there. Taken the gun off his lap and put it alongside the seat."

"Do you know what became of the shells?"

"The shells were there in his lap with the gun."

"Do you know what became of the shells later on?"

"I have no idea. But the way the shells was lying in his lap with his feet spread out, and the bottom of his coat flew up jerking the body out. Some of the shells might have dropped to the bottom of the car or as I say jerking it out might have rolled in the seat."

"Where did you go then after you disposed of the body?"

"After I disposed of the body I came back to work."

"Did you go right straight to work?"

"I did."

"How did you drive back?"

"Drove back by Mercer Road and the Ironwood Road."

"What did you do with the gun?"

"I threw the gun in the river."

"In what river?"

"Montreal River."

"Whereabouts?"

"About a mile from the city limits."

"Do you know about where it is?"

"Yes, sir. Right there by the water power plant. Old water power plant."

"Do you believe you could find it there?"

"I could."

"Do you know whether you got any blood on your clothes?"

"I don't remember. I never looked. I was very careful."

"Do you remember any blood.... Was there a seat cover on the car?"

"There was a seat cover on the car."

"What kind of material?"

"It was a..I don't know. I would call it overalls stuff. Denim or whatever you call it."

"Was it dark?"

"Was it dark? It was."

"Did you notice whether any bloodstains on this cover?"

"I did not."

"Did you look for them?"

"I did not."

"Where did you drive your car to when you went to Hurley?"

"Drove back to the New Central where it was always standing when I was not using it."

"Didn't drive the car to any different place than before?"

"No, sir."

"What did you do?"

"Went back to work."

"Work all day?"

"I worked all day."

"Did you go to the Gogebic Hotel that day?"

"I went up there for dinner."

"Have any talk with Mrs. Sigler?"

"Not any."

"What did you do in the afternoon?"

"I worked all afternoon."

"Where were you that evening?"

"I was home that evening."

"What time did you get up next morning?"

"Five thirty. Same as every morning."

"Now the next day was Saturday, was it?"

"Yes, sir. It was."

"Do you remember what day of the month it was?"

"It was the third of May."

"What was the first thing you did in the morning?"

"I went in and cleaned up the place and sat around."

"Then what did you do? Where did you clean it up?"

"I cleaned up the inside of the building."

"You mean the New Central?"

"The New Central."

"What did you do then later?"

"I sat around. Didn't have nothing else to do. Read the newspaper."

"What else did you do? Did you buy a new automobile about that time?"

"I did on a Friday night."[11]

"That was the day before?"

"The day before."

"What kind of car did you buy?"

"Bought a Ford sedan or coupe from Point's Garage in Ironwood."

"You say a Ford coupe?"

"Ford coupe."

"What did you pay for it?"

"Sum of two hundred twenty five dollars."

"Out of what money did you pay that?"

"Paid that out of money she had given me."

"Mrs. Sigler?"

"Mrs. Sigler."

"Where did you keep the new car?"

"My new car was standing on the outside of the building. That is, on the side street."

"In the meantime had you heard at all from Mrs. Sigler?"

"She did that Saturday morning call me up."

"Where did she get you by phone?"

"I have no idea where she was."

"Where were you?"

"I was at the New Central at the present time."

"What if anything did she say?"

---

[11] Andy bought the car on Thursday night, May 1. He used the old car to move the body on Friday, May 2 and drove the new car to central Wisconsin on Saturday, May 3.

"She says 'burn my overcoat and leave town for awhile.'"

"You say 'my'? Whose overcoat?"

"I asked her if it was mine or whose overcoat. I asked her that. She said 'burn your overcoat.' Told me to burn my overcoat."

"Say why you should leave town?"

"Did not."

"What did you do?"

"I took my car, went over to Ironwood, got filled up with gas and oil and left for parts unknown."

"Tell us what parts unknown? Where?"

"I drove first... drove from Hurley to Ironwood, got filled up with gas and oil. Drove to Wakefield. Drove through to Marenisco, Winchester, Tomahawk Lake and Rhinelander."

"Where did you stop that first night?"

"In Rhinelander that night."

"Register in a hotel?"

"Yes, sir.

"Where did you go from Rhinelander?"

"I got up Sunday morning. Drove around town awhile. Around the lakes and left for Antigo."

"Where did you stop the second night?"

"Didn't stop any place the second night. That is, no hotel. I stayed right in the car."

"Where did you go then?"

"Drove on. Oshkosh, Neenah-Menasha, Fond du lac. All along the line."

"Why did you make these various towns?"

"Why, just to move along. Something to pass the time."

"Did you get to Green Bay?"

"I did get to Green Bay."

"Did you ever stop at the Beaumont or Bellmont Hotel at Green Bay?"

"Never heard of it. Never did."

"How long you spend in Green Bay?"

"I spent in Green Bay approximately two hours."

"What did you do during those two hours?"

"My car was parked on one of the side streets while I was looking around. Down looking things over and seeing where they were putting construction of concrete and a bridge or viaduct that was there. Spent about half an hour looking things over."

"Then where did you go?"

Then I have taken my car and left for Sturgeon Bay."

"How long did you remain at Sturgeon Bay?"

"I remained at Sturgeon Bay one day."

"Then where did you go?"

"Then I came back."

"Was your money getting low?"

"It was getting low."

"Did you see any newspapers?"

"I did see the newspapers."

"Relative to anything that happened at Hurley?"

"I did."

"Well, what did that cause you to do?"

"The accounts I seen in the newspapers caused me to return. That they wanted me for the murder of Andrew Sigler."

"So you got back to Hurley, did you?"

"I did."

"Do you remember what day it was?

"I have no idea."

"Where did you leave your car?"

"I had taken my car, driven it off an old road."

"And walked to town?"

"No. I stayed around at the Scott and Howe roundhouse."

"Yes. And then?"

"Then the next morning I appeared."

"Where did you report?"

"At first I reported to the New Central. I went in there and got some tobacco, and cigars and a few drinks."

"Liquor?"

"Liquor."

"Then where did you go?"

"Then I went direct to the sheriff's office."

"What time was it that you knocked at the door of the jail?"

"I have an idea it was about five thirty, five o'clock."

"Who met you at the door?"

"Mr. Joe Volant, the sheriff."

"The sheriff?"

"The sheriff."

"What did you say to him or what did he say to you?"

"I says, 'Good morning Joe. I see you want me.' He says 'yes, welcome to town'. So I went in, we sat around. He didn't say anything nor I said anything. He had taken me and locked me up."

"Who was the next person you saw?"

"Mr. Foster, the district attorney."

"How soon after you reported there at the jail did Mr. Foster get there?"

"I think he flew over there with an airplane."

"What makes you say that?"

"He was right over there in no time after I was locked up."

"What did he say to you?"

"He says, 'Good morning, Andy... or Gudleski."

"What did you say?"

"I says 'Beg your pardon?'"

"What did he say then?"

"He says 'How come?' And I told him."

"Tell us the conversation you had with the district attorney."

"The conversation with the D.A. I had in the sheriff's office. He was telling me of the evidence that he had on me and other odds and ends he heard around town."

"Tell us what he said to you and what you said."

"He asked me what I knew about the shooting of Andrew Sigler or murder of Andrew Sigler. I told him 'nothing.' He says to me I must know something about it. I says 'nothing.' He took down some names or had some names there on paper. I didn't see it. I saw him scribbling away there on paper and he told me that the way things look it leads me to the entire outfit."

"Did he tell you what it was that he had on you?"

"He told me that he had a car that was full of blood and my leaving town."

"Did he say anything about certain people?"

"He did not."

"Well, what did you say when he told you those things?"

"I didn't say anything."

"Why didn't you tell him what you know?"

"It wasn't proper for me to tell him what I knew."

"You didn't think it was?"

"I didn't think it was."

"What was the next thing that happened?"

"He didn't want to listen to me anymore and I told the sheriff, Joe Volant, to lock me up with the rest."

"When you say he didn't want to listen to you anymore...what do you mean by that? What did he say?"

"Couldn't get hide nor hair out of the story. Couldn't get anything on me."

"Did he get impatient with you?"

"He did."

"Well, were you locked up?"

"I was."

"Were you locked up alone?"

"There was four or five others. Or a half dozen or so."

"In what part of the jail did he lock you up in?"

"In downstairs part."

"How long did you remain there?"

"I was there for about an hour."

"What happened then?"

"Mr. Joe Volant had taken me upstairs and put me in a separate cell."

"Was anybody else up there?"

"There was nobody at the time."

"How long were you alone up there?"

"I was there for pretty near a month and a half. Two months."

"Was there a time when you were locked up with a Finlander?"

"There was."

"Where was that?"

"That was in the bullpen in the other department."

"Was that before you were locked alone?"

"Yes, sir. After."

"How did anybody come to see you again after that?"

"Mr. Foster did."

"When was it he came to see you then?"

"He, I think, came to see me. Then there was another fellow came there. Supposed to have been locked up for a burglary and a few other crimes that was committed."

"Before that did Foster come to see you again and talk?"

"He did."

"What did he tell you?"

"A few odds and ends he heard around the streets from one joint to another. From a few critical people."

"What did he say to you about it?"

"He asked me what I knew about it and why I didn't want to tell him."

"What did you say then?"

"I didn't say anything about it."

"Did he say anything about a woman and a gun?"

"He did not."

Did he later say something about having got the woman and gun?"

"He did not."

"What was the next thing after he questioned you there? What was the next thing he did?"

"While he was there he got kind of aggravated or disgusted with me and didn't want to listen to me anymore."

"You say a man was brought in and locked up with you?"

"Yes, sir."

"Did you see him before he was brought into the jail?"

"I did see him before he was brought into the jail."

"Where was it you saw him?"

"First I seen him was when Mr. Dick Kalliomaa, the undersheriff's car had stopped in front of the jail. I saw Mr. Foster get out one side of the car, Dick on the other side and the stranger beside Dick."

"This stranger turned out to be one Joe Hayes, did he?"

"Yes, sir."

"How could you see him?"

"Through the window."

"From upstairs?"

"From upstairs."

"What thing or what conversation did you overhear as you were in that jail upstairs as these three men came in and were downstairs?"

"I really didn't hear anything of their conversation downstairs, but on entering the upstairs Dick Kalliomaa says 'We have got the god-damned fool that carried the guns.' Mr Foster downstairs which I know his voice plainly had made the same remark and 'we will get a few more of them.' The man that was locked up with me was Mr. Hayes."

Andy denied much of what Hayes said about their jail time together. He said that Hayes had fabricated many of the incidentals about the murder. He told Zabel that Hayes told him he would "see him through" a jail break and about the note he had written to Emma. He denied ever telling Hayes that he had killed Sigler. He also claimed that he had written $100 in the note and Hayes or someone had changed that amount to $1,000. Zabel questioned Andy about the the note.

"What were the circumstance under which you wrote that note on this letter on the sides and on the back of it? Explain to the jury just who got you and how you came to it."

"Mr. Hayes had persuaded me and told me to write this note and said he was going to be out on a Monday morning before the judge to pay his fine for carrying concealed weapons and that he would see me come through this thing. That he would help me break jail and get out and that he would bring me up if he could get this money with a gun and a few other odds and ends like saws and pliers to break jail."

"Had you and he, prior to that time, talked about any person here to whom he might go for money?"

"He said...he asked me if I had any friends in town. I says 'a lot of them.' He says 'one in particular that I might get money from?' I says 'I'm not certain.'"

"Did you mention who it was?"

"I did."

"Who was that?"

"Emma Sigler."

"Then what did he say about writing notes or letters?"

"He then had me write that....I refused to write the note and he kept on persuading me until I did write it and he dictated it and I wrote it."

Zabel produced the note, Exhibit 4, and Andy verified that it was the note, in his handwriting and that it was the note he had given to Hayes.

"After giving it to him what did you do or say to him with reference to that note?"

"I didn't really say anything except that I wanted to get some paper from downstairs to recopy it. That is, not to take Cadigan and Cadigan stationery out and then he had refused to give me the note back."

"You had asked him to give it back?"

"I say I was to get paper from downstairs to recopy the note."

"He refused to give you the note back? What did he say about it?"

"He says 'it is good enough.' He says 'everything is clear on there and it will pull through. I notice, among other things, the letter states 'I need about $1000.'"

"Beg your pardon?"

"That is what it states here."

"The statement is wrong."

"Did you write $1000 in there?"

"I did not write $1000. I wrote $100."

"When you handed this note to Mr. Hayes it stated $100?"

"$100 when I left that note in Hayes' hands."

Zabel passed the note to the jury who took note of the change in the amount; it appeared that another zero had been penciled in just to the right of the $100 amount Andy had originally written.

"Well, then, in the meantime, had Mr. Foster been there to see you?"

"He was not up there then after giving this Hayes this note."

"By the way, what name did he give you as his name?"

"He really did not give me any name. Mr. Hayes did not."

"Was he dressed with stand-up collar, fancy clothes or otherwise?"

"Well, I'd call him a common tramp, bum, blithe looks of him when he came in there. Dirty."

"Then after giving him that note, after he refused to return it, then what took place?"

"He went out that morning. On a Monday morning."

"Before he went out were any arrangements made about signals?"

"He had told me that if everything was okay between Mrs. Sigler and myself and him that he was to come down here at the cemetery on the Ironwood side that he was to wave to me that everything was okay and was to see me after. I understand by 'if everything was okay' that he was to wave it through out there and I was to see it from the window."

"And what did you understand?"

"That he got the money for me."

"Did he come back to the jail?"

"He came back that night."

"Came inside?"

"He did."

"What time did he show up?"

"I have no idea, but I presume about midnight."

"Had you slept?"

"I was asleep at the time."

"What did he say? What did you do?"

"They unlocked the door and he called me. I didn't make out this call and then he hollered a little louder and I got up and went over to the door."

"You were drowsy?"

"I had been sleeping. I was astonished. Stunned at the appearance of Mr. Hayes."

"How did he look?"

"He was all dressed up."

"Well, what did he say?"

"He says to me, 'Andy, tell these gentlemen the story you have told me.' I says 'none.'"

"Had you told him any story?"

"I had not told Hayes any story."

"And was the letter...the writing of the letter all that you have stated?"

"The writing of the letter is what took place in the conversation."

"Then you told him 'none,' what did he say?"

"Then Mrs. Sigler had come up. They called for Mrs. Sigler to come up. I did not see the woman come up the first time."

"What next was asked of you and what did you say?"

"They asked me to explain to them who killed Sigler and who asked me to do it. If I done it."

"What did you say?"

"I didn't say anything. I was stunned at the time."

"Did anybody ask you how much money you got for killing Sigler?"

"They did."

"What did you say?"

"I told them $2,000."

"Had you received $2,000?'

"I have got to see it."

"Have you killed Mr. Sigler? Did you?"

"I have not."

"What did you do then?"

"They were standing there talking and finally they all went downstairs. Mr. Foster came up and took conversation with me."

"What did he say?"

"Came up with a smile and a grin on his face as though he had the world by the crown and he made a few suggestions to me that finally brought me to take the whole responsibility on my shoulder."

"What were those suggestions?"

"Those suggestions that Mr. Foster had made to me to take this responsibility. That he was to see me through this case from one to seven years and was to give me a jury trial."

"Did he tell you what would happen if you didn't take the responsibility?"

"If I didn't do that I was to take a life penalty and stay in prison."

"Well, then, what did they do?"

"He was there talking with me for awhile and finally he says, 'Andy, do you realize that I am your only last friend you got besides your wife and family?' He says 'I can do more for you than any lawyer in this state or county.' I never says anything. I refuse to make any effort."

"Then what happened?"

"He told me he would give me a jury trial and see me through this thing if I stuck with him in convicting this Mrs. Sigler in this case. I never made any suggestions."

"He wanted to convict this woman?"

"He wanted to convict this woman in the worst possible way."

"Did he ever talk to you about Mr. Sigler's conduct toward her?"

"He did. He told me that Sigler had an awful temper and that he himself would not trust himself. Mr. Foster would not trust himself with Sigler and knew about his conditions."

"Well, this party that awakened you in the dead of the night. What did they do then?"

"They all left."

"What happened the next day?"

"The next morning..."

"Wait a minute. Did Mrs. Sigler and this Hayes come around to the jail someplace?"

"They were to come around to the back."

"Before this meeting that night?"

"They were to give me a signal that was to be given but they were not around the jail that night."

"You didn't see them?"

"I did not see them around the jail that night."

"You said there was a Finlander up there?"

"There was."

"How long was he locked up with you?"

"He was locked up with me four or five day."

"Was he a man that could talk and understand English?"

"Why, no."

"Do you remember that night when the party came and after Mr. Foster and those others. That is, Mr. Hayes had asked you these questions. What, if anything Mrs. Sigler exclaimed to you?'

"I do not."

An objection of hearsay was raised by Lameroux that was overruled by Judge Foley.

"Did you hear her say 'Andrew, or Andy, did you kill my husband?"

"I did not."

"At that time were you nervous?"

"Nervous and hysterical."

"Stunned?"

"Stunned at the time."

Andy denied ever telling Hayes much of anything. After Andy testified, nine-year-old Robert Sigler testified to the beatings he was given by his father.

Friday, January 30, 1925

As on the day before, Emma was dressed in the same black dress she had worn to Sigler's funeral. The pink flush of excitement was gone from her cheeks, and a grey pallor spread over her face as she related the story of how she had shot Sigler in self-defense. She dabbed her eyes with a dainty pink handkerchief as the story unfolded. For the first time, Emma lost her composure. The ostrich plume in her black and grey hat drooped as her shoulders heaved with great sobs. The small figure seemed to shrink within the folds of her gray and black coat as she told the jury all the gruesome details. A tense gasp broke the stillness of the courtroom as the audience realized that Emma admitted what she had done. The murmur of people whispering swept from the back of the courtroom to the front, growing to a crescendo.

Emma was very nervous, but appeared calm and collected. Several times during her testimony, she asked for a glass of water and resumed her customary calm pose.

Unnoticed by the spectators, and sitting apart from Emma, her father, Robert Shroth, slumped in his seat when Emma told the new version of the slaying. During the course of her testimony, his hands worked spasmodically, and he shook his head despairingly from side to side. His heavy brows furrowed over eyes that rested constantly on his daughter. Dressed in a dark brown suit, a drab figure in a well-lighted courtroom, he was a picture of desolation.

When Emma took the stand, Zabel smiled at her and led her by the hand to the witness chair. Her hands were shaking, and she felt her knees buckling.

"Don't worry, Emma. Just tell the truth, and you'll be fine," Zabel whispered to her as she sat down on the witness chair.

"What is your name?"

"Emma Sigler."

"How old are you?"

"Twenty-nine past."

"Andrew Sigler was your husband?"

"Yes."

"And when did you get married to him?"

"August 22, 1914."

"Where did you get married?"

"In Milwaukee, Wisconsin."

"Have you any children as a result of your marriage to him?"

"Yes."

"Where are they?"

"Robert...."

"That is the boy that was on the stand here?"

"Yes."

"How old is he?"

"He will be ten in August and the next one, Junior, will be five in June, and the twins, Lester and Leslie will be three in March."[12]

"You have been locked up in the county jail since what? July?"

"June 23, 1924."

"Now where were you born, Mrs. Sigler?"

"At Washburn, Wisconsin."

---

[12] Robert was born on August 15, 1915, Junior on June 17, 1920, and the twins on March 3, 1922.

"And went to school?"

"Yes."

"What school?"

"Do you mean how far? What grade?"

"Yes."

"Seventh."

"Then what did you do?"

"I stayed at home, helped on the farm, helped with housework and then I worked in private homes at a few different places in Washburn."

"Worked for a living until you got married?"

"Yes."

"And continued to work for a living after that?"

"Yes."

"When did you come to Hurley?"

"About 1918 or 19."

"When did your husband start the restaurant and hotel down here on Silver Street?"

"About 1919."

"Was the place as large as it is now?"

"No. That is, the frame part was but the rooms weren't there."

"What changes, if any, were made from time to time?"

"In the part that was know as the butcher's icebox, that was fixed into three stories, adding twelve rooms. To the rear was a shell that was fixed into rooms. The hall known as KC Hall was made into nine rooms and the steam heat put in all rooms."

"Were your children born here in Hurley?"

"The three little ones were."

"Now, these changes and extensions in the building, did that necessitate taking on different mortgages?"

"Some of them. Yes."

"What did you do when you bought this business? What part of the work did you do?"

"We were always, more or less, short of help. I had to help with everything. Taking care of the children, cooking, washing, doing bedroom work, waitresses."

"While pregnant with child how close to the birth of the baby did you work?"

"Up to the last day, always."

Emma asked for and was given a glass of water. She was sobbing uncontrollably. Spectators, especially older women, cried along with her. Emma sipped her water and gave the glass back to Zabel, who handed it to the clerk. She wiped the tears from her cheeks and eyes with her handkerchief.

"Your children live here? There with you?" Zabel continued.

"Yes. Up to the eighth month, that is, just before the twins were born, I cooked for 22 boarders for three weeks and put out the short orders also."

"Do you know how tall you are?"

"About five foot three and a half or four."

"Do you know how much you weigh?"

"About 115."

"That has been your general weight all these years?"

"No, sir. I weighed 148....148 at at the time of marriage."

"And did you and your husband get along together up to the time you started the Gogebic Hotel business?"

"The first year we had little quarrels. Didn't amount to much. He didn't show much of a temper the first few months and from the time, oh, shortly before the first baby was born he commenced to show temper, got impatient with me when I complained of different things. After the first baby was born he complained that the baby kept him awake nights. He got impatient with the baby and wanted to strike the baby. Robert, when he was three years old he took him out from the bed and threw him down a flight of stairs. I tried to make him understand that was wrong, That the baby must cry to expand his lungs. As much necessary for baby to cry as a grown person to exercise. Couldn't make him understand that. From time to time after he was getting worst. Showed more of a temper until, finally, he commenced to beating."

"What was his conduct to you whenever you found yourself in pregnant condition?"

"Very bad. And he didn't approve of my having children after the first baby."

"Now tell us what he did at the time these children were born. What he said and what he did to you."

"At times when I mentioned I had a little boy... After the little boy was about a year and a half old, I often remarked how nice it would be to have a little girl. My mind was all set on having a baby girl. He said, 'No, if any more damn kids come into this family I will leave.' I said, 'I supported myself all these years I can support the second one.' I said. After being pregnant with the second baby there is almost five years between Robert and Junior. All this time he felt pleased there was no children. When I became pregnant with Junior he became very violent at times. Struck me and said, 'I will kick it out of you.' I left him for three weeks, went to Washburn to my folks. Didn't tell my mother what for. Told her just for a rest to get away from business and excitement."

"You didn't tell your mother your troubles?"

"I didn't."

"What was his conduct when the little twins came?"

"Then after I was down in Washburn. I was about four to five months pregnant with Junior. Then I went down to Washburn and stayed for three weeks. He phoned four or five times and asked me to come back. Said he would be good. I didn't come back and he came down after me. Cried and pleaded for me to come back and said 'I cannot manage that business up there alone.' I came back. After I came back he was alright for a while. I started making baby clothes and I sat at the sewing machine. He said 'Let that damn stuff go. Got no business to make children's clothes like that. Other work has to be done. Can't have a bunch of kids around in the business.'"

"When the baby finally arrived what did he do?"

"The second baby? Junior? At the time of his birth while the doctor was there he cursed me. Dr. Urquhart said, 'Andrew, have patience. This woman is in great pain. We don't know how things will turn out. Don't you realize,' the doctor says, 'there are two human lives at stake and if she sees you carrying on like this it is going to discourage her and she is going to lose.' I can't recall the word he used but courage is what he meant. And the doctor would not let him come near the room."

"Instead of being glad at the arrival of this little boy, he acted this way?"

"Very much disgusted and said he didn't care to have a little goat around."

"How soon after that did you find yourself in that condition again with these twins?"

"Junior was 11 months old when I became pregnant."

"When you broke that news to him, how did he take it?"

"He went to the drugstore and got stuff for me to take to get rid of it."

"What did he say?"

"I said, 'No, we got two boys and perhaps this time we'll have a girl.' I says, 'I can sew and do fancy work and there isn't no reason why I can't have the pleasure of dressing a little girl.' He got the stuff. It was a cotton root and wild cherry."

"Did you take it?"

"No."

"What else did he say to you about what was you doing?"

"When I was four months pregnant with the twins he got into.... His people had been over from Austria at the time. At that time four months. He got into a violent temper that day and struck his brother. His brother was then 19. And broke a broom handle over his back. His brother was in such a condition that he was hardly able to walk. His brother did not strike him back. He said, 'I didn't come over here to hit my brother.' That same day, he struck me. He says, 'I'll show you. You wouldn't take that stuff. I will beat it out of you. Kick it out of you.' He kicked me. At that time there must have been fifteen black and blue marks on my body. Eventually those two little boys arrived. That night and the following week his brother slept in bed with his father and mother for fear that Sigler, after his argument, would kill him."

"When were the twins born?"

"The twins were born March 3. Well, it is three years ago. 1921." (sic)

"What physician attended you?"

"Dr. Maccani."

"Was Mr. Sigler glad? Joyful?"

"Mr. Sigler tore his hair and walked back and forth from the parlor and the kitchen. He says, 'God damn you. Isn't it bad enough they come one at a time? Now they come two at a time. What are we going to do with two? Another one sucking the bottle yet.' I made an attempt to nurse the baby and he says 'You run yourself down nursing the baby and you can't work around here when you got two babies dragging on you. Put them on the bottle.'"

"Did he make some reference about that time to cats?"

"He said, 'You might as well do as you do with cats.' He said, 'that little one is crippled now. It will never do anything. If you don't I will.'"

"How old were the twins at that time?"

"Only about two or three months."

Emma was crying uncontrollably again. She asked for another glass of water and the clerk brought her one from the pitcher on the prosecutor's table. She continued after she drank the water and wiped her tears.

"He said, 'Might as well bring in a pail of water and dump one of them into it. Nobody will know the difference.'"

"What did you say?"

"Mrs. Nelson took care of me at the time."[13]

"How did that talk affect you?"

"Made me nervous and put me in a very critical condition. As weak as I was I was afraid to fall asleep when he was near for fear he would take one of the babies. He poked fun at me making an attempt to nurse both babies."

"How did he treat the children when they grew up?"

"I asked him several times. He came in and looked. I had the babies in a wash basket alongside my bed. I says, 'Andrew,

[13] Verbatim. This is the only reference to "Mrs. Nelson" in the trial transcript.

isn't this nice? Isn't it an honor to think we should have twins and three babies within the time of eighteen months and all boys. You ought to consider this an honor.'"

"What did he say?"

"He says, 'The hell with them.'"

"Did he have any affection develop between him and these four little children?"

"What do you mean?"

"Was he nice and kind to the children as they grew up?"

"He very seldom spoke a decent word to them. He always made an attempt to hit them. When Robert would fuss he said "Oh, get out of my road.' He had a great habit of putting his hand this way (Emma raised her left hand and swatted it out toward Zabel) when he made an attempt to strike him. Robert was nervous, and when he started to fuss he had no time for him."

"Did he use any particular expression toward those children you remember?"

"God damn little snots. Damn brats. Always in the road. No god damn place for kids."

"Do you remember what happened on Christmas Eve a year ago?"

"Robert passed some little remark. He says, 'What did you say?' and Robert put his hand up. Andrew put his hand up and says, "What did you say?' Robert crouched together and Robert didn't speak, and he took Robert by the hair. He banged him back and forth on the wall. The boy fell to the floor. After he was down, he took a piece of board from a box and struck him over the back. I went to defend him and he hit me."

"When he got through with the child on that Christmas Eve what was his appearance?"

"I picked the boy up took him on my lap in the room and rocked him and tried to comfort him. Robert was crying bitterly. I noticed the marks all over his face. That night when I put him to bed I undressed him. His little back was all covered with black and blue marks."

"Was that child sent away to Superior?"

"The following day he still threatened on the boy. He says, 'You don't get any Christmas presents for this.' We had bought a guitar and a pair of boxing gloves and a few other presents for him. He says, 'You don't get any presents for this'. I got the guitar down from upstairs. He forbid me giving it to him. He says, 'I will make you black and blue if you give him those presents.' Next day I sent him to Superior with Mrs. Fall so he would not strike him again. After the little boy got to Superior, my mother asked him what was all those marks on his face."

"Did he still have the marks when you sent him away from home, Mrs. Sigler?"

"Yes."

"Was that the only time you say he struck little Robert?"

"Oh, no. Many times."

"Well, tell us was that the most brutal way he ever struck him?"

"No. Often jumped him out of bed. Pulled him out of bed at night if the babies would cry. The twins. Robert would be in the same room. He says, 'You are in the same room here. I have to come way downstairs,' he says. 'Why don't you get up and give them their bottle and cover them up."

"Expected the little boy to do that?"

"Yes, sir."

"What would he do?"

"Pulled him out of bed and jerked him over to the crib where the babies were laying. Would curse, say, 'Damn kids around here. Four in the room. I suppose if the room was bigger next year she'll have another one in here."

"How did little Bobby talk to his father?"

"Never spoke to him. He was always afraid of him. Bobby often said 'Mama, when I get big papa is not going to hit you no more.' He said to Mrs. Fall 'When I get big I will shoot him.' In answer to that little Robert says, 'Yes, I will help you.'"

"Where did this take place?"

"Over in Mrs. Fall's. Robert's house."

Foster moved to have the last paragraph stricken and it was stricken from the record.

"How did he treat Junior?"

"He was more brutal with Junior than with the other three."

"Tell us some of the things he did to Junior. Can you recall some of the things he did?"

"Yes. When Junior was only a few months old and I would want to take him out in the buggy to get the air he says, 'There is other work to be done. Big stack of dishes to be done over there. Put them out in the yard and let them stay there. That'll give them air enough.'"

"Did you ever see him kiss any of his children?"

"He used to kiss Robert the first year but I never remember seeing him kiss either Robert or any of the other three afterwards."

"Just the first year?"

"Yes."

"Do you remember the first time he ever beat you?"

"Yes. Robert was about two months old. He grabbed a slipper off his foot and threw it at me into the next room. It didn't strike me, and I started out the back. I took the slipper and threw it out the upstairs window. And he wanted to compel me to go down and get the slipper. He says, 'You threw it there and you can go down and get it again.' I says, 'I had a right to throw it.' He took me by the back of the neck and pushed me. I held on to the banister so I would not fall downstairs. I went down and brought the slipper up again. He says, 'After this when I tell you to do a thing, you do it.'"

"You had given it to him?"

"He grabbed me by the throat when I gave him the slipper. I slipped to the floor. He says, 'Will you do the things I ask you to do?' When I says, 'Yes', he didn't hit me. I went in the next room and cried for a long time. He says, 'If you don't stop your crying I will come in there and give you something to cry for.'"

"Did he ever hit you with anything besides his hand?"

"If there was anything nearer, near to get besides his hand, he would save his hand and use a club or stick or anything. Coal."

"Ever throw anything at you?"

"Sir?"

"Ever throw anything at you?"

"Always. Often."

"So that the children would see it?"

"Yes. Within the last few years I don't think there was a week passed when he didn't beat me. Leave marks on my body. Black spots. This took place as much as three times a week. Sometimes oftener."

"What is the fact as to whether he ever knocked you to the floor?"

"Very often."

"Did it sometimes happen when other people were present?"

"Yes, sir. Many times. Being in public, there was always someone around there. I would run in the dining room if I was in the kitchen then with him thinking he would be ashamed to chase after me in the dining room. That didn't stop him at all whether man, woman or customer in the dining room. He would still beat me."

"Do you know a man named Clifford?"

"Yes."

"Do you know where he is now?"

"I don't know. Out of town?"

"Was he ever present at one of these beatings your husband gave you?"

"Yes. One time he had been beating me all morning. Every time I came at a distance from him he would throw things at me. I didn't want to leave the house. Didn't want to leave the children for fear that he would abuse them. He often passed remarks about those children to abuse me because he knew it hurt me. I went to the back door and called one of the girls and asked them if they wouldn't get my cap and coat for me. I was cold. I went to the back. When this girl gave me this cap and coat then I had no chance to get it on. He chased after me."

"What did Clifford do?"

"I ran out between the electric shop and the Office Saloon. There is a little pathway. There is a space leading to the main street. When I got about five feet from the main street he grabbed me. I fell down. He got on top of me, put his knee on my chest, one hand on my throat and with the other hand he pounded me on the head. Tore my hair out. Ben Clifford and

Joe Charbonneau were across the street. Ben Clifford ran over, pulled him off of me, held Sigler and says, 'Now run.' Says, 'Make a getaway.' I ran up to Mr. Lennon's office up the front stairs. I was afraid if I would go into my part of the place that he would catch me there again."

"Mr. Lennon was mayor at that time, was he?"

"Yes."

"He is a lawyer also?"[14]

"I went in there to have the girl brush the snow off me and get warmed up a little bit. My back and shoes were all full of snow. I was cold. There was snow on the back of my neck and all over my face. I took off my hat. Hat was all crumpled up from the scuffle in the snow. I put it on my head when I was going upstairs."

"Were there any other times when boarders...."

"I took my hat off. I took off my hat and drew my hand through my hair and handfuls of hair came out. Had two bald spots. One in front and one in back."

"Who pulled the hair out?"

"Andrew."

"Do you remember the time when Mr. Lennon was called downstairs to subdue your husband?"

"Yes, Found him in the back swinging chairs around in a wild manner. In the room off the kitchen. He dumped my sewing machine over. I took pleasure in doing sewing for the children. Their underwear and coats. He knew it would hurt me if he would destroy my sewing machine. Tipped it upside down. Broke the drawers out of it. I was sewing dresses for the little babies or suits and pants and I had put them in it. He tore

[14] Emma didn't answer the question, but continued with her narration.

it up. I had crocheting in the room somewhere. Crocheting four inches wide. I was making them all a set for sheets and pillow slips. I had a yard and a half of it. He unraveled almost all of it."

"What happened then? What did he do toward you?"

"In this room there was a big mirror on the wall. He swung the chair onto that. Swung it at me. He struck the mirror and the mirror smashed."

"Did you stay in the room?"

"He took an electric iron. I had that set up to do some pressing on the babies' clothes. He took that and started at me, so I dodged out. Mr. Lennon was coming through one door, and I went through the other door."

"You got away from him that time?"

"I ran upstairs then. Fixed myself up and went out."

"Were you ever driven out of the house?"

"At that very moment I'm speaking of now I went out of the house. Went up to the Burton Hotel and registered. Rested there in the afternoon. In the evening I stayed there. Went to bed about sometime between quarter to nine and nine. When I got home the next morning he says, 'Where were you out all night? I suppose you were out jazzing all night.' I says, 'I wasn't. I was up at the hotel.' He says, 'You had somebody up there with you.' I says, 'I was not. You can ask the man I took the room from.'"

"Were you ever obliged to flee out of the house nights or in the morning early?"

"I was put out of my bed many times during the night."

"Do you remember one morning seeing Mr. Varda, I believe his name is?"

"One morning about three o'clock when he closed he came upstairs. I was sound asleep. Woke me up. Started to chew the rag about the register being short. I wasn't taking care of the girls. I was letting them knock down on the income. At that time I was sick. I was not able to be disturbed. He says, 'What have I got you here for?' I explained the condition that I was in. Told him I was not able to. He says, 'That makes no difference.' He took his foot, put it in my back and forced me out of bed. I went in another room, the children's playroom to dress. He says, 'You come back in bed here. What the hell are you married for if you don't want to come across?' I begged and pleaded with him. Told him that I was not able to. I was putting on a stocking. He knocked me off the chair. I said, 'I am going downstairs.' He says, 'You are not. You will come back in bed and do what I want you to.' I didn't get the stocking on. He started throwing things at me. Threw a wash basin at me that I was using to wash my babies. I ran down the front...through the hallway down the front steps by the door."

"You ran outside the building?"

"Outside. It was in November."

"Bare feet?"

"Yes, bare feet. And in my nightgown. He chased me down the steps. I ran out as far as the corner of the Office Saloon. I saw someone coming up the street but didn't know who it was. Later on I heard it was Jimmy Sommers. I called loud, 'Help!' I don't know where the officer came from, but he came from where the police booth is now. He came running. He says, 'What is going on here?' I felt cheap out there without any clothes on. I says, 'Will you come upstairs and protect me until I get some clothes on?' On the way up he says, 'What is the matter?' I says, 'Andrew is after me. Chased me out.' As we came in the door there was an iron pipe about a foot long from the gas stove at the foot of the steps in a skirt dress. I says, 'Look what that is what he threw at me.' After we got upstairs at first he didn't know the officer was there. He jumped out of bed and ran towards me. Then he saw the officer. I jumped behind the officer. Officer says, 'You cool down now. You get back in bed.' He says, 'You come back in bed here,' Sigler says."

"Did you dress?"

"I dressed then."

Zabel continued to question Emma about the abuse that Sigler inflicted. She cited many more instances where he had thrown things at her. He asked what other implements or utensils Sigler threw at her.

"Forks, cleaver, butcher knife, tin cans." She showed the jury a three inch fork mark on her right arm. She showed the bald spot on her head. She said that Sigler had urged her to have her hair bobbed so he could "have a better hand hold."

Emma was on the stand for another several hours before Zabel finally got around to asking Emma about the details of the morning and afternoon of May 2, 1924, the day Sigler was killed and her dealings with Hayes. Finally, Zabel questioned about her arrest.

"Where were you arrested," Zabel asked.

"In my place. I was in my kitchen when Foster and the undersheriff, Dick Kalliomaa, came in the front door. I walked toward them."

"What orders did Foster give to the undersheriff?"

"Foster says, 'You are under arrest, Emma.' He says, 'Put the cuffs on her.'"

"Foster says that?"

"Yes, just like that."

"Do you know whether he was afraid you might hurt them?"

"From appearances, I must have looked mighty big to them."

"They put the handcuffs on you?"

"Yes. At that time I remarked I thought they were small."

"When they had these cuffs on your hands where did they take you?"

"Over to Foster's office. My sister went over."

"With the cuffs on you?"

"Yes."

"You had the cuffs on your arm up in his office?"

"Yes."

"Did you have the handcuffs on your hand while he questioned you?"

"Yes."

"There were a bunch of men for protection for him, wasn't there?"

"There was the undersheriff and Mr. Foster and Mr. Hayes."

"Who was there with you?"

"I don't remember whether my sister was asked to leave the office first. I don't remember how long she stayed during the time they questioned me."

"All that time you were being questioned by these men they had the handcuffs on you?"

"Yes."

"What questions did Mr. Foster ask you?"

"First thing he says, 'Did you get your insurance?' I said, 'No.' He says, 'Why didn't you?' I says, 'I wasn't in any hurry for it. I haven't inquired about it.' He says, 'Why didn't you get your insurance?' I says, 'I know why. At least I thought that you had stopped it.' He says, 'That is a true fact.' I says, 'I don't think so.'"

"Well, what else?"

"How?"

"What else did he ask you?"

"He says, 'Where were you this afternoon?' I says "At home.' He says 'Were you over to Ironwood this afternoon?' I says, 'No.' I don't remember if he asked me if I was over in the evening or not. I denied a few of the questions that he asked me there and he opened the door and Mr. Hayes walked in the room and he says, 'Do you know this man?' I said 'Yes.' He asks, "Who is it?' I says, 'I think it is a detective.'"

"What else did he ask you?"

"Then he asked me again if I had been over to Ironwood and if that is my writing on that sheet of paper and if that was my envelope and what was in it."

"Did you admit it?"

"I admitted it then."

"Tell him that you had given him the money?"

"Yes. He asked me what for."

"Did Mr. Foster tell you anything about who had done the killing?"

"Well, I don't remember word for word what took place, but he questioned me. He asked me why I had sent that money to Andy. Why I hired attorneys for him."

"Did he tell you that Anderson had killed your husband?"

"He says, 'You knew Andy had killed your husband. Why did you make an attempt to help him?'"

"What did you say?"

"I guess there is a cause for everything."

"When he told you that Andrew had killed your husband what did you say?"

"I says, 'No, Andy didn't kill my husband. No one could ever make me believe that.'"

"Did you at that time, at any place, or to anyone ever admit to say that Andrew Anderson killed your husband?"

"No. Never."

"Then after that, where did they take you?"

"Down to the jail, through the front door and into the parlor."

"Leave the handcuffs on you?"

"Yes."

"Where did they take you in the jail?"

"Into the parlor. Mr. Foster spoke to me."

"What did he say to you there?"

"I don't remember. Something in regard to the case. He was asking me questions. He said then that I had hired Andy to do the killing. I says, 'I never.' and he said, 'Could you face him?' I says, 'Yes.' He said, 'If we brought you up to face Andy could you look at him square in the eye and say you had never hired him to do the killing?' I said, 'Yes.' They brought me up before Andy. He had been crying. I says, 'Hello, Andy.' He says, 'Hello Emma.' I says, 'Andy, did you kill my husband?' Andy never answered. The detective says, 'Come on and tell us, Andy that she paid you $400 for killing her husband.' Andy never answered. He got rough. He says, 'Come on and tell us. We got the goods on you. Come on and tell us.'"

"Anything else?"

"He says, 'She did not.' He says, 'Where did you get the $400 from?' He says, 'There's other places to get the $400 besides from her.' I walked down and says, 'Andy didn't kill my husband, and neither did I hire him to do it.' First the detective says, 'Take her away. Take her away.' I says as I turned, 'Andy didn't kill my husband. Neither did I hire him to do it.' Hayes says, 'Take her away.'"

"Yes? They locked you up?"

"No. They took me down in the parlor and questioned me."

"Did they lock you up that night?"

"Yes."

"Been locked up ever since?"

"Yes."

Lameroux started his cross-examination of Emma. He blustered and looked at his pocket watch, noting the time. It was getting late, but he was confident he could wrap it up that evening.

"What did you do when you first came here?"

"My husband was working at the Adams House, and I came up here to visit. I stopped at the Senate House. At the time I was there Mrs. Lewis was called away on account of her mother being sick in New York. They asked me to work, which I did."

"You don't need to make a long story of that. Just answer the question. What did you do here?"

"I stopped at the Senate House."

"Were you in business at all before you acquired the property you are in now?"

"Yes."

"What business were you in?"

"Running a restaurant."

"Running a restaurant?"

"Yes."

"Had no roomers?"

"No."

"When did you acquire this property and open your business there where you were? This Gogebic Cafe?"

"About 1919."

Lameroux asked Emma about starting the business and when they started selling liquor. Emma denied she ever sold liquor to anyone but admitted that Sigler had. He asked her about rooms and roomers. Then he got to prostitution at the Gogebic Hotel.

"When did you begin keeping women there?"

"I never began keeping women there."

"Did your husband?"

"Yes."

"How many times did he have.... How many did he have there at a time?"

"One, mostly."

"When did that commence? That business."

"Are you referring to women of prostitution?"

"Yes. Prostitutes. When did you begin keeping prostitutes in your place there?"

"A little after a year after we were there."

"A year after you started?"

"Yes."

"That business has continued more or less ever since, hasn't it?"

"Yes."

"You knew what was going on?"

"I did."

"And took frequently the money from the women?"

"I did not."

"You mean to say you never took any money from any women?"

"No."

"Didn't you look after taking the money generally in the place when your husband was away?"

"Not for prostitution."

"You never received any of that?"

"No."

"Did you refuse to receive it?"

"I had nothing to do with the prostitution part."

"Isn't it a fact you solicited girls to go into that business there yourself?"

Zabel objected to the way the testimony was going, and Judge Foley sustained the objection. After a brief consultation with Foster, Lameroux tried a different tactic. He began to attack her testimony about the abuse that Sigler had given her and the children. It was his intent to discredit her for not leaving Sigler.

"Now, Mrs. Sigler, why was it you remained in a place like that to raise these children?"

"Because I had no other place to go."

"Didn't you have anywhere? A father or a mother?"

"I was not supposed to bring my family to my father and mother."

"Didn't you have a father and mother with a home?"

"I did."

"You felt that you couldn't get away possibly from this place?"

"I went away several times and was called back."

"You didn't feel you could get away permanently?"

"Not to stay."

"And you felt that it was necessary, under the circumstances, that you raise these little children under the conditions that you have described?"

"I did not feel that it was necessary."

"Then why didn't you quit?"

"I thought it was necessary to try to clear the place. To clear it."

"To clear it?"

"Yes."

"Were you making any headway?"

"Didn't make much headway. Made many attempts."

Emma's remark caused the spectators to burst out in laughing. Judge Foley was laughing, himself. He had to finally call for order by banging his gavel loudly and yelling out "Quiet!"

"Getting work all the time?" Lameroux continued.

"I couldn't say work. There was one girl there. Sometimes two."

"Who handled your bank account?"

"At first it was for Sigler in the name of the Gogebic Cafe. Since he broke that man's arm, crippled him for life, it has been in my name."

"Crippled him for life? How?"

"His arm and hand is crippled for life. It is stiff."

"His arm is stiff?"

"His hand is."

"Then it was in your name."

"Yes."

"How long has the bank account been in your name of that business down there?"

"About a year before my husband's death."

"About a year before his death?"

"Yes."

"Now, coming down to the time of your husband's death. What were you doing the day before your husband's death?"

"Working around the place."

"What was he doing?"

"He was out in the backyard most of the time cleaning up the yard and helping the men with the garage building."

"Helping what?"

"The men were building a garage in the back."

"For your place?"

"Yes."

"Was he in and out of the building?"

"Yes."

"Did you have any difficulty with him that day?"

"No."

"Who were there in the building besides you and your husband working there or living there?"

"Mrs. Rice and Mrs. Mason."

"Mrs. Rice at that time had been ill for some period, hadn't she?"

"For two weeks."

"About two weeks?"

"Yes."

"What was Mrs. Mason doing during those two weeks and at this time?"

"Nothing in particular."

"Wasn't she helping you?"

"She gave a hand at washing dishes once in a while."

"Didn't she take care of the children?"

"No. I never permitted her to even touch the children."

"Sure of that?"

"Yes. I wanted her to keep away from the children."

"This very night didn't she put one of those children to bed?"

"Didn't put him to bed. Just took him upstairs."

"You permitted her to do that?"

"She went upstairs that day to turn on the light."

"When did you last see your husband?"

"Alive?"

"Alive."

"It was about between 6:30 and 7."

"What date?"

"May 2."

"When did you last see him before that?"

"At about half past midnight."

"Upstairs in bed?"

"Yes."

"When did you last see him before that?"

"About eight o'clock the evening of May 1."

"Where did you see him?"

"At the end of the counter downstairs."

Lameroux asked more questions about the comings and goings of Emma on the night of May 1 and what she remembered about Sigler leaving, She testified to seeing Sigler in his bed at midnight. Lameroux tried, in vain, to get Emma to admit that Louise was downstairs on the morning of May 2, and that Sigler had been killed on the night of May 1. Emma didn't vary from her testimony to Zabel earlier in the day. She handled herself quite well under Lameroux's grilling, in spite of her nervousness.

When the testimony was closed shortly after 5 o'clock, the Court announced that the arguments would not be limited. Judge Foley said that in such a case as this he would not feel justified in limiting counsel.

Judge Foley called for a night session. It appeared that Foster and Lemoroux had another ace up their prosecution sleeve.

Helen Bailey of Alfa, Mich., employed in Ironwood and then living in Montreal, testified that she was employed at the Gogebic Cafe about six weeks and was questioned as to Mrs. Sigler's conduct with her husband.

"She was always quarreling with Mr. Sigler," she responded.

Lempi Luoma was called and testified about a remark that Andy once made to her when Mrs. Sigler passed them.

"There goes a woman who would pay me lots of money to kill her husband."

"Did he say to you, 'Somebody ought to kill the son-of-a-bitch'?"

"Yes sir."

"When did he make that statement?" Lameroux asked.

"That statement was made once when Andy and I went for an automobile ride to Cary Location and returned."

Zabel on the redirect tried to discredit Miss Luoma.

"Are you married?"

"No," she replied.

"Any children?"

"Yes, I have one."

Then came questions regarding a shortage of 30 cents from the cash register for which Miss Luoma was blamed by Mrs. Sigler. She said that Emma took the 30 cents out of her paycheck.

Joseph Volant, former sheriff,[15] was recalled and testified that Andy told him that Emma had agreed to pay him $400 for the job and that he said he had been paid $400 the day after Mr. Sigler was killed.

"Did he say Mrs. Sigler hired him to kill Sigler?" he was asked again.

"Yes sir," he replied.

[15] Volant chose not to run again and Robert Erspamer became the new sheriff in the November, 1924, election. Kalliomaa ran for sheriff and was defeated.

Saturday, January 31, 1925

The courthouse in Hurley once again was crowded to capacity and Undersheriff Simon had the unpleasant duty of barring the outer door of the building to admit no more spectators. Most of them were disappointed for they had heard Foster argue to the jury on other occasions but they had not previously heard Zabel.

Promptly at 8:45, Zabel opened his argument. He assailed the district attorney at times, challenged the testimony of Hayes, and charged the state with an "unquenchable frenzy to send Emma to state's prison."

"Prostitutes, thieves and detectives. How well they go together!" he shouted as he named various witnesses who took the stand for the state. At one time, the audience was visibly moved when he declared that "the brutality disclosed in this case has challenged the annals of time." The jury, however remained stolid.

When he started to cite the case of "Dogface" Johnson, that of a man named Lang in Kenosha County who was sentenced for a crime he did not commit and another case of a similar nature, Judge W.R. Foley interrupted the argument and declared counsel would have to confine his efforts to the case in question.

Berating Hayes, Zabel referred to "his little speech — it was pretty. Just like a phonograph record. What a miserable picture he presented. He was evasive. He wouldn't come down and toe the mark." He stressed the fact that Hayes, on the witness stand, changed slightly his story of the shooting as he said it was related to him by Andy. The version of whether the automobile was moving or was stopped when the shooting took place was the point.

"And they would have you send this woman to prison upon the testimony of a man who doesn't care any more for an oath than that. No! No!

"You've been asked to convict her on testimony that you wouldn't convict a yellow dog on. Are you going to gamble with her life and the lives of four children on such testimony?" he asked.

He emphasized the fact that the state failed to bring anyone in to testify that he heard the shots out on the lonely highway the night of May 1, when Anderson, according to the story by Hayes, shot and killed Sigler.

"But if they were fired in that dark and dingy room in the hotel, nobody would have heard it." Again laying stress on the testimony of Hayes, he declared that Hayes "wasn't at all interested in getting a confession. If that's true, then he wasn't a detective, but a defective.

"Hayes has testified, however, that a confession was more than he had hoped to get. But he had hoped to get certain information that would finally unravel the mystery.

"There wasn't any reason why he shouldn't sign it (the confession) if he gave it," said Zabel.

"But Hayes had testified that when Anderson told him the story of the killing he (Hayes) was in disguise and Anderson didn't know his identity."

Justifying Anderson's going to prison, he said, "It was only a manly instinct" and "it wouldn't hurt him so much. In time the prison gates will open for him when the truth becomes known." He referred to "Mr. Hayes' manufactured confession" and how the state "had to snip little pieces from the seat-cover of the automobile in order to establish whether there had been any blood spilled in the car." That point was brought out to stress the contention of the defense that the body had bled considerably before it was put in the automobile.

Zabel assailed the state for a direct attack on the character of W.C. Lennon, mayor of Hurley.

"Is there no limit to the depth they will go. Was it because Mr. Lennon was a political opponent of Mr. Foster for the office he now holds? Oh what a diabolical thing that was. How they must have gloated over it when they told it."

He challenged the state for failure to prove there no bullet holes in the room where Emma claimed she shot her husband, and said a bullet hole would have shown in the Gudleski car if Sigler had been shot when seated in the automobile.

"Ordinarily, a man's head does not reach the height of that part of the top extending down on the side." No testimony was introduced to show that Anderson's automobile had side curtains.

"What a beautiful trio they make," he said. "Lempi Luoma, Mrs. Mason and Joe Hayes." He referred to them as "Faith, Hope and Charity."

"Are you going to send her to prison because someone (turning and pointing to Foster) wants to put laurels on private detectives? How well they fit together."

He referred to that part of the letter from Sigler written at Superior in which he said his wife had been true to him and termed that a "priceless jewel."

"That woman, I say, is clad in untold riches, and Mr. Foster would even rob her of that jewel. She paid the price of womanhood to have him banished. But you know Mr. Foster didn't do that. You know he wasn't bribed."

He quoted the DA as saying that if she had killed him herself, "she would have done a commendable act."

Ridiculing Louise Mason, he said, "she comes in here dressed like the Queen of Sheba. She neither toils nor spins, yet she can afford to powder and paint and rouge. She prefers the company of dogs to that of children." He said the slight discrepancies in the stories of Anderson and Mrs. Sigler were all the more in favor of the defense, for "had the stories been exactly alike in detail it would have invited suspicion."

"What is this? A political lawsuit?" he shouted. "Why I never got into such a thing in my life."

* * * *

In his closing argument, Foster challenged the jury to consider the testimony of the defendant and Andy as nothing but lies. He made a strong argument for the state, covered highlights of the case and disclosed numerous discrepancies in the testimonies of the witnesses for the defense.

Foster closed by referring to Andy as "this gallant Sir Walter Raleigh who has life imprisonment before him, and who shoulders the entire blame in the killing of Sigler just because he wanted to shield Emma Sigler and give her a chance to carry on for her four little boys.

"The defense is just a part of the scheme to defeat justice and deny on the part of Anderson that he had anything to do with the murder except to haul the body away in the cool, clammy manner that he testified to. This man, Andy Anderson, is fighting for a release, naturally. He's been down there in Waupun, now, and is willing to tell anything — anything, Ladies and Gentlemen — to get out of Waupun and free himself of the murder of Andrew Sigler to which he voluntarily confessed."

Foster pointed his finger at Emma.

"The only possible defense was fighting — fighting in the family, and then they see how preposterous it is, and they turn to her because they feel that through sympathy she would be justified in killing her husband, because if she killed him there would be a possibility of her being justified. Yet from June 23 on, no such claim was made and she was apparently satisfied to let this innocent man suffer at Waupun at hard labor. Does that sound reasonable to you — that this affair took place under the circumstances which the defendant claimed."

Warning the jury against being carried away by emotion, Foster declared that "neither she nor her husband were fit to bring up children in such an environment. They'll get better care in an orphan asylum than in such a place.

"Could you see one thing about that man's testimony to indicate he wasn't telling the truth?" he asked in referring to Hayes. "Not a thing."

He covered the admission of Andy in the Ashland Circuit Court and asserted the defense had made no effort to obtain a witness to impeach the detective's testimony. He called Andy a "confessed liar".

"His conduct on the stand indicates he isn't normal.

"The defense failed to refute the story that Anderson and the defendant met on the street in Hurley either the day before or the day after the shooting as testified by Emil Erickson. They failed to show who the man was who called for Sigler early in the morning of May 2, that part that led to the quarrel and shooting as claimed by the defense, Mr. Zabel was unable to explain how Mrs. Sigler shot her husband in the side and from the left when he came after her with a cleaver. He declared the empty cartridges that Anderson told he had picked off the floor wouldn't have been in a little pool of blood but would have been back of the bed if Mrs. Sigler fired while standing on the bed as she testified she did."

As he closed, his voice was pitched so low that it was hardly audible to the jury.

"Thank you ladies and gentlemen of the jury. I believe in my heart that you will not be swayed by any sympathy for this woman."

* * * *

Judge Foley's instructions to the jury were comparatively brief. The Court warned the jury to give much consideration to the defendant's testimony "as you think it should have. In determining the credibility of the witnesses you must consider their interests."

Foley instructed the jury to disregard Andy's testimony as not factual and to take the testimony of Hayes "lightly."

"You should return a verdict of not guilty unless there is proof beyond a reasonable doubt that is sufficient to call her guilty. Now, ladies and gentlemen of the jury, the charge is that Andrew Anderson was found guilty and the defendant hired him to kill her husband. The defendant has pled not guilty to the charge. You, the members of the jury, must distinguish between three charges.

"One: If Mrs. Sigler killed Andrew Sigler and hired Andrew Anderson to dispose of the body, she must be found guilty.

"Two: If Andy Anderson killed Andrew Sigler and Emma Sigler did not hire him, she is not guilty.

"Three: If Emma Sigler hired Andy Anderson to kill Andrew Sigler, she is guilty."

* * * *

At 12:20, the jury started their deliberation. The first vote was eight to three for conviction with one blank vote.

At 3:15, the jury asked for a testimony in the cross-examination of Mrs. Sigler regarding when and how she found out where Sigler had hidden the pistol. They also asked when Mrs. Mason came to the Gogebic Hotel.

At 5:22, the jury again came in and foreman William Miller asked the Court for a .32 automatic Colt to indicate to some of the jurors how an automatic revolver throws the empty cartridges. There was no weapon found and none was introduced in the evidence, said the Court, and consequently he had no right to give them a revolver.

"Then there was no evidence as to how far the ejected shells would go?" asked the foreman.

"I don't think there was," replied the Court.

The jurors deliberated into the evening, and they were allowed to spend the night at the Curry Hotel in Ironwood. Before they left for the night, Judge Foley cautioned the jury not to speak to each other about or to read any newspapers about the case.

Sunday, February 1, 1925

Emma said she slept soundly on Saturday and was ready to accept the jury's decision. In her mind, though, she did not expect to be convicted.

Only a few people were in the courtroom. The jury filed in at 10:00, and the foreman asked Judge Foley for the day off so the jury could attend church services.

"No, you will go to the jury room and resume deliberations. You must reach a verdict," Foley told Miller.

The jury voted nine to three for conviction as soon as they were ushered into the jury room. The three holdouts were for acquittal; two were leaning to convict, but one person believed Emma's testimony that she had killed Sigler in self-defense and was not guilty. After a great deal of badgering, the three jurors caved in and voted for conviction.

It had been a difficult two days for the jurors because every member felt pity for Emma. All knew what a tyrant Sigler had been. None of the jurors could understand why Emma should be found guilty, but the law stated that she was guilty because she had confessed to killing Sigler, and she hired Andy to dispose of the body. Judge Foley had mentioned nothing about self defense.

Shortly before 4:00 pm, after 17 hours of deliberation, the bailiff was instructed to inform the Court that the jury had arrived at a verdict. When foreman William Miller was asked what the verdict was, he replied, "Guilty."

Zabel immediately filed a motion for a new trial but it was denied by Judge Foley, who asked Emma if she had anything to say.

"Yes, sir, I killed my husband in self-defense and not Andy Anderson. All he did was take my husband's body away."

“Mrs. Sigler, you have been judged guilty of being an accessory to murder in the first degree by a jury of your peers, and it is the sentence of this court that you spend the rest of your life in the State’s prison at Waupun at hard labor with June 24 of each year in solitary confinement.”

Emma asked that she be given until Thursday to arrange her affairs. The request was granted.

Wednesday, February 4, 1925

Emma is confident that she will again walk the streets of Hurley. She believed Zabel when he told her that her case would be brought to the attention of Governor John B. Blaine in an effort to obtain a new trial. Just what her attorneys have planned she does not know, she told a reporter for the Ironwood Daily Globe.

"How do you feel about going to prison?" the reporter asked Emma.

"I'm anxious to get down there, for I know I'm not going to be there for long."

"Did you kill your husband even though the jury convicted you of being an accessory before the fact?"

"Yes, it was me who killed Sigler, and I did it in self-defense. I was justified, because I had endured tortures at the hand of my husband only too long."

"What about the jury, Mrs. Sigler? Did they do you justice?"

"The jury took my case so lightly that I heard members of the jury singing 'It Ain't Gonna Rain No More' just before they announced to the bailiff that they were ready to bring in their verdict. One member of the jury had openly stated before the trial that if he were to be chosen he would be certain to vote for my conviction."

"Do you hold it against them?"

"I hold no grudge against the jury. I say as Jesus said when his enemies nailed him to the cross, 'God, forgive them for they know not what they do.'"

"Anderson is in prison for murder. Why is that?"

"If Andy Anderson took a life sentence for murder, he took it for another murder and not for killing Sigler."

"Why, then, didn't Andy tell the story earlier?"

"I didn't think Andy admitted to my killing Sigler because I thought they were trying to trap me. They kept the newspapers away from me until the preliminary hearing so I didn't know what was going on. Andy told his wife that all the time she was blinded in this case. 'Stick to that woman' he told her.[16] I thought Andy was trying to shield me and figured that if I helped him and he broke jail the killing of Sigler never would be solved and it would be better for the children."

"Did you tell anyone earlier that you had killed your husband? Anyone other than your attorneys?"

"I told Foster and Volant right after the killing that I had done it, and they laughed at me."

She skipped from one part of the testimony to another and without emotion told time and time again that she killed her husband. She explained that Sigler was shot in the side and not from the front because the bed on which she stood was in one corner of the room. As he broke open the door, she was to the left of him and it was then she fired, she claimed.

"Louise heard those shots, and she wouldn't come clean," she said.

"She even tried to pump me, and said she saw Sigler's reflection in a mirror. But I played the game and didn't tell her anything."

"What about the note Andy wrote to you? What can you tell me about that note?"

"That note from Andy when he was in the jail was originally intended to ask for $100, and Hayes changed the figure to

---

[16] Emma could not have heard that from Andy, because he was in Waupun Penitentiary.

$1000. It looked like there was an erasure, but an erasure would not be necessary to add another cipher. It was changed anyway."

"Why did you telephone Andy and advise him to leave town?"

"I tipped off Andy to leave town because I thought the buttons that were found, were from his overcoat and not from Sigler's."

"What did you tell him to do? Didn't you tell him there was blood on his overcoat?"

"I said, 'Burn your overcoat and beat it.' He said, 'I got you.' Do you think I would be foolish enough to mention blood over the telephone?"

"How much did you pay Cadigan and Cadigan to defend Andy?"

"The story that Cadigan and Cadigan had been offered $12,000 to defend Andy came from Hayes. He got that impression when he stayed at the hotel the first few days of his work in Hurley. Hayes told me that I was sitting pretty with Sigler out of the way and I had a good business. I told him 'Yes, sitting pretty and with a $12,000 mortgage on the place.'"

"Are you in touch with any of your husband's relatives?"

"Well, the only one is his brother Bill. He sent me a letter saying he felt sorry for me because he knew what I had to put up with."

"Are you coping then, Mrs. Sigler?"

"Since the trial I've looked at life like one who is yet to be free, and I smiled when I left the courtroom, and I looked the judge straight in the face when he sentenced me. I came back here to the jail, and I slept like a log. I couldn't have slept better if I had been acquitted."

Thursday, February 5, 1925

Early in the morning, Emma was escorted from her cell to the waiting car of Sheriff Bob Erspamer and taken to the train for the trip to the penitentiary at Waupun. A deputy dragged Matt Waarala to the car. He was to become an inmate at the Northern State Hospital for Insane at Oshkosh. "Well, my little home away from home, I will say goodbye to you now," Emma said as they were driving away.

Mrs. Erspamer met them at the depot where a demonstration of sorts awaited them. A huge crowd of people, most of them Emma's friends, were there to see her off. Many were crying, but they were not as sorry for Emma as they were for her four children.

As Cora Erspamer guided Emma to the platform, Emma turned to the crowd and shouted, "I'll see you all again very soon."

Emma sat with Cora, and Bob kept a close eye on Waarala.

After they were settled in their seats, Cora and Emma chatted.

"I wonder what my children are doing. Do you have any idea?" Emma asked.

"Luella Trier will be appointed their guardian. You can't ask for a more wonderful person than Luella, Emma."

"Yes, I know, Mrs. Trier. The children will be taken care of well, but she's pretty old, don't you think?"

"Yes. I doubt if she will take them in. They will probably be sent to the orphanage in Superior."

Emma started to cry.

"Your children will be well cared for at St. Joseph's. Now, don't you worry about it."

"My babies, my babies, my babies. Placed in an orphanage." Emma sobbed.

"It was the only way, Emma. There was no one else who was willing to care for them."

"I'm confident that I'll get pardoned. Mr. Zabel is working very hard for me. He said he'd bring my case to the Governor's desk."

"Emma, is it true that you are going to have a baby?"

"Yes. I'm due in the late spring or early summer."

"Can you tell me?...Who is the father?"

"He's a city official. That's all I will tell you."

"If that's the case, it will strengthen your request for a pardon."

Emma sat pensively for the rest of the trip looking out of the train window. Cora read a book. Finally, when they were at the outskirts of Waupun, Bob Erspamer looked over the seat at her.

"So you are headed to Waupun to spend the rest of your life in prison, Emma. How do you feel about that?" Bob asked.

Emma gave him a profound answer.

"I've been in jail all my life and won't mind it in prison at all."

EPILOGUE

Criminologists in the early 1920's were quite sophisticated. In investigating crimes, police often rely on forensic experts. After any serious crime, the scene was combed for fingerprints, bullets, fibers, and other trace evidence that could be taken to a lab and analyzed.

There is no indication that any of these things were done after the death of Sigler. Sheriff Joseph Volant and Undersheriff Richard Kalliomaa were at the scene shortly after Sigler's body was found, about eight hours after he was shot to death by Emma (or sixteen hours if he had been murdered by Anderson the night before). Their investigation of the crime scene was superficial, to say the least.

Dr. Urquhart never said how long Sigler had been dead. Although difficult to estimate, even in 1924, medical doctors could reasonably estimate the time of death to within an hour based on temperature reading of the corpse. Rigor mortis sets in by three to six hours, usually. There is no indication that these critical forensic measurements were ever taken.

Had they investigated thoroughly, they surely would have found Anderson's footprints among those of La Fave and their own. They probably would also have found tire tracks from Anderson's automobile.

There was no search for either the .32 caliber revolver, probably the murder weapon, which Anderson claimed to have thrown in the river or the .38 that Anderson claimed to have given to his brother-in-law. Had this been done and the guns found, fingerprints could have been taken.

They had the bullets and shell casings, yet there was nothing but cursory ballistic evidence taken. They knew the murder weapon was a .32 caliber because they found the bullets where Sigler's body had been dumped. They also found one slug still in the body at the autopsy. There is no testimony that the bullets were analyzed for signature evidence.

No blood was found at the scene where the body was found, and apparently the "thorough search" of the hotel didn't include Room Seven, which would have revealed blood spatters on the walls and floor.

A search for neither the meat cleaver nor the revolver was undertaken. Nobody asked Emma what might have happened to the cleaver, and the gun was not introduced at the trial.

Andrew Sigler's coat would have had bullet holes if Andy had shot him. The coat was not introduced as evidence.

* * * *

When Emma arrived at the state penitentiary, she was examined to determine the extent of her pregnancy. Physicians discovered that Emma was, indeed, pregnant and notified Warden Lee who immediately notified Governor Blaine. Joe Fuller, an investigator assigned by Governor Blaine, went to Hurley and obtained statements and names of all persons who visited Emma at the Iron County jail from the date of her incarceration to the time she was sentenced.

Newly-elected Sheriff Bob Erspamer, Warren Foster, Dan Reid, chairman of the county board, and Rev. C.L. Harries pastor of the Hurley Presbyterian Church, left that night for Madison to answer to what Emma had told them about her pregnancy. Mayor Lennon was summoned to Madison by Governor Blaine to tell the investigative panel what he knew. On February 10, Governor Blaine began an investigation. The governor himself went to Hurley on February 14, to question city officials, including former sheriff Volant, Foster, Mayor Lennon and Dick Kalliomaa. There apparently was no reason to suspect any of these men as the father of the child. A statement was issued by Governor Blaine:

> Report has been received by the governor that Mrs. Emma Sigler of Hurley, recently convicted of being an accessory to murder, when delivered to the prison at Waupun was found in a delicate condition and the governor has instituted an investigation. To prevent obstruction of justice, no information will be given out until the facts warrant official action.

There were no answers to Emma's medical condition by February 28, and it wasn't until April 21, 1925, when State Senator Walter Palakowski, a member of the prison inspection committee demanded an explanation from Governor Blaine.

On May 14, Palakowski received a sharp letter from the governor. The governor wrote:

> I regard it as against the public interests, and it would intend to defeat the ends of justice if I would give publicity to such information as I have in this case and therefore I must decline to divulge any information which would defeat the ends of justice until I have come to a final conclusion in the matter, when all information that I have will available at the executive office to you or any other citizen who has a public interest in this matter.
>
> The responsibility in this matter is an executive responsibility, and I shall discharge that responsibility within the time and in the manner that the case warrants, notwithstanding your demands and threats, and I want to advise you now I shall not be driven into a position by intimidation on the part of anyone, that may defeat the ends of justice or the public's interest in this matter.
>
> I want very frankly to advise you that when I come to a decision, that decision will be based on the facts and not as a result of intimidation or bludgeoning. I also want to advise you frankly that I am going to satisfy no demands of curiosity. The demands of justice and the public's interest are higher than the demands of curiosity.

Senator Polakowski requested a hearing with the governor and the two met on June 3, 1925, as a part of a senate probe into graft, vice and corruption at the executive level. The governor told Polakowski that the legislative action would be deferred "until after the arrival of the child."

Emma was subpoenaed to appear before a senatorial committee led by Chairman William A. Quick on June 3, 1925. Quick said the committee wanted "first hand testimony only." As a result of her testimony before the investigative committee, Governor Blaine issued an executive order to have Emma examined further at the Wisconsin Psychiatric Hospital on June 12, 1925.

It was through the efforts of Emma's defense attorney, Winfred Zabel, that she was transferred from Waupun to the hospital. Emma had a choice of having her baby in Taycheedah reformatory or at the hospital.

"Consideration of welfare of prospective child is paramount," the governor said in a telegram. "If child is born, she and child will be temporarily transferred to Taycheedah, established for such cases, until medical authority deem it proper to separate child from its mother, when child will be cared for under the law and Mrs. Sigler returned to prison." Emma was eight months along by this time, and the baby was due on or about July 1.

She was sent to Taycheedah for an x-ray examination. On June 12, Dr. J.J. Bowen, prison physician, stated that the charges that she was to become a mother were unfounded. On June 15, 1925, Governor Blaine officially announced that Emma was not pregnant. The results of the x-ray showed an "absence of shadows which are present after the fourth month."

Emma's pregnancy is a matter for speculation. When she was admitted to Waupun State Penitentiary, she claimed to be four months along in her pregnancy. In June, she would have been in her eight month of pregnancy.

The trial testimony and the investigation of Governor Blaine pointed to the father of Emma's child as a city official. If that was true, there is no indication of who the man may have been.

Well into the eighth month of her pregnancy, there could be little question that Emma was pregnant. She was a small woman, and her pregnancy would be quite obvious. Yet, when she was transferred to the woman's prison, suddenly a single medical doctor determined that she was not because he could see "no shadows" on her x-ray.

* * * *

On November 25, 1925, Zabel filed an appeal to the Supreme Court. Apparently, the appeal depended on raising several hundred dollars to cover the cost of printing a record of the brief and to pay for a transcript of the trial.

Zabel was assisted by P.J. Zisch who said in a letter to Iron County: "Mr. Zabel and I have concluded to appeal the Sigler case to the Supreme Court in view of an opinion from the court. I think there is sufficient material in the record of the case to warrant the court to apply the rule as laid down in the case quoted.

There is more than a grave doubt as to whether Anderson killed Sigler at Mrs. Sigler's instigation. Certainly the jury failed to accord her the benefit of that doubt. If, on the other hand, she killed her husband, as it was claimed, the record contains sufficient evidence to warrant the finding of justifiable homicide.

Taking either view of the case, we are satisfied that the Supreme Court cannot distinguish between the case quoted and Mrs. Sigler's case, and I believe that Mrs. Sigler should have the opportunity of having her case appealed to the Supreme Court.

Mrs. Sigler communicated with us a few days ago, in which she petitioned us to appeal this case in her behalf.

If her attorneys were successful in Emma's appeal, there is no record that can be found in the Wisconsin court system.

On February 6, 1929, Everis Reid, Iron County district attorney, represented Iron County at a parole hearing held with Governor Walter Kohler. Emma's parole was denied.

In June, 1936, Emma was again denied clemency by Governor LaFollette while she was in the Northern State Hospital. Again, in May, 1938, she was denied parole. In March, 1941, she sought a pardon from Wisconsin Governor Heil while she was at the women's prison at Taycheedah. Warren Foster was consulted by the parole board and he let his views be known. She was denied parole once again.

Finally, on August 20, 1942, Emma was granted outside privileges and was released for 11 days to allow her to visit her sister. On October 26, 1942, she was paroled to her sister, Mrs. Nick Sklavenitis of Elkhorn, Wisconsin.

In the years immediately following her release from prison, Emma became a shrewd business woman. She bought four old properties in Duluth and renovated them into rooms and apartments that she rented out. One of these she named "Noah's Ark Hotel" and it was quite successful. Her husband, George Zink, who she married in 1944, her brother, and her son, Junior, helped with the renovation of the dilapidated buildings.

Several factories closed in 1951, and her hotel businesses began to decline. She made plans to take in transients, but that fell through.

In the fall of 1951, her husband died suddenly, and Emma was very distressed. Because of remarks about her past, Emma requested a post mortem examination on George's body; he died a natural death.

In 1953, Emma became a member of the Spiritualistic Church in Duluth and attended services at least three times a week.

After selling her real estate holdings in 1954, Emma opened a thrift shop where she sold her furnishings from the hotel business, and moved in with an invalid, Mr. Asplund, becoming his 24-hour nurse and housekeeper.

The last contact Emma had with her parole officer was on March 20, 1956, when her sentence was commuted. In her March 27, 1956, case closing summary, Emma's parole officer wrote that "Emma Sigler Zink has lived at 409 W. 50th Street, Duluth, Minnesota, since December 1954, where she has been employed as a housekeeper. She has been in Duluth nearly 13 years and for much of that time operated rooming houses in Gary and West Duluth.... She is an energetic, ambitious individual. She has been receptive to supervision and seems to be well adjusted. There are no special problems at this time." At the time she was formally released from custody, Emma had been just the second woman in the history of the Wisconsin penal system to be given a life sentence for murder.

Soon after her release from parole, Emma moved to Indianapolis, Indiana, where she died in April, 1986.

* * * *

There is no doubt that Emma was a battered wife because the trial testimony bears it out. In 1925 the term "battered woman's syndrome" was not in the legal vocabulary. It wasn't until the late 1970's that the battered woman syndrome became admissible to aid juries in assessing a defendant's perception of danger posed by the abuser.

* * * *

Winfred Zabel tried unsuccessfully to get Emma off with a plea of self defense or justifiable homicide. Governor Blaine suggested that her case be presented to the Supreme Court as worthy of justifiable homicide, but that did not happen. Although he was unsuccessful in his many attempts to free Emma, Zabel continued to represent her pro bono until 1941.

* * * *

Emma's children were placed in a Superior orphanage immediately after her conviction. In the 1930 census for Barksdale, Bayfield County, Wisconsin, Robert Sigler was living with the George and Anna Anderson family. Joseph, who was called "Junior" and the twins, Lester and Leslie, now dubbed "Hans" and "Fritz", according to the 1930 census record, lived at the St. Joseph orphanage in Superior, Wisconsin.

* * * *

Robert married in the early 1940's and owned a woodworking business in Washburn. It was not successful, he was unable to pay his bills, and his machinery was taken. With no job and no money, Robert, his wife and four children moved into one of Emma's apartments in Duluth. Emma told her parole officer that Robert acted like his father, Andrew, because he beat his wife and threatened Emma. Robert worked on his own, making jewelry and selling novelties, but that business fell into ruin. He was unemployed for much of the time he was in Duluth. His wife left him, and he eventually got a job with the railroad and nothing more was heard from him, nor from any of his children.

Family problems, especially from Robert, plagued Emma throughout the years, and she cared for his two oldest daughters for nearly two years after Robert and his wife separated.

Joe Sigler, Junior's son, told me that he and his father may have encountered Robert in Duluth in the 1960's.

* * * *

After he left the orphanage, Joseph (Junior) became a member of the Civilian Conservation Corps and then served with the 2nd Armored Division in Europe during World War II; Emma received an allotment of $30 per month from Junior. After his discharge in October, 1945, Junior helped Emma and George repair Noah's Ark Hotel. He married in early 1946, and he and his wife moved into one of Emma's properties on Ramsey Street in Duluth. He died in 1991 in Iron River, Wisconsin. Junior's son, Joe, lives in Fort Worth, Texas.

* * * *

Leslie joined the Merchant Marine as a cook aboard ship. He died in New Orleans in 1984.

* * * *

Lester was wounded in action in World War II. He lived in Ashland where he owned and operated four motels. At the time of this writing, he was in a nursing home. His daughter, Vicki, lives in Colorado.

* * * *

Andy was never cleared of the charges brought against him, nor did he ever talk about the crime. According to his parole officer, "I always had this idea that Andy was covering up for someone." Andy was released from Waupun on June 4, 1941, and went to work as a mechanic for the Ben Anderson Company in Madison. In 1943, Andy remarried. His son, Andrew, knew nothing about his father's past. He told me that Andy "was an excellent carpenter and mechanic and had built a home and garage by himself in Tomahawk, Wisconsin." Andy Anderson had spent most of his life in a prison of one sort or another: eight years in the reform school in Waukesha and two years at the Green Bay Correctional Facility. It was the only home he really knew. When he married Lillian Randa in 1920, he had been out of prison for only two years. By all reports, Andy was a congenial guy who did not dwell on his past. He was happily married and enjoyed Hurley's wide-open atmosphere. Whether he had a "crush" on Emma Sigler is not known, but he certainly knew her quite well because he worked next to the hotel for Friola Electric and just about a block away at the New Central. Andy liked children, and the Sigler children were no exception. The trial testimony indicates that he rescued them from Andrew Sigler's tirades on more than one occasion.

Lee Wagner, Andy's parole officer from Merrill, Wisconsin, first saw Andy in the early to mid 1970's. He was a "real nice guy" and "very talkative." He told me that he "thought the world of Andy" and that Andy had an "excellent personal parole profile." He was "the kind of guy you could trust to report in on time and on the right day. No, I never had a bit of trouble from Andy in all the years I was his parole officer."

Andy was given an administrative pardon on September 15, 1986, by the Governor of Wisconsin. He died in Tomahawk, Wisconsin, on July 10, 1991. His final resting place is in Greenwood Cemetery in Tomahawk.

* * * *

Lillian, Andy's first wife, died on May 10, 1953, in Ironwood. She never quite recovered from the shock of Andy's arrest and the death of their son, Randall, a crewman on a B-17 in the WW II European Theater. His plane was shot down over the English Channel on December 10, 1943. His body was never recovered.

* * * *

After the trial, Louise Mason returned to Chicago and never returned to Hurley. She is not listed in the 1930 census. Louise claimed that she lived at 1705 Fourteenth Street in Superior, Wisconsin, with Mrs. Barrett. Checking a few years before and after 1923, I couldn't find anyone by that name listed at 1705

N. 14th Street. Louise also claimed that she lived at 4714 Kenwood Avenue in Chicago, and that is where she could be reached to testify at Emma's trial, but the Chicago directory indicated that Louise did not live there. No other records have been found relating to Louise.

* * * *

Joseph P. Hayes died on November 8, 1953, of a kidney ailment, at the Veteran's Hospital in Wood, Wisconsin. He was 58 years old. His wife, Mary Rockford Hayes, said that he had a "tough, seamed face which fit well into his frequent role as planted criminal." He spent many weeks of his life in jail cells throughout the Midwest, always with a cellmate whom police and district attorneys had been unable to crack. "Many, many times," she related, "we took Joe out in old clothes on the highway and dropped him off." Shortly he would be picked up by the police as a vagrant and thrown into jail. "One of the toughest cases he broke was the Sigler case," his wife said.

* * * *

At Emma's trial in January, 1925, the testimonies of both Andy and Emma indicate that Emma killed her husband. Even though she confessed to murdering her husband in self-defense, there are many who still believed that it was really Andy who killed Sigler. The Daily Globe had much to do with the myth as it published the day-by-day story of the Sigler murder. The account reads much like a tabloid, details embellished and facts distorted.

* * * *

In his book Hurley: Still No Angel (Northwoods Publishers, Ann Arbor, Michigan, 1954, pp.65-72), Lewis Reimann got some of the facts wrong. For example, he wrote that Andy testified at the trial that it was he, not Emma who killed Sigler. Andy might have done that at Emma's preliminary hearing, but he told a different story at her trial six months later. Reimann wrote that Emma "engaged an expensive lawyer, W.C. Zabel" when, in fact, Zabel defended her *pro bono*. He wrote that Ray Rice's stomach was destroyed in formaldehyde by a pathologist at the Madison State Hospital. Those who read the book believed what Reimann wrote, and the myth was perpetuated even further.

* * * *

Zabel told True Detective (June, 1932) magazine that after Andy related his story to him at Waupun State Penitentiary, "the whole thing was as clear as day to us now. And what a botch they had made of the whole affair! We doubted our ability to untangle the mesh that had them so thoroughly ensnared. Had they been truthful about the whole affair in the first place and not tried to hide the crime, they would both have been freed and probably without the formality of a trial. The panic of fear that had seized them in the presence of death had proved their undoing. Mrs. Sigler's attempt to keep the truth hidden from her children, and [Andy's] gallant offer to help her was what tightened the net of circumstantial evidence around them.

"Here was the knotty legal problem that faced us. [Andy]'s pardon could only be secured by conviction of the actual murderer. Therefore, we must first convict Mrs. Sigler of the murder of her husband to free [Anderson] and then turn around and make an attempt to clear Mrs. Sigler of murder on the basis of self-defense."

* * * *

The precise circumstances of Emma's pregnancy, the deaths of Andrew Sigler and Ray Rice, and the question of Emma's pregnancy will never be known. The answer went with Emma to her grave. They will forever remain a mystery of the past when criminals, prostitutes, and saloon owners kept watch over Hurley.

APPENDIX

Hurley

(Originally written in the *Ironwood Daily Globe**, February 3, 1925, this editorial points out how and why the seedy atmosphere of Hurley was intolerable to the people of neighboring Ironwood)*

The recent murder trials in Hurley are eloquent of the fact that conditions across the Montreal River are desperate. It is preposterous to presume that these conditions of vice are unknown to the average citizen in Iron County. The only presumption to be drawn is that the citizenry of Iron has become so case-hardened to these conditions that there is no outcry for a change, even after the testimony given in either the Santini and Sigler murder trials.

We have no fault to find with the outcome of either trial. It is another of those queer twists of justice which sent Mrs. Sigler, the mother of four children, to prison for life and permitted Santini his freedom on bail on the technicality of a disagreement among jurors. Mrs. Sigler is a victim of circumstance and environment. So, too, is Santini in a large measure.

Had Mrs. Sigler married a man in another part of Wisconsin, she would not have been surrounded by the temptations which eventually led to her downfall. She might not have seen how easy it was to sell moonshine without direction. She might not have been called upon to permit her home to be used as a house of prostitution. But because it was possible to "get away with it" in Hurley, she assented. It looked like an easy living for herself and her husband. Others were acquiring wealth in that way. Why not the Siglers? And so they fell. And the fall was into a trap they helped to make.

But Mrs. Sigler is not the only person to blame. The people of Hurley, the County of Iron, the State of Wisconsin, and the United States of America are all partly to blame for the conditions in Hurley. To be sure the greatest measure of guilt lies among the people of Hurley. They have the power to change conditions for better or worse. And since things invariably are "worst", the only deduction which can logically be made is that the majority of Hurley people want the present condition of things.

The present term of Iron County circuit court was called upon to try two murder cases. Both cases originated in Hurley. The testimony brought out conditions of vice so clearly there is no way for officers of the City of Hurley or the County of Iron to deny the existences of these vices. One bit of testimony related by the inmate of a house of prostitution is of unusual interest. It told how she was requested by city authorities to leave town. There was no arrest of her, or better yet, of her employer. And she returned to Hurley in due time to resume her nefarious trade.

It is inconceivable how an honest enforcement official can continue in office in Hurley or in Iron County. It is beyond understanding how an official, honest when he is inducted into executive office, can turn over the duties of his office one, two or four years hence and say he has performed these duties to the best of his ability and in an honest and upright manner. Perhaps it can be done, but it seems impossible.

There isn't a man, woman or child in Hurley who doesn't know about the row of saloons and dives on Silver Street. The sheriff and district attorney of Iron County, the chief of police in Hurley, the county and municipal judges, the mayor of Hurley and the chairman of the Iron County board know of these saloons and dives the same as everyone else knows about them. Yet there is no action toward removing these ulcers of society. And perhaps no action can be expected because it seems apparent the people of Hurley and Iron County are satisfied with these crime-breeding dives and illegal business institutions.

Even Governor Blaine knows of them. The Capital Times of Madison gave him a splendid word picture of Hurley about a year ago and called upon the governor to clean up this wicked spot. Governor Blaine came into Hurley last August seeking votes in his primary campaign, and he received these votes. And Hurley is still Hurley.

So as there can be no misunderstanding, the Daily Globe, through this remonstrance, does not expect that any action will be taken by anyone concerned in Hurley's welfare, whether it be for good or evil. It's going to take something heaps stronger than printer's ink to remove the dark stains on the reputation of our neighboring city. The kind of ink we use isn't black enough to be noticeable on the dark record which Hurley has forged during the past thirty-five and more years.

But through this comment, we do want to make clear the fact that although we have been in close touch with Hurley for five years, we are still not so case-hardened to happenings across the river that we do not appreciate how vile conditions are over there. We do not want our readers to mistake our position. We know there is nothing we can do to remedy the situation. But we do not want our readers to think we are sitting supinely by while this kind of lawlessness goes on under our noses. At least we can remonstrate. There are scores of people in Hurley who would remonstrate with us if they dared.

The people of Hurley and Iron County have it within their power to remove the vices and crimes which now parade themselves so shamelessly and brazenly to public view. The people across the Montreal have the authority in their own hands to make Hurley a synonym for everything that is good instead of a byword for vice and crime.

Printed in the United States
34226LVS00002B/172-210

9 781598 580181